Finally Home

Hayden Falls

Book Seven

Debbie Hyde

Cover Design by: Debbie Hyde
Couple Photo by: prostooleh @ Depositphotos
Background Photo: Carrie Pichler Photography (Facebook).
Photographer Website: https://carriepicherphotography.weebly.com

ISBN: 9798864488461

To all the men and women in our Armed Forces, whether past, present, or future. Thank you from the bottom of our hearts for your service. YOU ARE TRUE HEROS!

Chapter One

Aaron

Happy Birthday to me. Not. In about twenty minutes, I'll enter the one town in this country I never planned on seeing again. It might even be the one town I hate the most in the world. That might not be true. I've seen some messed up little villages during my overseas tours in the Army. I never wanted to see this town again, but it's nowhere near as bad as some places I've seen. We'll stick to this being the worst town in the US.

I didn't leave Hayden Falls, Montana, nearly ten years ago with the intent of never coming back or hating it. Life threw me a curveball. One that landed between my eyes and has left me senseless for a decade. I try not to think about the dagger that was plunged into my heart ten years ago. I'm not looking forward to this visit at all. This will definitely be my last time here. I wouldn't be here now if the town council weren't forcing me to show up.

My dad died nine years ago. You never expect a man in his late forties to have a heart attack. I have an aunt here, but the city officials wouldn't let her handle the legal matters of my dad's estate. I wouldn't call an old farmhouse an estate, but apparently, lawyers do. Mayor Martin is not my favorite person right now. His son, Quinn, seems nicer. It's probably a ruse to get me here.

Only my aunt knows I'm coming. As much as I dislike the Mayor, I figure he can make room for me in his schedule when I show up at City Hall on Monday morning. Am I being mean? Why, yes, I am. Their stupid ordinance letter disrupted my life. I could care less if they had no warning when I'd show up. I knew one day I'd have to come and deal with this, but I wanted to do it on my terms, not theirs.

About ten miles outside of town, a huge billboard comes into view. That's new. This one is lower to the ground than the ones you see on the interstate. It looks like they're working on it. A small pickup and an SUV are parked on the side of the road. The SUV's back passenger door is open. Thank goodness it's on the field side and not the highway. The sight of a woman holding a baby concerns me. Maybe they aren't working on the billboard. She might have car trouble. I'm not about to leave a woman and a baby on the side of the road. I pull over and park in front of the two vehicles.

Getting out, I pull my ballcap low over my eyes and walk toward her. I don't see anyone else out here. "Ma'am, do you need help?"

"We're fine." She smiles as she pats the baby on the back. The little guy is cute. He looks to be under a year old.

I pause at the front of the SUV and stare at her. She has long wavy light brown hair, blue eyes, and a sweet smile. Wait. I know her. What's her name? Her eyes widen, and her mouth falls open.

"Aaron Bailey?" She's as stunned as I am.

"Yes, Ma'am." I didn't think anyone would recognize me. I'm not the same scrawny boy who left town ten years ago.

"Oh my gosh. I can't believe you're back." She walks closer to me.

I know her. Sadly, I can't remember her name. I don't want to have to ask. It would be rude of me. Right? A man pops up from the other side of the pickup. The truck isn't on a jack, so he's not changing a tire. My gaze drifts over to him. Now him, I know. Seeing this fool makes my blood boil with rage.

"A A Ron! Good to see you!" Four shouts.

I hate it when he says my name like that. Too bad we aren't in a Middle East country right now. I'd pop this jerk between the eyes and call it a day. There's nobody in the world I hate more than Mick Calhoun.

I look at the woman and baby again. She's beautiful and looks smart. She's wearing a wedding ring. Surely, she didn't marry this fool.

"E, did the Hayden Sisters send dessert?" Four asked.

E? Oh my. I do know her. "E Hayes?"

I'm stunned. Did she hit her head or something? Perhaps she was in a car accident and had brain trauma. There's no way she married Four and had his kid.

She smiles sweetly at me. "Well, it's Maxwell now." She turns toward Four. "Of course, they did. The basket I gave you is full. You'll be fine."

"Thanks." Four grabs a plastic crate filled with paint from the back of the truck and starts toward the billboard. "See you around, A A Ron," he shouts over his shoulder.

I shake my head and ignore the idiot. He's sadly mistaken if he thinks I'll be seeing him around town. He'll be safer if I don't. It's best I help E and her baby. The little boy is really cute. I can see her in him, but he's definitely a Maxwell.

"Which Maxwell?" Brady is her age, but she had a crush on Aiden. The last I heard, Aiden was working with a country band in Tennessee.

"Aiden." She smiles with a faraway look in her eyes. Yep. She's madly in love. It's good Aiden came home.

"What are you doing out here?" I glance toward the billboard and back to her.

"The Hayden Sisters packs Four an all-day basket when he works on the billboards. No one else was able to bring it out here today." She shifts the baby to her other side.

"What's up with the billboards and Four?" I refuse to look in his direction again.

"The Town Council put billboards up on the main roads into town. Mick paints them for town events, festivals, and holidays." She leans closer and lowers her voice. "It keeps him from tagging the buildings around town."

I roll my eyes and shake my head. This crazy town put up billboards to keep this idiot from spray painting nonsense on the store walls. There are four major roads into Hayden Falls. At least this keeps Mick out of everybody's hair and benefits the town. I still don't like the idea of E being out here alone with him. I don't think Mick would hurt her, but I don't like him. Besides, what would Aiden think? I'd be livid if my wife and baby were out here with Mick.

"You sure you don't need any help?" I motion toward her SUV.

"I'm sure. I was just dropping the basket off. Caleb and I are heading home now." She leans in and puts Little Caleb in his car seat.

"I'll follow you." I get in my truck and wait for her to pull ahead of me.

E holds her hand up and waves when she turns onto the road toward H. H. Maxwell Ranch. It makes sense for her and Aiden to live at the ranch. Her family owns the only bed and breakfast in the area. I started to book a room at The Magnolia Inn, but doing so would have announced my arrival. I'm not ready for everyone to know I'm here. If I'm lucky, I'll be out of here in two or three weeks and on my way back to North Carolina.

Staying with my Aunt Susie might feel a little crowded, but she assures me we can make do for a few weeks. Her two youngest children are still in high school. Tucker, her oldest, is on his own. Marley is in college in Missoula. She only comes home on the weekends. If I have to sleep on the couch, it'll be fine.

There are a lot of people in this town I never want to see again. Mick Calhoun sits at the top of that list. Wouldn't you know he'd be one of the first people I ran into? I'll have to avoid him like the plague for the rest of my visit, or I'll end up in jail.

There's another person I'll need to avoid while I'm here, but for different reasons. My heart can't handle seeing her again. If I had known going into the Army would cost me her, I never would have enlisted. I would have been happy working on one of the ranches around here or at a dead-end job in town if it meant I'd have her forever. Sadly, I was looking at the money situation and not listening to my heart. My Dad needed help financially to keep the house, and I thought joining the Army would give my future family a better start. I was wrong.

I rub the heel of my palm across my eye and shake the memories away. I can't think about Dad or her. Within a year of leaving, I lost them both. Dad's gone and never coming back. I was on an assignment and didn't receive word he had a heart attack until two weeks later. I didn't even make it home for his funeral. If he's looking down on me, he probably hates me.

She's still here. My aunt's store is near her shop on the square. Avoiding her is going to be hard. I'll have to do it, though. If I see her, I know every feeling I've buried of her will resurface. I still love her, but I won't admit it. There's nothing I can do about it anyway.

Needing to get my mind off her, I pass the lake and turn toward the mountain. My dad's old house is out here on Mountain Trail Road. You'd think the people in this town could come up with better street names. The house is why I'm here. I paid it off years ago. I pull into the driveway and stare at what was once my home. It's overgrown with weeds and bushes. It's seriously in need of some repairs. I don't know why I kept it. City Hall demands I do something about it, so here I am.

After walking around the place the best I can, I head to Aunt Susie's house for dinner and to get settled in. I'm not going to City Hall until Monday morning. I have three days to lay around and do nothing. Only I won't. Tomorrow and Saturday, all the stores will be open. I'll wander around town, hiding in the shadows. Yeah. I'm going to try and catch a glimpse of her. My heart's a fool. He's not listening to my head. Since I'm here, I might as well twist the jagged knife in my heart a little deeper.

Chapter Two

Kennedy

Fridays can be more hectic for me than most people's Mondays. Owning the only beauty salon in town is awesome and tiring. Actually, other than counting the restaurants in Hayden Falls as a group, every store here is one of a kind. Fridays can be crazy for the salon. It's surprising how many women call or show up, believing we can work them in. Those ladies always have an emergency linked with a sad story. If any of my girls have an opening, we fall for it every time.

Yesterday afternoon was booked solid for us. Today is Senior Day at the high school. The girls had us working past closing this week with new styles, cuts, perms, and highlights. This year's Senior girls are going dressed to impress. Their parents paid handsomely and tipped on top of the regular fees. My girls and I aren't complaining.

Peyton and I overslept this morning. We didn't have time to fix breakfast. I can't send her to school without something to eat. We'll run into the diner to get her a sausage biscuit and a hashbrown. She can eat in the car on the way to school. I called the elementary school and let them know Peyton would be late. It'll only be an hour, so it's not a huge deal. There's only one more week of school, and my daughter doesn't want to miss any days. The third grade may not sound like a big deal to most of us, but it is to Peyton. She's working on getting a perfect attendance award this year. Being late is better than skipping an entire day.

Peyton quickly unbuckles her seatbelt once I park the car on the square across from the bookstore. This is one time a drive-thru would be handy. She grabs my hand, and we run across the street to Davis's Diner. I called Miss Cora with our order before we left the apartment. We hurry inside and rush to the front counter.

"Jeffrey!" Peyton shouts and runs across the dining room.

We don't have time for her to run off. I spin around to find my best friend, Tara, having breakfast with her husband and their son. Jeffrey is in Peyton's class. Looks like we're not the only ones running late this morning. I pay for our order and hurry over to their table.

"Can we join them?" Peyton has already climbed into the chair next to Jeffrey.

"We're running late, Pumpkin," I remind her.

"We are, too," Jeffrey said.

"Slow down, little Mama," Phillip smirks and takes a sip of his coffee.

"What's the rush? The school won't mind if Peyton's a little late." Tara pats the empty seat next to her.

I'd love to join them, but I can't. Why couldn't today be Saturday? I hate rushing.

"Mama is going to miss an appointment," Peyton explained.

Tara raises an eyebrow. I drop my head back and take a deep breath. I was an idiot to agree to an early appointment at the salon. Mrs. Douglas talked me into moving her afternoon wash and style to nine this morning. She has a doctor's appointment in Missoula just after lunch. I told her I would try to get to the salon a few minutes before nine.

Tara grabs my wrist. "Slow down and breathe." She lightly laughs. "We're running late too. The school is fine with it. I'm sure you've already called them."

"Yeah." I nod and take the to-go cup of coffee Miss Cora brings over. I left it on the counter. She sets Peyton's orange juice on the table in front of her.

"We can take Peyton to school with Jeffrey," Tara offers. "You can relax and head on to the salon."

Relax? That's not happening. The one time I agreed to an early appointment, I overslept. My day will only go downhill from here.

"You don't mind?" This will really help me out.

"Not at all." Phillip ruffles Peyton's hair. "We've got the little lady."

"Uncle Phillip." Peyton laughs and bats his hand away.

Phillip Crawford is not my daughter's biological uncle, but he accepted the position. Phillip has always been polite to Peyton and me. While he and Tara were apart, I only spoke to him in passing and only if I had to. Since they've gotten back together, Phillip has proven he's not the jerk we all believed him to be.

"Dad." Jeffrey slaps his hand on the table, not too hard, though. "You don't mess with a girl's hair."

Tara and I laugh. Jeffrey may be small, but he watches everything.

"My son is very wise." Phillip wiggles Jeffrey's black baseball cap around on his head. He smiles at Peyton. "I'm sorry, little lady."

"It's okay, Uncle Phillip." Peyton smiles up at me. Her eyes drop to the takeout bag in my hand.

"Right." I hurry and pull her food from the bag.

"Here you go, sweetie." Miss Cora brings Peyton a plate.

I set her biscuit and hashbrown on the plate. She needs ketchup. I grab the bottle from the table next to them.

"Bye, Pumpkin. I'll see you after school." I kiss the top of her head.

"Bye, Mama." Peyton waves and turns back to Jeffrey. He's her best friend. When they're together, she hardly notices me.

"Thank you." I hug Tara and wave to Phillip.

Yes, my friends gave me the extra time I needed this morning. I still hurry down the sidewalk to Kenny's Kuts. Mrs. Douglas is one of my best customers. She comes in every Friday for a professional wash and style. I don't want to lose her. I have about fifteen minutes until she arrives and at least an hour until we officially open. The other girls will be here by then.

I love the warmer months. We open at ten and close at five. During the winter, our hours are eleven to four. Of course, there are always exceptions. Sometimes, we take late appointments, and emergencies do happen. Trust me. An unsupervised kid with scissors can do a lot of damage. Special occasions also have us staying late.

Thankfully, people move out of my way as I rush down the sidewalk. I practically skid to a stop in front of the salon's door. Juggling my coffee and takeout bag, I dig through my purse for my keys. It's not an easy task. A sigh of relief rushes out as I finally push the salon door open and still have everything in my hands. I quickly set everything on the reception desk before rushing back to lock the door. I'm okay with letting Mrs. Douglas in early, but not anyone else. If the people roaming around town see me in here, they'll want in just to gossip. My girls and I try not to participate, but you'd be surprised at how much gossip you hear in a beauty salon.

A cold chill runs down my back as I flip the lock, causing me to shudder. I'm not superstitious or anything, but that felt weird. Without opening the door, I look out the front windows. People are moving around the town square as they usually do. I don't see Mrs. Douglas yet.

My eyes drift across the street to the Gazebo in the center of the town square. People are crossing the square, but nothing looks out of place. My eyes catch on a man dressed in a black jacket walking away. He crosses North Main Street, the opposite street from my salon. I watch as he disappears between the bank and the barbershop.

Is he why I had the strange feeling? I huff out a laugh and shake my head. I'm being ridiculous. There's nothing wrong with someone wearing a black jacket and blue baseball cap. Blue baseball cap. I close my eyes and cover my mouth with my hand. I hate it when memories sneak up on me like this. Blue baseball caps aren't forbidden around here. A few guys wear them from time to time. I'll just put a black cap in my bag and pass it on to the guy if I see him again.

A light tap at the window pulls me from my thoughts. Mrs. Douglas is a few minutes early. I hurry and let her in.

"Thank you so much for doing this." Mrs. Douglas smiles sweetly.

"It's not a problem," I assure her. She doesn't need to know how my morning has gone so far.

I'll wash her hair and eat my breakfast while she sits under the blow dryer. Hopefully, the rest of my day will go much better. It definitely will when I pick Peyton up after school. I glance out the front windows again. The man in the blue cap is long gone.

Chapter Three

Aaron

Coming here was a mistake. A huge mistake. It's just as bad as my decision to join the Army right out of high school. My dad tried to talk me out of it. I wish I had listened to him. Sadly, I knew everything back then, and no one could change my mind. I was an idiot who knew nothing. Why I stayed in for six years is an even bigger mystery. Well, no, it's not. I had nothing left. After my first three years, military life was all I knew, so I signed up for another three. When it was over, I had no reason to come back to Montana. One of my Army buddies was from a little town in North Carolina. I followed him home. I've lived there for four years, and it still doesn't feel like home.

I planned on walking around town yesterday to see all the changes. Surprisingly, there were a few new shops on the square. Beth's Morning Brew serves the best coffee in the state, or so I hear. I never made it inside. The bookstore, Page Turners, is on the corner of South Main Street and a couple of doors down from my aunt's shop.

Kenny's Kuts is on the other corner of the street. About four years ago, the beauty salon started showing up in town celebration photos my aunt sent me. Seeing Kennedy Reed run down the sidewalk and rushing inside was all I could take of the town yesterday. Pain tore through my heart at the sight of her. It was harder than I imagined it would be. Immediately, I turned and walked away.

Tonight, I'm here to drink my troubles away. A man pulls out the chair across from me. Without being invited, he makes himself comfortable. I groan. I didn't want company.

"You're being a creeper." Tucker Wallace, my cousin, narrows his eyes at me. He's a little upset. His mom didn't tell him I was coming to town.

"I'm just being me." My eyes flick past him to the dance floor.

If I thought my few minutes in town yesterday were hard, coming to Cowboys tonight is an even bigger mistake. Apparently, I managed to show up on a Girl's Night Out or something. A huge group of women are line dancing together. Their tables are across the dance floor from me and in the other corner.

Somehow, I managed to get the one table on the dance floor level no one wanted. Even though this little table is close to the stage, it's the only one between the steps to the upper level and the stage. There's a stool against the wall between the stage and me. I'm not sure why it's there. Maybe the performers use it from time to time. This table might be for them. If I'm not supposed to sit here, Jake Campbell hasn't said anything.

"If this is the new you, you need to lighten up. What you're doing is bordering on stalking." Tucker sets a beer in front of me and twists the top off his own.

"Trust me. I'm not stalking." I open the beer and take a sip.

"You sure about that?" Noah Welborn grabs the stool and joins us.

"Yeah." I lean slightly to the left to glance over his shoulder at the dance floor.

"You're wrong, man." Noah leans to block my view.

"About what?" I give the bar owner my full attention.

"Lots of things." Noah crosses his arms over his chest.

"You wanna be a bit more specific?" I don't know why he's coming down on me like this.

"Let's start with the fact you didn't tell anybody you were coming to town." Noah jabs his finger in my direction. "And that's not your biggest screw-up."

"I don't have your number," I mumble. It's a lame excuse.

"That's because you changed your number and deleted everybody here from your life but your family." Noah's mad. I knew he would be.

Noah and I were best friends growing up. Up until the eleventh grade, he was my only friend. It was the year Mark Bevins' family moved to Hayden Falls. Mark's grandfather owns a software and technology company in Denver. His Dad was here to test a remote site for the company. It didn't work out. According to Aunt Susie, Mark's family moved back to Colorado a year after I joined the Army.

Mark was in my homeroom and nearly every class I had. Noah and Mark didn't get along. For some reason, they didn't trust each other. I haven't talked to Noah since I left for boot camp. The last letter I got from Mark said Kennedy Reed was pregnant and getting married. It was the day my life changed forever.

"I don't have his number." Tucker leans back in his chair.

Noah's eyebrows nearly hit his hairline. The only person in this town with my number is Tucker's mother. At one point, I even threatened to never speak to Aunt Susie again. It wasn't my proudest moment. She's my dad's sister and all I have left of him. Well, her and a rundown house.

"You wanna tell us what happened to you? Why did you cut us all off?" Noah pops the top of a soda. He must not drink alcohol when he's working.

I huff and shake my head. This is Hayden Falls. Everybody knows everybody's business. It doesn't take a rocket scientist to figure out things. Noah and Tucker are smart men. They can put two and two together. I don't need to explain anything.

"Come on, Aaron. You need to give us something here." Noah waits for an explanation that's not coming. I stare at him like he's crazy. He turns to Tucker.

Tucker shrugs. "I have no clue."

"You guys can't be that stupid." My eyes drift past them to the dance floor again.

Both men look over their shoulders. My old high school girlfriend is drinking, dancing, and having the time of her life. Lucky her.

"You should go talk to her," Tucker suggests.

"Are you insane?" I gawk at my cousin.

"No," Noah replies. I wasn't talking to him. "You *need* to talk to her."

"I have nothing to say to her." My voice drops low and hard.

Noah and Tucker share a knowing look. Yeah, they were here and saw the whole fiasco play out.

"You might be wrong on that." Tucker strums his fingers on the table. It's annoying. Still, I don't know why he thinks I'm wrong.

"You should let her explain," Noah said.

"You both need to explain," Tucker adds.

"She got pregnant and married someone else." I toss my hands up. "What's to explain?"

"All of it," Tucker replied.

Noah looks over his shoulder again to the happy group of women on the dance floor and back to me. "Yeah, we know that's what happened." He lowers his voice. "But nobody knows the details."

Tucker nods. "Something's not right about it."

I huff out a breath and close my eyes for a moment. "Of course, something's not right. The woman I loved cheated on me weeks after I left, got pregnant, and had to get married."

I know we're Small Town USA here, but even these two fools can figure this one out. None of us mentioned she got divorced in less than a year. I called my aunt a few weeks after the divorce was final. Aunt Susie told me about it. It's the only conversation I regret having with my aunt. I told her if she was going to talk about Kennedy, then I was never calling her again. My aunt hasn't mentioned Kennedy Reed in almost nine years. Yeah, she slips in photos with Kennedy or her shop in the background. I don't say anything. It's best to stay quiet.

"No." Noah shakes his head. "There's more to it than that."

Tucker's nodding again. I don't care what these two think. I know all I need to know. However, I don't understand how everybody here doesn't know all the details. You can't keep secrets in this little town.

A shout comes from the pool tables area. Noah groans and drops his head back. Everyone else acts like it's a typical Saturday night. Maybe it is. Four and Pit are playing pool. I noticed them when I walked in. I've been avoiding looking in their direction.

"I don't think I've ever seen those two argue with each other," Tucker said. They're definitely disagreeing about something.

"When they're drunk, anything can happen." Noah looks to the upper level. He motions with his head toward the pool tables.

One of the Barnes brothers nods and walks over to Four and Pit. I'm not sure which Barnes this is. It's either Lucas or Leo. Both were interested in becoming deputies in high school. I think it's the same Barnes who was watching me on the square yesterday morning. I can't be sure, though. I never could tell them apart. Four shouts something obnoxious, but the good deputy settles him down quickly. I glance at Kennedy again. She hasn't noticed me yet. She's not paying any attention to what's going on at the pool tables either.

"How can she stand being here when he is?" I don't want to be anywhere near Mick Calhoun.

"None of us like it when Four gets drunk. He didn't used to be so mean," Tucker replied.

Mean? I don't like the sound of that. If I have to witness Mick being mean to someone, I'll end up in jail for sure.

"I have to throw him out at least once a week now," Noah said.

Four breaks out into some crazy dance with the pool stick. Even Pit looks mortified. That's it. I can't take any more of this fool. I shouldn't have come here tonight.

"I'm out of here." I stand to leave.

Noah stands and grabs my wrist. "Give me your number." I raise an eyebrow. He's not asking. "Come on, man. You were my best friend. You're not shutting me out again."

I sigh. Reconnecting with people here wasn't part of my plan. But he's right. We were best friends. He deserves answers. I'm just not ready to give them to him. It's a bad idea, but I give Noah and Tucker my number. To be honest, I've missed these two. Tucker was an automatic brother and best friend since birth. He's only a year younger than me.

More shouts come from the pool tables. I don't bother to look, but I see a couple more men heading in that direction. After telling Noah and Tucker goodbye, I duck my head and use the upper level to slip out of the bar. Going across the dance floor would have taken me by *her*. I'm trying not to get too close to her.

Chapter Four

Kennedy

"Hey, Miss Susie!" Peyton runs into Enchanted Stitches ahead of me and wraps her arms around Miss Susie's waist.

"Hey, Pumpkin. How are you?" Miss Susie hugs my overly excited daughter.

"It's the last week of school. I'm so excited!" Peyton claps and bounces on her toes.

"Are you ready for your fitting?" Miss Susie asked.

"Yes!" Peyton shouts a little too loudly.

Peyton has been super hyper since I picked her up at school an hour ago. The elementary school has an early release at one o'clock for the last week of school. I swear the teachers loaded the kids up on sweet snacks before sending them home. We even stopped at our apartment for thirty minutes before coming here. She's still bouncing off the walls.

Mrs. Wallace goes into the back of the shop and returns with Peyton's dance costume. She's told us all to call her Miss Susie. I struggle to do so. The younger kids don't have a problem with it. She's a special lady and well-loved in this town.

Peyton's dress is beautiful. It's a simple design. It reminds me of a sundress with a flared skirt. Of course, there's a pair of matching shorts underneath it, in case she twirls enough to lift the skirt too high while she's on stage. The dress is red, white, and blue. The shorts are blue.

"Did Jeffrey get his costume yet?" Peyton is always looking out for her best friend.

Peyton wanted to take dance classes so badly, but she refused to do anything if Jeffrey couldn't do it with her. Next school term, they're going to play in the school band. She wants to play the clarinet, and Jeffrey will play the drums. It was his father's idea.

When I mentioned during the adult dance classes how disappointed Peyton was, Hannah quickly found a solution. Jeffrey was born prematurely and has asthma. He was a very sick baby for the first few months. For the most part, he's now a happy, healthy little boy. He just can't play any sports because he gives out of breath. Peyton and Jeffrey take private classes on Saturdays from Hannah. Yes, they do this at the same time. Hannah can monitor Jeffrey's activity and slow him down if needed. Jeffrey and Peyton are Hannah's only child couple dancers. They're performing on stage during the Memorial Day Festival.

"He should be here any minute." Mrs. Wallace opens the fitting room door. "Do you need help?"

"No, ma'am. I can do it." Peyton steps inside and closes the door.

Mrs. Wallace walks over and hugs me. "It's good to see you."

I lightly laugh as I return her hug. "You see me every day."

We do see each other every day. Our shops are on the same side of the town square. Sometimes, we wave to each other through the front windows. Other times, we stop and talk for a few minutes on the sidewalk. Talking to her is hard sometimes. She's Aaron's aunt. Half the time, I don't know what to say to her. She's never mentioned Aaron to me since he left for the Army. Several times over the years, I wanted to ask her about him, but I never did. His wife wouldn't like his old girlfriend checking up on him.

We're coming up on the tenth anniversary of Aaron leaving. It's the worst day of my life. Well, that's not true. The worst day was when his friend told me Aaron had fallen in love with someone else and never wanted to hear from me again. I couldn't care less about how Aaron Bailey is doing. That's a lie, too, but I'll never admit it. It doesn't matter anyway. He's never coming back to Hayden Falls. The bell over the door jingles, pulling me from my thoughts.

"Aunt Kennedy!" Jeffrey runs across the shop to me.

"Slow down, Buddy," his Mom calls out.

It's only a short distance from the door to me. It shouldn't set off his asthma, but Tara worries about him no matter how short it is. I can't say I blame her. He's had a couple of asthma attacks since they moved to Hayden Falls. They scared me so badly I wanted to call 911. Thankfully, Tara was there and knew exactly what to do. Jeffrey isn't my blood nephew, but I love him as if he were. I hope the little guy never has another asthma attack.

"Hey, Buddy." I wiggle his baseball cap on his head and smile at his Mom.

"Here you go, young man." Mrs. Wallace comes out with Jeffrey's costume.

Tara and I move to the viewing area while Jeffrey enters another dressing room. Naturally, his costume matches Peyton's. He has blue pants, a white shirt, and a red bow tie. He's not happy he has to give his black baseball cap up while he's on stage. Hannah can't get him to take it off during practice. Phillip wears one, too. Jeffrey wants to be just like his father. I used to believe Jeffrey looked like his mother. After seeing him and Phillip together, I can honestly say I was wrong. He's Phillip's little mini-me.

Peyton bursts out of the dressing room. "Mama, look at me." She rushes to the mirrors and spins so fast it makes me dizzy.

Wow. The skirt of her dress flares out in a way I'd never imagined it would. Mrs. Wallace did a fantastic job on it. The dress is white with red and blue panels in the skirt. You really see those when Peyton spins. Of course, the top has jeweled embezzlements. Peyton told Hannah she wanted to be flashy—her choice of words, not mine. I have to laugh. My child is so silly sometimes. She will flash, though. The sunlight will catch on those rhinestones. I hope the pictures and videos capture their sparkle so she can see it.

The front door flies open as Phillip rushes in. "Did I miss it?"

"No. He's getting dressed now." Tara wraps her arms around his waist. "You didn't have to be here today. It's just his fitting."

Phillip looks at his wife like she's crazy. "Of course, I had to be here. It's his first fitting. I can't miss it. Besides, I promised him."

Who would have thought Phillip Crawford would be a loving family man? I sure didn't. Two-thirds of this town would have never believed it either. Since Phillip found out about Jeffrey last fall, he's proved us all wrong. He became more than Tara could have hoped for. They got married a few days after Christmas. I'm happy for them. I really am.

"What about me, Uncle Phillip?" Peyton drops her head and slides one foot back and forth.

Immediately, my heart breaks. She wants what Jeffrey has. Jeffrey thought his father didn't want him. Tara and Jeffrey didn't know Phillip's parents hid the fact he had a son from him for eight years. Peyton hasn't said anything to me, but I see it. She wants her dad, too. It's the one thing I can't give her. Surprisingly, Phillip stepped up and has included Peyton in everything he does with Jeffrey. My father and brother are there for her, too. I'm grateful for all they do, but it's not the same as the love of a father would be.

"Of course, I'm here to see your fitting, too, little lady." Phillip hurries over to and takes Peyton's hand. He twirls her under his arm and helps her onto the wooden pedestal in front of the mirrors.

"It's beautiful." Peyton giggles.

"You're beautiful. Without you, it's just fabric." Phillip twirls her again so she can see the skirt flare out. His words almost have me in tears. Tara's blinking back tears, too. Naturally, Peyton eats his words up.

"Thank you, Uncle Phillip." She wraps her arms around him.

"This feels weird." Jeffrey frowns as he looks down at his costume.

Phillip and Peyton grin at each other and share a knowing look. Phillip winks at her, and Peyton nods her head. What is that about?

"But you look so handsome." Peyton hurries to Jeffrey and grabs his hand. She pulls him over to the wooden pedestal and steps up beside him. "See how great we look together?"

Jeffrey grins at her in the mirror. She's a little taller than him, but he doesn't seem to mind. "Yeah. We look good."

Tara, Phillip, and I laugh. They do look good together. I'm so glad my best friend's son is best friends with my little girl.

A loud crash comes from the back of the shop, drawing our attention. Mrs. Wallace hurries behind the curtain to check it out. She has a few ladies working for her. I hope they're okay. Phillip gets the kids' attention back to their costumes. For some reason, my gaze stays on the curtain to the back room.

"Are you okay?" Tara whispers.

"Yeah. Of course, I am." I have no clue why she asked me that. I didn't drop anything.

Before I can ask my friend if something is up, Mrs. Wallace rushes back into the room. She makes a beeline to Peyton and Jeffrey. My eyes are still glued to the curtain. I can't explain the strange feeling that's come over me.

As the curtain falls back into place, I catch a glimpse of someone in a blue baseball cap hurrying out the back door. I gasp and slowly move to the curtain. It can't be. I push the fabric aside and see no one in the back workroom. I turn, and my eyes lock with Mrs. Wallace's. She can't hold my gaze. She bites her lip and turns back to the kids.

Tara's eyes bounce between Mrs. Wallace and me. Phillip seems clueless. He's praising both kids, and that's perfectly fine with me. Tara and I need to talk, though. By her reaction and Mrs. Wallace's, I have no doubts that Aaron Bailey is indeed in Hayden Falls.

Chapter Five

Aaron

Yesterday was another mistake. Showing up at City Hall to annoyingly surprise the Mayor completely backfired on me. The wonderful Mayor Martin wasn't in his office. Mrs. Barnes made me an appointment for today so I could speak with the Mayor and his son. I arrived five minutes early. Wouldn't you know it, the Mayor is already ten minutes late. Punctuality isn't a thing here. Instead of me annoying them, they're seriously ticking me off. There's no doubt in my mind that this meeting will be a disaster. I should just get up and leave.

I left City Hall yesterday and surprised my aunt at her clothing store. Yeah, I used the back entrance to keep from being seen. After today, hiding in the shadows will be pointless. Most of the townsfolk probably already know I'm here. It's impossible to hide in this town for two weeks. I was hoping for a little more time, though.

Aunt Susie opened Enchanted Stitches before I was born. It was a dream she and her mother had. The store officially opened the first week in June after Aunt Susie graduated from high school. My aunt and grandmother prepared for a year for their Grand Opening. Aunt Susie is a wonderful seamstress, but all the clothes she sells aren't made here. She does special orders for people all the time. She stays booked with prom dresses, weddings, baby clothes, cheerleading outfits, and costumes for Halloween, the church, and schools. Now she has dance costumes because of the new dance studio.

Leave it to me to show up at my aunt's shop on the day Kennedy Reed's daughter has a costume fitting. Aunt Susie tried to hurry me out the back door before they entered. Stubborn me didn't realize what she was doing until it was too late. I didn't know Kennedy's baby was a little girl. When I cut ties with this town years ago, I refused to listen to anything if it didn't pertain to my family members. I didn't get a good look at the little girl, but she had her mother's long light brown hair.

Jumping back into stalker mode, I peeped through the curtains separating the front of the shop from the work area. Mainly, I just listened to everything going on in the shop. My aunt seems to love Kennedy's little girl. Pumpkin is a cute nickname. Pumpkin pie is my favorite dessert.

Hearing Phillip Crawford being overly friendly with Kennedy and her daughter pissed me off. I peeped through the curtains several times. From the looks of things, he's married to Tara Adams now, and they have a son. Phillip isn't a problem. Still, hearing him praise the little girl made my blood boil. I had to get out of there before I did something stupid. I did something stupid anyway. In my haste to leave, I knocked a container of sewing tools to the floor. The loud crash had my aunt bursting into the room. I don't know what all the tools were, but she insisted everything was fine. I turned and bolted for the door before I could make things worse.

The door to the Mayor's office finally opens. Quinn Martin steps out. Guess I'm seeing both Martins today. Quinn is the town lawyer. If he's needed, maybe I should have brought a lawyer too.

"Come on in, Aaron." Quinn motions for me to enter the office.

"Good to see you, young man." Mayor Martin stands and shakes my hand over his desk. "Glad you're in town.

The Mayor sits back down before I can speak. The man acts like it was a great inconvenience for him to stand up and greet me. Quinn motions for me to take a seat. He sits in the chair next to me.

"I didn't have a choice." I hold up the letter I received from City Hall.

"Ah, yes. We've been working on cleaning up Hayden Falls," Mayor Martin said.

I nod as though I understand. I get it, but they could have let me handle things remotely. Aunt Susie could have handled the in-person visits for me if those were necessary. This little town is small, but it can't be that far behind in times.

"What exactly do you want me to do?" I ask.

"Clean it up," the Mayor replied harshly.

How did this man ever get voted into a public office? He didn't use to be this rude. Maybe politics has gone to his head. By the Mayor's attitude today, this is one field I never want to go into.

"Yeah. I get you want that, but why did I have to come here? Aunt Susie could have taken care of most of this. The rest I could do online or over the phone." I don't mean to snap, but his attitude is setting mine off.

"It's not your aunt's responsibility. It's yours. Clean it up or sell it," Mayor Martin demanded.

Before I can reply, which is probably not wise right now, a knock comes on the door. Judge Morgan opens it and sticks his head in. "Can I see you in my office?"

"Sure thing." Mayor Martin starts toward the door. "Quinn, handle this." With that, he's gone.

I rub my hands over my face. The man insisted on seeing me, and then he ditches? It makes no sense. His son now has to clean up this mess. I turn to Quinn and wait. If his attitude is anything like his father's, we should go ahead and call the Sheriff's Office.

"Forgive my Dad." Quinn rolls his eyes and shakes his head. It's very unprofessional of him and not what I expected. "He's forgotten how to talk to people."

"Really? I couldn't tell," I say dryly.

Quinn chuckles. "Yeah." He points to the envelope in my hand. "My father forgets to tell people the reason those were sent out. A couple of years ago, several teens were going into abandoned places. Not all of them were homes. A couple of the boys got hurt. It was mostly cuts, scrapes, and bruises. The worst was a broken leg. The parents freaked out and demanded the Town Counsel do something."

Okay. I understand why they're doing this. Teens with nothing to do can get into a lot of trouble. Hayden Falls doesn't offer a lot of recreational activities for them. My friends and I used to check abandoned buildings out when we were in middle school and early high school. The last couple of years of high school, we all discovered girls and found a whole new line of trouble.

Quinn continues, "The town offers to buy the properties with back taxes if the owners don't want them anymore."

"I pay the taxes," I point out. I don't know why I do. I just couldn't part with the place. It's all I have left of my dad.

"I know. You're one of the few who has paid them. You can clean it up and sell it if you don't want to live there. If the house isn't worth saving, you could also bulldoze it down and sell the property," Quinn suggested.

"I stopped by there on my way into town. The place is seriously overgrown. The best I could tell, it looked pretty sound." Bulldozing it down will be a last resort.

Quinn nods. "Miles checked it out last year. He thought the same thing."

Miles Hamilton wanted to be a firefighter. He was a good guy from what I can remember of him. Did he get his dream career? If I hadn't joined the Army, becoming a firefighter was next on my list.

"I'll figure it out." I stand. This meeting was pointless.

"There is another option." Quinn stands as well.

"Yeah?" Of course, there's another option. I have several going through my head.

"You could fix the house up and move back," Quinn suggests.

I raise an eyebrow. "You want me to move back to Hayden Falls?"

"I do," Quinn replies. "You'll always be a part of this town. We'd love to have your family here."

That's strange. He knows every member of my family. "My family already lives here."

Quinn's eyebrows draw together. He's thinking hard about something. Finally, he nods. "Okay. Well, we'd love to have you back. People miss you, man." His voice drops, but I hear him. "A couple needs you."

That's even stranger. I'd love to know what he means, but I'm not discussing my personal life with anybody here. It would be on their little gossip blog before sunset. Yeah, I know all about Hayden Happenings. I don't feel bad about not sharing my life with Quinn. I don't even tell Aunt Susie everything.

"For now, I'll just start cleaning the place up. I'll figure out the rest as I go." I need to get out of here. I grab the door handle.

"Aaron?" Quinn calls out. I turn to face him. He's holding a couple of business cards. I already have his number. "Wade Lunsford has a landscaping business. He might be able to help with the cleanup. If the house is still sound, Sawyer Gibson remodels and builds houses. I'm sure he can help."

"Thanks." I take the cards. "I'll call them." The more help I get, the faster I can get out of this town.

Quinn holds his hand out. "Thank you for your service. We're all proud of you." I take his hand. He's nothing like his father. "For what it's worth, I hope you decide to stay."

"Thanks, man." I nod and hurry out the door.

Me? Stay in Hayden Falls? I drop my head back and laugh as I walk down the front steps of City Hall. Quinn seems genuine, but he's insane. I have no intention of staying in this town.

Chapter Six

Aaron

Since everyone probably knows I'm here, I might as well see if Beth's Morning Brew really does make the best coffee in Montana. A good cup of coffee will help lift my grumpy mood after dealing with the Mayor. I hope the people in this town wise up during their next election and vote for somebody with a brain. This trip was a waste of time and money.

Walking into the coffee shop was another mistake. My list of mistakes is getting longer by the minute. I can't keep up with them anymore. Kennedy Reed just paid for her order and moved to the lower counter to wait. I'd turn around and leave if it wouldn't be obvious to everyone I'm avoiding her. I may still be mad about what happened between us, but I don't want to be outright rude. The people in this town can be brutal with their gossip and guilt shaming. Then again, why should I care? She's the one who cheated. Still, I mind my manners and get in line to wait my turn. The door jingles when a new customer enters. I don't turn around.

Beth Murphy steps up to the cash register. “Aaron Baily, welcome home.”

“Beth.” This isn’t home, but I won’t tell her that. She’s smiling, and I don’t want to take it away.

“What can I get you?”

“A medium regular coffee with lots of cream and two sugars.” I pull my wallet from my back pocket.

“No charge.” She pushes some buttons on the register, and the price falls to zero.

“Uh. Why?”

“Thank you for your service, Aaron. We’re all proud of you.” Beth smiles. She sounds like Quinn.

“I can pay for my coffee,” I insist. Sure, there are guys out there who look for discounts. Every soldier deserves it, but I’ve never been comfortable with people giving me stuff. I prefer to pay my way.

“You can pay for the next one. This one is on me.” Beth reaches for a to-go cup.

Okay. This won’t be an everyday thing. I can handle that. Still, I want to do something. “Then I want to pay for the next customer’s drink.”

I step aside and motion for the woman behind me to step forward. Beth glares holes into her. Welcome to another bad idea. It’s the story of my life lately.

“Um.” The woman seems unsure.

“Please, I insist.” I’m not earning any brownie points with Beth, but it’ll be all right. I’m not collecting points, and it’s not like I live here.

“What can I get you?” Beth’s words are cold.

“A medium Strawberry Refresher with coconut milk, please.” The woman drops her eyes from Beth’s hard gaze.

I swipe my credit card and move to the lower counter. There’s a customer waiting between Kennedy and me. Her drink arrives first. Great. Now I have to stand here between my ex-girlfriend and the woman I bought the drink for. I glance at both women from the corners of my eyes. Both are fidgeting. I get why Kennedy isn’t comfortable, but I don’t know what’s up with Karlee Davis.

“Here you go, Kennedy.” Hadley Lunsford slides a drink across the counter.

“Thank you.” Kennedy snatches the cup up and turns toward the door. For a moment, our eyes meet. I don’t move. I can’t. “Aaron.”

“Kennedy.” I give her a firm nod and look away. So much for not being obvious.

Beth sets mine and Karlee’s drinks on the counter. “Have a great day, Aaron.” She fake smiles at Karlee but doesn’t speak to her.

Karlee takes her drink and gives me a genuine smile. “Thanks for this, Aaron. And thank you for your service.”

The front door slams shut, startling a few customers. It’s a wonder the glass didn’t break. Everyone in the coffee shop looks out the front window. Kennedy is storming across the square toward her salon. What’s her problem? She’s got no right to be mad.

“You’re welcome, Karlee.” I hold the door open for her. “Have a great day.”

She hurries down the sidewalk, past the bakery, toward her grandparents’ diner. The man coming out of the bakery is one of the two men I need to see. I left him a voicemail before going into the coffee shop. He spots me and grins.

“Aaron Bailey.”

“Wade Lunsford.”

I don’t get a handshake from him. Instead, Wade gives me a bro hug. He’s so odd. I hope the rest of the men in this town don’t hug. It’s uncomfortable.

“I got your message. I can definitely help you clean your dad’s place up,” Wade said.

Well, that’s good to know. It’s one thing marked off my to-do list. Even though I’ve owned the house for about eight years, it will forever be my dad’s place to the people around here.

“Thanks, man. When would you like to look at the place?” I’m ready to get off the street. The looks I’m getting from people passing by are unsettling.

“How about we meet up there this Saturday around lunchtime?” Wade suggested.

"Yeah. Sounds good." It's a horrible idea. I prefer to get this over with today. Saturday means I'm staying in town longer than I want to.

"Sawyer has that day free, too. I called him a few minutes ago. I'll let him know to meet us there," Wade offers.

I need Sawyer Gibson, too. "Once we agree on terms and a price, can you do this without me being here?"

"You're not staying?" Wade looks shocked.

"Nah, man." I press my lips together and shake my head. "I wouldn't be here now if the Mayor hadn't insisted on seeing me."

"But…" Wade glances toward the beauty salon. "I thought…" He shakes his head. "Never mind. Not my business."

I nod. If he thinks I'd hang around for Kennedy Reed, he's got another thing coming. Coming back for her is in the past. I don't want a woman I can't trust. It's best we don't talk about her.

"If you get an opening before Saturday, let me know." The quicker I get out of here, the better it will be for everybody.

"It's doubtful, but sure." Wade offers me his hand. "We're all meeting at Cowboys Friday night. Hope to see you there."

"Maybe." I shake his hand and walk to my aunt's shop. Going here is too close to Kennedy, but I parked my truck behind Enchanted Stitches.

As I reach the door, I notice Tara Adams, now Crawford, running from Petals Florist. She spots me and comes to a halt outside the beauty salon. She glances into the salon and back at me. Tara huffs and shakes her head. Her eye roll was loud. Yeah, you can't hear eye rolls, but I did on that one. With one final glare of disgust at me, Tara rushes into Kenny's Kuts.

What is up with the people in this town? It makes no sense for them to be mad at me. I went away to fight for our country. My girlfriend cheated the moment I was gone. How does that make me the bad guy? These people are insane. I can't deal with this nonsense. I need to get back to North Carolina. If it weren't for the meeting I set up with Wade and Sawyer on Saturday, I'd get in my truck and leave right now. For the next four days, I'll have to stay out of town.

Chapter Seven

Kennedy

"Uh!" I storm into the salon and throw my cup of coffee across the room. Thankfully, there's only one customer in here.

"Kenny, what's wrong?" Savannah Edwards, one of my stylists, rushes to me and grabs my upper arms.

Lindsey Peterson, another one of my girls, runs to the front door. She flips the sign to *'closed'* and locks the door.

I scream again and push past Savannah. My body heaves with each breath I take. I'm standing in front of the display of professional shampoos and conditioners. Lindsey, Savannah, and Hope Gibson don't know what to do. I don't know either.

"Uh!" I scream again and push the display over.

Jade Walters, my stylist in training, wraps her arms around me from behind. I'm pinned down and can barely move.

"Calm down," Jade orders.

"Take deep breaths." Hope stands in front of me. I am breathing. Can't she see it?

Andi Crawford, our only customer at the moment, frantically digs her phone from her purse. She agreed to be Jade's test model for a wash, trim, and highlights today.

"Tara, get to the salon now," Andi says quickly. "Don't bring Jeffrey. It's bad."

Tara must have been in town. She gets here in less than five minutes. Hope locks the door behind her. My best friend takes one look at the mess I made and sighs. I wiggle to get out of Jade's hold, but she's surprisingly strong. It's probably best she doesn't trust me right now. The last thing I need to do is break some of the equipment in here. This stuff is expensive.

"We don't know what's wrong," Lindsey tells Tara.

"Oh, I saw what's wrong standing on the sidewalk just now." Tara moves in front of me. "What did he do?"

"He…" I take several quick breaths. Tara nods, encouraging me to continue. "He was at Beth's."

"That tells me where he was, not what he did." Tara cups my face in her hands. "He did something to upset you. Tell me what that is."

Well, it's obvious he upset me. I've never thrown a fit like this, not even when I lost him ten years ago.

"He bought Karlee Davis a drink." I finally get the words out.

Tara leans back in shock. "Okay," she says slowly. "I don't know why he'd buy her anything, but Aaron isn't crazy enough to get tangled up with Karlee."

"Aaron Bailey's in town?" Hope is as shocked as everyone else is.

"Yes." Tara looks each of my girls in the eye. "But nothing said here can leave this salon."

My four girls nod. Even Andi agrees. She's Jade's best friend and Tara's sister-in-law. If she spreads any of this around town, Tara and Phillip will handle her. Andi is actually turning out to be a better person than we all thought, just like her brother Phillip.

"Why did he buy her a drink?" Savannah scrunches up her face. Yeah, I'm disgusted about it, too.

"Beth gave him his for serving in the Army." I hiccup. "He bought the next person's."

Tara sighs and drops her head for a moment. Her eyes lift to mine again. "He didn't buy Karlee's drink because he likes her."

"He was paying it forward," Lindsey said.

"Everybody's doing it. It's all over social media right now," Hope adds. It doesn't make me feel any better.

"I don't care. It's Karlee," I cry. "She'll read more into it."

The girls look at each other. They all know I'm right. If a man is kind to Karlee, she'll chase after them. The thought of her with Aaron makes me sick. I wiggle again, but Jade doesn't release me. When the tears start to flow down my cheeks, Andi hands Tara some tissues. I don't know how I've held them back this long.

"Forget Karlee right now." Tara wipes my tears away. "Did Aaron say anything to you?"

"He just said my name in greeting. I did the same," I say between sobs. It was the coldest conversation I've ever had with him.

"You need to talk to him," Tara whispers.

"I can't." I shake my head and cry harder.

"It won't be easy, but you *need* to." Tara's eyes plead with me.

Tara is the only one who knows everything. She knows the truth. Everyone else, including my family, believes the lie. One lie that was meant to save me turned into my biggest mistake.

"No, Tara. I can't." I sniffle. "He hates me."

"You haven't seen him in ten years. He's the one who left and never came back. You should be the one hating him." Tara pulls a chair over. Jade releases me so I can sit.

"Trust me. He hates me." I take a ragged breath. "He won't look at me. Well, our eyes met for a moment. His hate for me was unmistakable."

"Do you have any appointments this afternoon?" Tara asked.

"No." I blow my nose. It's not ladylike, but crying does this to me. "I was supposed to supervise Jade's appointment with Andi."

Tara looks up at Jade and Andi. "Y'all need to reschedule that."

"I'm free next Tuesday if you can reschedule," Andi tells Jade.

"Are you sure?" Jade really needed this appointment. I hate she's even considering rescheduling because of me.

"Yeah." Andi waves her hand like it's no big deal. If she were still under her mother's influence, she'd be throwing a temper tantrum. I like this Andi much better. "I'd like to have it down before the Memorial Day Festival, though."

"Andi Crawford." Tara playfully narrows her eyes. "Are you trying to impress someone?"

"Oh, please." Andi rolls her eyes. "I'm trying to impress everyone."

The girls laugh. I try, but it's more like a choked cry. Andi might be fooling the others, but not me. I know the twinkle in her eyes all too well. She's got her sights set on somebody. She has nothing to worry about. I'll make sure Jade has her looking fabulous next week.

"Next Tuesday is fine with me." I point to the front desk. "Jade, reschedule Andi now before we're booked up."

"You should take the rest of the day off," Hope suggested.

"We can handle things here." Lindsey grabs a broom. "Right after we clean up."

"I'm sorry, guys." They shouldn't have to clean up my mess.

"Don't worry about it. We all have bad days," Savannah said.

"Where's Jeffrey?" I look out the front windows. I don't see Phillip with him on the swings.

"He's at Petals with Katie." Tara takes my arm and pulls me to my feet.

"I can walk Jeffrey over to Phillip," Andi offers.

"You don't mind?" Tara hands me another tissue.

"Of course not. I love my little nephew, and he loves me. I'm his cool aunt." Andi grins.

"You're his only aunt," I point out.

Andi flips her wrist. She doesn't care. Tara gives her instructions. My friend worries too much. Andi literally only has to walk Jeffrey across North Main Street, and they'll be at the bank. Phillip won't mind if Jeffrey comes and hangs out with him. Tara even calls Katie to let her know it's okay for Andi to pick Jeffrey up.

"I'll lock up. If you need tomorrow off, let me know," Savannah offers. She's a true blessing to me. She has a set of keys and has opened and closed the salon many times.

Tara walks me out to my car and takes my keys. I should have parked behind the salon today. At least a dozen people noticed I'd been crying.

"Did Aaron's wife come to Montana with him?" Tara glances at me from the corner of her eye as we drive to my apartment.

My mom has Peyton for a few more hours. I really need a little time alone with my best friend before I pick up my daughter. I hate how much seeing Aaron has messed me up.

"I don't know. He was alone when I saw him." I want to cry again.

Aaron Bailey is married to someone else. I don't want to meet the woman he chose over me. When Aaron left for boot camp, I thought our relationship was solid and strong. Apparently, a skinny little blonde with big blue eyes proved me wrong.

Chapter Eight

Aaron

Going to Cowboys is the last thing I want to do tonight. Wade invited me, and since I need his help, here I sit. Only this time, I'm not in the little corner between the steps and the stage. Tonight, I'm on full display for everyone. My cousin could have gotten us a table on the upper level where most of the men are. Most of the women sit at tables across the dance floor from us. My eyes drift to Kennedy way too often.

Noah comes over and joins us when he can spare a few minutes. Wade and Sawyer are on the way. I wish they'd hurry up. I need a distraction before I walk across the dance floor and do something stupid. Seeing my ex laughing and having a good time ticks me off.

It ticks me off even more that Kennedy is still beautiful. After what she did, I shouldn't be watching her, but I do. Why couldn't she have gained three hundred pounds and lost some hair or teeth? It's a gross thought, but maybe it would keep me from staring at her. No matter how much I fight it, I think she's beautiful. Memories of dating her have plagued my mind for days. If I'm being honest, memories of her have snuck up on me for ten years.

"Staring is rude," Noah says as he joins us.

"Why don't you just go talk to her?" Tucker asked. If only it were that simple.

"No." I grab a beer and glare at my cousin.

"I hear she really freaked out after running into you at Beth's." Noah opens a can of soda.

"What?" I snap my head in Kennedy's direction.

She was angry when she left Beth's, but I haven't heard anything about her freaking out. She didn't used to be highly emotional. Whatever happened must have been bad for Noah to hear about it. I shouldn't care, but I don't like the thought of her freaking out.

"Yep." Tucker nods. "It's all over town."

I cut my eyes at my cousin. "I haven't been in town since Tuesday."

One run-in with Kennedy was enough for me. I've spent my time between my aunt's house and my dad's place. I decided to put my anger to good use. Uncle Darren loaned me his tools. I managed to clear a path to the front and back doors of the old house. It'll make things easier when Wade and Sawyer stop by tomorrow.

I don't know why Kennedy freaked out. I only said one word to her. She has no right to be upset. She should be apologizing to me. Only I don't want to hear her apology. It'll just rip open old wounds. Wounds I let heal years ago. I rub my hand over my chest. Maybe they haven't healed. I'm not ready to analyze what I feel, though.

"Just talk to her," Noah insists.

I toss my hands up. "Why does everybody keep saying that?"

Noah lowers his voice. "Because they need you."

They need me? I've heard that more than once. Who are they? Are people referring to my family or Kennedy and her daughter? Do my friends and family want me to take care of another man's child? Could I raise another man's child? I could, but knowing Kennedy cheated on me and conceived the child makes it hard for me. Yeah, it makes me sound like a jerk, but I can't help how I feel.

It's not the little girl's fault things are this way. It's not the little girl's fault her parents are divorced, either. Her father is across the room right now. Surely, he takes care of his daughter even though he's no longer with Kennedy. I highly doubt it, though.

Noah leaves when one of the bartenders shouts for him. My eyes, once again, drift to Kennedy. The sight before me has my blood boiling. Four has left the pool tables and is now dancing around Kennedy and her friends. I stand, but Tucker grabs my wrist and shakes his head. Fine. I'll leave it be for now.

Aiden Maxwell stands and shouts, "Keep moving, Calhoun!"

Everyone goes quiet except for Jake Campbell and his band on stage. The dancers keep dancing, but their eyes bounce between Aiden and Four. Noah is behind the bar, shaking his head. Aiden pays him no mind.

Four turns to face Aiden. "I am moving, One Arm!" He does some type of crazy wiggle. He probably considers it dancing. It's anything but dancing.

Aiden slams his palms against the table and leans forward. "Get away from my wife!"

Whoa! Somebody is about to die. Aiden Maxwell just became my new best friend. Well, nobody can take Noah and Tucker's places, so Aiden is now my third best friend. Being here tonight might not be so bad after all. Watching Mick Calhoun get beat down by Aiden would be awesome. It would be the best thing I've seen in years. I should probably video it.

Four grins and does his crazy little wiggle to the other side of the tables. I growl low and deep. Now, the fool is dancing next to Kennedy. She laughs and tries to cover it with her hand. She sits shoulder-to-shoulder with Tara. Four continues to wiggle in front of them. Phillip Crawford just stood up next to Aiden. All three of us may cross this dance floor tonight.

I can't watch this nonsense anymore. This night is back to being a mistake. If Kennedy wants this fool back, who am I to stop it? I don't care what she does. I should look away, but the idiot in me doesn't. Four says something and offers Kennedy his hand. I'll break his legs if he dances with her. Hasn't she learned her lesson with this fool? Kennedy's eyes flick to me for a moment. She shakes her head and leans back against her stool.

Four caught her movement and turned to face me. He notices me for the first time tonight. I've seen him a few times since the day at the billboard. I turned and went in the other direction to avoid him. Unfortunately, the fool is now wiggling his way across the dance floor. This night is about to be an even bigger mistake.

Four wiggles a little too close to a couple of ladies. Their dance partners shove him away. Too bad they don't shove him out the front door. The path he's on right now is going to get me arrested. Why he thinks it's a good idea to come anywhere near me is a mystery. He has to know I hate him.

"A A Ron." Four clamps a hand on my shoulder. "Good to see you again. How bout a game of pool? Winner gets $200."

He's a bigger idiot than I thought. I shove his hand away and slowly stand. There's no way I'd ever play pool with him. Never mind that it would be an easy two hundred bucks in my pocket. I don't even want to be in the same room with this man.

"Go away," I demand in my deepest voice.

"Don't be like that." Four continues his insane dance.

Tucker stands and grabs my wrist over the table. "Don't, Aaron."

I haven't done anything yet, but I'm about to lose it. Noah slides a mug of beer to a customer and rushes from behind the bar. I hear several chairs on the upper-level slide against the wooden floor. Kennedy hops off her stool. My eyes stay pinned on Mick's. Sadly, the fool doesn't get it. Four wiggles and hip bumps me. It was the moment my night went from bad to worse—much, much worse.

My blood burns as hot as lava. I swear there must be steam coming off the top of my head. I draw back and punch the fool in the face. The shouts and screams don't register. The next thing I know, I have Four flat on his back on the dance floor, pounding him repeatedly in the face.

"Aaron, stop!" Noah shouts and grabs me under one arm. I don't listen.

"Aaron, stop!" Tucker does the same on my other side.

Both men try to pull me off Four. I hit the fool one more time for good measure. I shouldn't have come here tonight.

Several more men get involved. A few pull Four across the dance floor and out of my reach. Lucas and Leo Barnes stand in front of me. Lucas, I believe, has his hand against my chest. He's strong, but I can't hit him. He's a cop. It's a line I won't cross. Spencer Murphy and a couple of firefighters surround Four. Kennedy's brother, Devon, is one of them. Aiden stands in the middle of the dance floor and smirks at me. He quickly turns back into cop mode before anyone else notices.

Jessie Calhoun pats his brother on the shoulder. He stands and starts my way. Aiden holds his arm out, stopping him.

"I don't care if you were in the Army and served overseas. You can't show up in town and start beating people up for no reason," Jessie shouts.

"We're taking him to the Emergency Room in Walsburg," Devon said. He and Spencer lift a bloody Four to his feet. "His nose is broken, and I'm pretty sure his left cheekbone is too."

Lucas nods to Devon. He takes a deep breath before turning back to me. "I'm sorry, Aaron, but I have to arrest you."

"You're not on duty," I snap. Sure, I know it doesn't matter, but it's all I got right now.

"He's not, but I am." Chief Deputy Al Green dangles a pair of handcuffs from one finger. Where did he come from? He wasn't here a few minutes ago. "Turn around, Bailey. Hands behind your back."

"I didn't call them," Noah whispers and steps back.

I could protest. I could fight. But I don't. There are too many men here for me to win anyway. I glare at Chief Deputy Green. He smirks. This man has never liked me.

"You might want to listen." Lucas caught the moment I wanted to protest and do something stupid.

"Don't make it worse." Tucker releases my other arm.

I nod to my cousin and do as I'm told. I drop my head as the cold metal clamps around my wrists. This night is the second biggest mistake of my life.

"Let's go." Chief Deputy Green's hand clamps down on my shoulder. He pushes me forward with a hard shove.

I've made a lot of mistakes this week. What's one more? I glance at Kennedy. She's watching me with her hand over her mouth. Tara has an arm around her. Phillip stands behind them. Devon whispers something in his sister's ear. She swallows hard but doesn't break eye contact with me. Are the tears in her eyes for Mick or me? Why should I care?

Chapter Nine

Aaron

Every cop on the force seems to be here tonight. A few are in uniform, but most aren't. Guess I'm the freak show for them this week. Everyone in Hayden Falls will know about my arrest by sunrise. It'll probably be in their little gossip blog. I hate to admit it, but ever since my aunt told me about Hayden Happenings, I've looked the blog up a few times. Okay. A lot of times.

Noah and Tucker are here. They loudly protested when Lucas told them to stay out front in the waiting area. From what I hear, the waiting area is packed. I have no idea who all is out there. My friend and cousin, however, sit in chairs outside my holding cell. I sit on this cold, uncomfortable metal bench with my elbows on my knees and my head in my hands.

After three hours, we've gotten nowhere. I'm under arrest, but I haven't officially been questioned yet. The few questions the Sheriff and his sons asked through the bars go unanswered. I merely shrug and look away. I can't deny hitting Four. Everyone saw what happened.

Noah reluctantly handed over the security footage from the bar. I'm not mad at him. He had no choice. Sheriff Barnes has seen the video. I see no point in talking about what happened.

Aiden is acting weird. I can't explain it, but I believe he's stalling things. I'm not sure why. It makes no sense. Spencer seems to have caught onto whatever is going on. He's helping Aiden. I wish they'd tell me what they're doing. The Sheriff and Lucas seem to be losing their minds. Leo sits at a desk and watches me. It's how I know he's Leo. Leo was always the quiet Barnes.

Devon Reed is here, too. I don't like the looks he's giving me. I rarely look in his direction, but I feel his cold, hard eyes. Tucker had to go to the breakroom and get ice for my hand. The firefighter across the room wouldn't offer his help. Isn't that illegal? Not sure, but it's rude. I can't believe Devon took care of Four but refuses to help me. It's fine. I don't need him.

Shortly after midnight, Mick Calhoun enters the Sheriff's Office. We hear him long before we see him. Sheriff Barnes sends every available deputy out front to clear out the waiting room. They've seen and heard enough tonight.

"Where is he?" Mick demands.

Surely, this fool is not about to challenge me. Of course, he'd do it when I'm behind bars. He's such a coward.

"Mick, you should go home." Lucas stands in the doorway, blocking Mick's path to me.

"Nope. I wanna see him." Mick pushes his way into the room.

"Mick, come on. Let's go. We shouldn't be here." Jessie walks in behind his brother.

"That's far enough." Aiden stops Four about halfway across the room.

Mick glares at me. "My nose is broken, and my cheekbone is cracked." He's mad. I can see the bandages, but I couldn't care less. "Why, Aaron? What did I ever do to you?"

It's my turn to glare. He doesn't need me to answer that question. He's a fool. The fact cannot be disputed, but he knows what he did.

Noah stands. "You've been told to leave."

"No!" Mick jabs his finger at me. "He needs to explain."

Everyone turns to look at me. I roll my eyes and shake my head. They all live here. They know what happened. Nothing gets by these people.

"Now might not be a good time." Tucker stands next to Noah, forming a wall in front of me.

"I'm not leaving until he explains." Mick takes a step toward the holding cell. It's all Aiden allows. "Why, Aaron? I've done nothing to you."

I jump to my feet. "You destroyed my life!"

Every man in the room looks as though I just slapped them. They look at me like I'm the crazy one. I should have never come back here. I should have just signed the house over to my aunt and been done with it.

Mick holds both arms out. "How did I destroy your life? I haven't seen you in ten years."

I drop my head back and laugh. It's cold, not humorous. "You know exactly what you did. Everyone here knows."

"Aaron?" Surprisingly, Devon steps forward. He's shaking his head. "We don't know. What did Mick do? Why are you so mad at him?"

I gawk at Devon for a moment. "Why am I mad? You should be furious. I'm surprised you haven't already broken a few of his bones."

Devon narrows his eyes. "Everyone here will admit Mick's hard to deal with." He shrugs one shoulder. "Most of us just ignore him."

"Some brother you are," I mumble.

Noah and Tucker snap their heads in my direction. They look at each other and shake their heads. It baffles me how confused everyone looks right now. This town is utterly ridiculous.

Devon walks closer to the holding cell. "I have one sister. That's it." He holds up a finger. "I don't know what's going on with you and Mick, but Kennedy has nothing to do with this."

I grab the bars and shout, "Kennedy has everything to do with this!"

Jessie shoves his brother. "What did you do?"

Four shakes his head. "Nothing. I don't know what he's talking about."

Noah wraps his hand around my wrist through the bars. "What does Four have to do with Kennedy?"

I groan. This is not possible. "You are one of the smartest men I know," I say to Noah. He nods but still doesn't get it. "But since everyone in this town seems to have amnesia, I'll play along." I point to Four. "The moment I left town, you moved in on my girl, got her pregnant, married her, divorced her, and apparently, you don't take care of your daughter."

I jerk my wrist away from Noah and sit back down. With my arms crossed over my chest, I lean back against the bars. It doesn't escape me that you can hear a pin drop in the room.

"Aaron, look at me." Devon's voice is surprisingly calm. I glance at him without turning my head. He shakes his head. "I don't know why you think that, but Kennedy wasn't married to Four."

What? That can't be right. Now they have my attention.

Mick steps up to the bars. Aiden doesn't stop him this time. "Don't get me wrong. I like Kennedy, but not like that. I've never been with her."

Now, I'm seriously confused. I look to Noah and Tucker for answers. Both are shaking their heads. The cops in the room have gone totally silent. They're letting this little scene play out.

"He's not her daughter's father?" I ask Noah.

"Her father is from Hayden Falls, but it's not Mick," Noah replies.

"Why would you believe all that?" Devon asked.

"My friend told me. I got the letter in boot camp." I drop my head into my hands again.

"I never told you that. All my letters to you got returned unopened," Noah said.

"I sent everybody's back unopened. After getting the one about Kennedy cheating on me with Mick, I asked my Superiors to return everything from Hayden Falls. Any letters that got through were burned."

"He doesn't mean you." Tucker has figured things out.

"Mark Bevins." Devon practically spits the name out.

Noah growls and clenches his hands into fists. "Have you talked to him lately?"

I shake my head. "Not since that letter ten years ago."

Tucker huffs out a breath. "That explains a lot."

"Yeah." Devon runs his hand through his hair. "You need to talk to Kennedy."

"I got nothing to say to her," I mumble. Even though it wasn't with Mick Calhoun, she still cheated on me.

"Well, you can listen." Devon's eyes meet mine. "Just know, I'll be there for it. In fact, I'll set it up for you on one of my days off."

Noah and Tucker nod. Maybe I should listen since Kennedy's brother thinks I need to talk to her. However, I'm not sure if I can do it. Her inability to stay faithful while I was gone destroyed us. It sure did a number on me. I rarely trust anyone now.

"That's enough for the night, gentlemen." Sheriff Barnes gets everyone's attention. "You all need to go home. We have to finish booking Mr. Bailey and move him to a cell for the night. Hopefully, he can see a Judge in the morning. If not, it'll be Monday."

My life is, once again, a complete mess. I've been arrested in a town I never wanted to return to. Apparently, I've been lied to about some things. I'm not sure I want to know the truth. If I don't get to see a Judge in the morning, I'll miss my appointment with Wade and Sawyer tomorrow. That means I'll be stuck in this town even longer.

"That's not necessary." A man I've never seen before walks into the room.

Sheriff Barnes and Lucas narrow their eyes. Aiden and Spencer grin. The stranger's face shows no emotion. He's about my height but a little more muscular. There's no doubt he's ex-military. We can spot each other easily.

"What are you doing here?" Sheriff Barnes asked.

The Sheriff might not know why this man is here, but Aiden does. This night gets stranger by the minute.

Aiden holds his hand out. "Jude, good to see you."

"Aiden." Jude takes his hand and gives a sharp nod in greeting. He turns to Sheriff Barnes and hands him a piece of paper. "I'm here for Mr. Bailey."

Before the Sheriff can say anything, Quinn Martin walks in and hands him another piece of paper. "Judge Morgan just signed this."

As I said, things are getting weirder by the minute. No small-town Judge is going to sign papers after midnight. When the sun goes down around here, the people of Hayden Falls are done for the day.

Sheriff Barnes reads over both documents. He looks at me. "I didn't know you worked for Slone Security."

I didn't either. I've never heard of this security company.

"He's our newest recruit," Jude replies.

Yeah. New as in seconds ago. This Jude guy doesn't say another word or move a muscle. I understand and stay quiet. Without this man's help, I'll spend the night with Hayden Falls' finest. Jude can explain what's going on when we get out of here.

"Wait a minute." Jessie Calhoun steps in front of the Sheriff and points at me. "He can't beat my brother like this and get away with it."

"Mr. Calhoun." Jude offers Four an envelope. "Your medical bills tonight have been taken care of. Your aftercare with Doctor Larson here in Hayden Falls has been arranged. Your first appointment is on Monday. This is our offer for settlement."

Mick opens the envelope. His and Jessie's eyes widen. Mick is ready to accept the offer.

"We'd like to show this to our father," Jessie said.

"That's fine. Get with Quinn by the end of the day tomorrow." Jude looks at his watch. "Well, later today, that is." His voice remains calm and even. "Come Monday, that number drops."

The Calhoun brothers nod and leave the Sheriff's Office. None of this makes any sense. I don't know this man. How did he know I was here? I really should speak up, but I don't want to spend the night in a cell.

"Release him," Sheriff Barnes orders.

It ticks Chief Deputy Green off to have to unlock this holding cell and let me walk out. I want to rub this in his face, but again, I stay quiet. Noah and Tucker slap my upper arms when I step out of the cell.

"You're his cousin?" Jude asked Tucker.

"I am."

"Good." Jude gives another sharp nod. "Take him home to your mother. Aaron and I will talk tomorrow. It's been a long day. I have a room waiting at the Inn."

Jude glances at me. For the first time since walking into the room, one corner of his mouth turns up. His eyes practically dance. Yeah, the ex-military man owns me, and there's nothing I can do about it.

"Talk to you later, Bull." Jude turns and walks out the door.

It's a conversation I want to hear and one I don't. I have no idea where this security company is even located. I'd really like to know how a man I've never met knows my code name. Right now, I want out of this station. A lot has happened tonight. I need to figure it out. I say nothing and follow Tucker to his truck. I have no idea what direction my life just took.

Chapter Ten

Kennedy

Friday night's barroom brawl has been the talk of the town for days. Rumors have even made it to Willows Bend and Walsburg. Well, I should say Four's beat-down has our local communities buzzing. Aaron didn't give Four a chance to get a single punch in. No one can believe it. I saw the entire thing, and I'm still shocked.

As much as I hate gossip, it's been great for business. On Saturday, I had to lock the door at three to keep random walk-ins from wandering in. Hope placed a sign on the door with the salon's phone number instructing would-be customers to call for an appointment. We have been very busy with phone calls, and walk-ins still happen. My girls and I are booked solid for the next two weeks. These ladies aren't here for haircuts, color, or perms. Nearly every customer wants a professional wash and style. In other words, they're here for gossip.

This morning, I found a new surprise waiting for me. I arrive at the salon twenty minutes early to find a line of women from the front door to the corner of the street. Who knows, maybe they continue around the corner. I'm not checking to see. I should have parked behind the salon and used the back door.

Peyton is with me today. Sometimes, she spends the day with me while I work. It's a perk of owning your own business. Peyton wanted a muffin from Sweet Treats this morning. Sophie opens the bakery a couple of hours before the salon opens. Parking on the square was just easier. Until this nonsense dies down, I won't be taking the easy route again.

"Hey, Kennedy. I hope you can get me in today." Connie Green is first in line. The nosy heifer should be at the pharmacy working.

"We're booked," I reply loud enough for everyone to hear me. Several women groan. I don't care.

"I don't mind waiting," Connie says with a smile. Of course, she doesn't. Being sweet isn't going to help her today.

Before I can give her an outright no, the front door opens. Savannah pulls Peyton and me inside and flips the lock. She glares at Connie through the window before turning away. Everyone knows Connie is one of the biggest gossips in this town.

"Thanks, Vanna." I hand her the to-go tray from Beth's with everyone's favorite coffees.

"This is insane." Lindsey crosses her arms and glares at the women outside. They see her. They don't care, and they don't leave.

"We shouldn't have to work like this." Hope joins Lindsey.

The crowd outside continues to strain their necks to look through the front windows. It's ridiculous. The bottom of the windows are only three feet off the floor.

"We could get the Sheriff's Office to move them along," Jade suggested. "We'll have to use the back door until this stops." The other girls nod.

Jade already has Andi Crawford in her stylist chair. It's a good thing we rescheduled her appointment a week ago. I could take a few of the ladies on the sidewalk, but I won't. I blocked out the entire morning to help Jade. She's preparing for her licenses and really needs this training session.

"Even if the Sheriff's Office made them leave, more than half of them will be back in a couple of hours." Lindsey turns her back to the windows and walks away. She's not wrong. They would just come back later.

"Hopefully, it won't get bad enough we need the Sheriff's Office," Savannah said.

"I don't know. Some of those men are really cute." Hope wiggles her eyebrows, causing us all to laugh.

I get Peyton set up in the employee lounge and come back to the front room. "I'm surprised they're still going this strong over a bar fight. Usually, those die out by the end of the weekend." Why they're here is a mystery. I haven't seen Aaron in ten years.

"Oh, it's not just the fight." Jade presses her lips together.

"Here." Savannah hands me her phone.

One look at the screen destroys my entire morning. Hayden Happenings. I should have known our little gossip blog was involved. I've been so busy this morning and haven't had time to look it up. Yes, I've looked every day since the fight. Megan must be slipping. She usually posts her hateful articles the next day.

Barroom Fights – Oh My

Not all Army men are sexy. Well, he is, but sadly, he's got anger issues. Maybe some folks should never return home. Our local hero is definitely a bad boy and not the kind we want to cozy up to.

Of course, that might not be true for two of our local ladies. Our little beautician is going off the deep end and throwing tantrums after seeing her ex in town. She's got competition this time around. One of our town's troublemakers is swooning over the bad military man. Coffee will do that to a woman. May the best woman win. Ladies, be sure to sign him up for anger management before his fists talk to you, too.

"I'm going to kill her." I toss my hands in the air.

"That's my phone." Savannah snatches the phone from my hands and holds it against her chest. "I just upgraded. I can't afford to replace it."

I wave my hand toward the front windows. "And these imbeciles are here because of it."

"Do you want me to call the Sheriff's Office?" Hope asked.

"No. I'll handle this." I go to the reception desk and pull out a notebook. I quickly scribble a message on a piece of paper and grab the tape. "Vanna, go get the little table we use during the festivals."

"Um. Okay." Savannah hurries to the back storage room.

"Oh look, Andi. There's your mother and new sister-in-law." Lindsey points to the windows.

Sure enough, Roslyn and Brittney Crawford are looking at us and trying to push their way to the front of the line. Andi groans and glares at her mother through the glass. She goes to the window and pulls the blind down. It's more like a mesh screen. We use them to keep the sun out when customers complain. Hope does the same to the rest of the windows.

"I'm not related to them." Andi is related to them, but they disowned her. She takes a deep breath and turns to face me. "Please, don't make me reschedule again. The Memorial Day Festival is this weekend."

"Don't worry, girl. Jade and I are going to make you look fabulous. I promise." I'm not letting the vultures outside stop us today.

Savannah brings the table, and I open the door. Women begin to shout and plead for an appointment. I'm usually the first to give in to a sad story, but not today. Savannah sets the table up with the notebook and a cup of pens while I tape the message to the front window by the door. It's everything I'm about to tell them.

"Ladies." I motion to the table and handmade sign. "We are completely booked for two weeks. You can call during normal business hours to schedule an appointment. If you'd like to write your name and number in this book for a waiting list, we'll call you if we have a cancelation."

They aren't happy, but most of them are nodding their heads. Connie Green grabs a pen. I'm not done, though. I'm about to dampen their spirits even more.

"A professional wash, trim, and style package is $250 without a regular appointment. Thank you, ladies, for your business." I push Savannah inside and lock the door again.

Connie's mouth drops open. She's only halfway through writing her name. She quickly scribbles it out and tosses the pen on the table. Several women walk away. Surprisingly, more than I expected to write their names in the notebook. Of course, Roslyn and Brittney Crawford write their names.

Savannah grabs my arm and whirls me around to face her. "Girl, are you insane?"

"You're really going to charge $250 for a wash and style?" Hope's eyes are wide.

"To every woman on that list, yes, we are. That is if we even call them." I don't feel bad about overcharging.

"You go, girl." Jade gives me a high-five.

"We all know no one is going to cancel this week." Hope takes a sip of her coffee.

"Well, darn." Jade huffs. "I had my eyes on a couple of pairs of shoes at the mall in Missoula. I could get them easily with our new prices."

Savannah gasps. "There's a dress online I want. Two customers, and it's mine."

Lindsey narrows her eyes. "What kind of dress are you buying for $500?"

"Oh." Savannah flips her hand like she's rich. "I need shoes and a new purse to go with it."

We all burst out laughing, including Andi. She grew up rich, but she's not as bad as we all believed. She's been on her own since Christmas. Everyone sees the changes in her. Getting away from her family was the best thing to happen to Andi.

"Okay, bestie." Jade holds up a black cape with the salon's logo on it. "You ready to look amazing?"

"Beyond ready." Andi grins and claps her hands.

I glance out the window. Even through the blinds, I can see the line of women adding their names to the notebook. We'll have to let our appointments in when they come to the door. Until the madness outside dies down, we're keeping the door locked. Hopefully, things will be better by lunchtime. For now, Jade and I are going to work our magic on Andi. I'm pushing Hayden Happenings and Aaron Bailey as far from my mind as I can get them. I hope Aaron's okay. Has he seen the blog yet? Is he mad about it? I close my eyes and sigh. Yeah, I'm really bad at blocking things out.

Chapter Eleven

Kennedy

By lunchtime, things were a little better. At least we could unlock the door now. The line of women outside is gone. Several still stop by and read the note I taped to the window above the table. Most walk away, but a few idiots sign the waiting list. None of our appointments have called to cancel today. At least they can walk in now without being swarmed by gossipers. Roslyn Crawford tried to pay Mackenzie Hanson for her appointment time. I had Hope give Mackenzie special treatment free of charge for not giving up her appointment. We sent Mackenzie to Frozen Scoops, looking fabulous. She gave Peyton gift certificates for free ice cream for her and Jeffrey. Big win right there.

We called in our lunch orders at Davis's Diner. One of us will have to slip out the back door to go pick it up. There's no way I'll exit the front door while we're open. Even though there's no longer a line out front, women walk by and try to peep in the front windows. We still have the blinds drawn.

Every woman with appointments today has spoken to me. I'm polite to them. They are paying customers, after all. I give them nothing to feed their wagging tongues. I simply say I'm fine when they ask how I'm doing. Jade and Andi get my full attention.

I do have conversations with women I know and trust, like Mackenzie. All of these women aren't even from Hayden Falls. Rumors of the bar fight and gossip blog have spread to Willows Bend, Walsburg, and a few other little towns near us. It's fine. We happily give their hair the best treatment possible, take their money, and send them on their way. They all look great when they leave the salon. We never let anyone leave unhappy.

Well, little Emma O'Brien left unhappy last month. She used a pair of craft scissors on her head of massive red curls while her mother was fixing dinner. By the time I got her bouncy locks evened out again, they were just above her shoulders. She absolutely hated having bangs. It was a drastic change for the five-year-old little girl. Her mother was glad it didn't have to be shorter. It was the best I could do.

Just before noon, the doorbell jingles. My brother and Zane Gallagher walk in carrying bags from Davis's Diner. I wasn't expecting to see Devon today.

"Miss Cora said these belong to you, wonderful ladies." Devon sets the bags on the reception desk.

"Uncle Devon!" Peyton runs across the salon and throws herself at my brother.

"Hey, Pumpkin." Devon scoops her up. She's too big to be picked up, but my brother doesn't care. "How's my perfect niece today?"

"Perfect." Peyton giggles. "How's my crazy uncle today?"

Devon doesn't know it's a teasing jibe between Peyton and Phillip. Devon is her crazy uncle. Phillip Crawford, even though he's not blood-related, is her cool uncle.

"Crazy as ever." Devon tickles her side, and they both laugh.

"Oh, my gosh," Andi cries and ducks her head. "I don't want anyone to see me until it's done." Jade holds a towel up and helps Andi disappear into the back.

"Oh, come on, Priss! It can't be that bad!" Devon calls out.

"Go away!" Andi shouts.

"Uncle Devon, be nice," Peyton scolds.

"I'm only teasing her, Pumpkin." Devon walks over and picks up the to-go bag with a flower sticker. Miss Cora puts stickers on the kid's meal bags. "I think this is yours."

"Uh-huh." Peyton nods. "Cheeseburger and extra fries."

"That's my girl." Devon boasts. He's the reason my daughter loves cheeseburgers. "Let's get you set up in the employee lounge."

While Devon helps my daughter, Lindsey flips the sign on the door to '*out to lunch,'* It's the only way we'll get time to eat when we have full schedules. We don't book any appointments between noon and one o'clock. Of course, appointments have gone past noon a few times. The stylist always gets an hour for lunch, no matter when her break starts.

Zane passes out our lunches. All firefighters should be as sweet as he is. He's also a little flirty, but the women in this town don't mind. Miss Cora bags our orders separately and writes our names on the bags. She's way more organized than I am. Savannah takes Jade and Andi's orders to them. They must be hiding out in the shampoo room because I don't hear Devon teasing them in the lounge. He's busy making my daughter laugh.

"My girl is settled with her food and a *Disney* movie going." Devon looks proud of himself. He really does do a great job with Peyton.

"Don't you mean *my* girl?" I tease.

"Nope. She's mine too." He pulls a chair up next to mine. His expression turns serious. "We need to talk."

Oh no. My brother rarely talks seriously. When he does, Devon drops some hard truths on me. This time will be no different. I knew this was coming. I thought I had a few more days, though. I guess the fight Friday night and the gossip blog today moved things forward.

"Look. I've seen Hayden Happenings. You have nothing to worry about. You know Megan stretches the truth." I try to clear things up before he gets started.

"Yeah. I saw it too, but it's not what I want to talk about," Devon said.

I sigh and drop my shoulders. It's worse than I thought. He wants to talk about Aaron. I definitely don't want to have this conversation with my brother. Devon has been threatening to hunt Aaron down and give him a piece of his mind for years.

"Nothing is happening between Aaron and me." I cut right to the chase. "You have nothing to worry about there, either."

Devon rubs the back of his neck with his hand. "Uh, Kenny. I think you need to talk to him."

Wait. What did he say? There's no way I just heard those words come out of my brother's mouth. What's wrong with him? Did aliens land and take over his body? Devon would never tell me to talk to Aaron Bailey.

"Aren't you supposed to be at the station?" Deflecting is my strong suit. We're not going to talk about my ex.

"Yep." Devon nods. "We have an order in at the diner too. It's not ready. Yours was. We've seen pictures of the salon this morning and heard about your new high prices. Zane and I thought we'd save you, ladies, from leaving."

"And we greatly appreciate that." Savannah fist-bumps with Zane.

"You should go check on your order. I'm sure Chief Foster wants his lunch." I unwrap my burger and take a bite.

"You can't keep putting this off." Devon won't let me avoid the subject.

Hope, Savannah, Lindsey, and Zane watch us but stay quiet. We sit in chairs around the front room of the salon. Peyton is in the lounge. At least Devon was smart enough to start a movie for her. I don't want her to hear any of this.

I look my brother in the eye. "Aaron hates me for some reason. He's not going to talk to me. Besides, I have nothing to say to him."

"That's not true." Devon points at me. He's getting very serious. "Trust me. He'll talk to you."

I sigh and drop my head. "It's best I don't."

The doorbell jingles, announcing a new customer. Hope must have forgotten to lock the door. At the sight of our new customer, I slowly stand.

"Aaron, what are you doing here?" I flick my eyes toward Devon for a moment. Did he arrange this?

Aaron shoves his hands into his pockets. He looks everywhere but at me. "We need to talk."

"So I hear." I narrow my eyes at Devon. He did set this up.

"You shouldn't be here, Aaron." Devon ignores me.

"You said I need to talk to her or listen. I'm ready to get this over with." Aaron does look at my brother.

What did I do to cause him to hate me so much? Is his wife so jealous he can't speak to or look at his ex-girlfriend? I really hate his wife.

"I told you I would set it up on one of my days off. I'm off tomorrow and Thursday." Devon said.

"You two see me standing here. Right?" I snap.

"Fine." Aaron continues to ignore me. "Tomorrow then."

Devon finally acknowledges my presence. "My house or your apartment?"

I gawk at him. "Don't I get a say in this?"

"Yeah. My house or your apartment?" Devon repeats.

"*If* I show up, your house." I cross my arms and glare at Devon. There's no way I'm having Aaron Bailey in my apartment. The rumors would be far worse than anything I've experienced so far.

"I'll send you the address." Devon dips his chin at Aaron.

Reluctantly, Aaron nods and leaves. I have no idea what's going on, but I don't like this one bit. My brother should have no say in my life. He loves my daughter and me dearly, so I usually listen to him. He shouldn't have promised to plan this meeting without talking to me first. Of course, I don't have to show up tomorrow night. Problem solved.

"Uncle Devon!" Peyton rushes into the room and wraps her arms around his waist. "Can we go camping this weekend?"

Camping at the lake is a big thing around here, especially during the town festivals. Devon talked me into taking Peyton when she was four. She loved it. We go camping at least twice every summer. We park near the restrooms and keep Peyton away from the party field. It gets too wild out there.

"I'm on duty this weekend, Pumpkin." Devon shakes his head. He looks as sad as she does. "I can't, but we'll plan a trip on my next weekend off."

"Okay," Peyton pouts. She doesn't like it, but she understands. She goes to the front windows and peeps around the blind. Thank goodness there's no line outside. "Mama, Jeffrey and Aunt Tara just went into Petals. Can I go get a blue balloon?"

"Sure, Pumpkin. Go straight there." I wait until she's out the door to turn on my brother. "When did you become an Aaron Bailey fan? You know what he did?" He doesn't know everything, but he knows enough.

Devon shakes his head again. "I'm not his fan. You both have been lied to. You need to talk this out."

I cross my arms and huff. "I have no reason to talk to him."

Devon tilts his head. "Your reason just walked out the door."

My hand flies to my chest as I suck in a breath. "What?"

Come on, Sissi." Devon grabs my upper arms. "You can finally admit it."

"No." I shake my head. "There's nothing to admit."

"Kennedy." Devon leans closer. His words are stern. "You can't hide it. Her eyes. All it takes is one look into her eyes, and your secret is lost."

I cover my mouth with my hand and drop my head. He's not wrong. Why couldn't she have boring brown eyes like mine? It doesn't matter. Our story isn't like Tara and Phillip's. Phillip's parents hid his son from him. Aaron didn't want us. I can never tell Peyton that. Devon wraps his arms around me when my body jerks with the first sob. Aaron is here now, and the lie that was supposed to have protected Peyton and me is about to be exposed.

Chapter Twelve

Aaron

"Great," I grumble as I drop down onto one of the swings in the Gazebo.

That didn't go well. Nothing has worked out in my favor lately. My weekend didn't get better. Well, it got quieter, so I guess that's better. My week is starting out horribly. I did get to meet with Wade and Sawyer this past Saturday. The house and property weren't as bad as I thought. It just looked bad. Both men have been hired to clean the place up. I hope Mayor Martin is happy. It's costing me a pretty penny, but it'll be nice to see my dad's place returned to its former glory. Actually, I could blame all my troubles on the Mayor. If he hadn't forced me to come here, none of this bad stuff would be happening.

Jude Harrington is still a man of mystery to me. He was called back to the office for an emergency on Saturday. All I know is it involved a high-profile client, whatever that means. So far, I've learned Slone Security is based in Missoula, and I'm now an employee. Not of my choosing, by the way. Great. The last thing I wanted was another connection to Montana. My dad's house and my aunt's family were enough. It looks like we're throwing a job into the mix now.

I've spent the past three nights at The Magnolia Inn. Jude's room has been reserved until he returns and says he doesn't need it anymore. I was told to use the room until Jude returns, and we will sit down and talk about my future with his company. My career with Slone Security will end the minute I work off the debt I owe them for getting me out of the mess with Mick Calhoun. Jude Harrington doesn't look rich, but he's throwing a lot of money around for a man he doesn't know. It makes no sense.

I plant my feet on the floor to stop the swing from swaying. I bend forward and drop my head into my hands. I have control of nothing in my life. I don't want to be here. I want to go home. Home to what? I don't know. I don't even have a dog. I do have my Army buddy, Cade, back in North Carolina. He's been the closest thing I've had to a friend for the past ten years. Still, I've kept him at a distance. He doesn't know everything about my life here in Hayden Falls. I've been doing my best to forget this place. It hurt too much to try and talk about everything I lost here.

Truth be told, Noah will always be my best friend. I should have never cut him off like I did everyone else. It was wrong of me. I was so hurt back then. I didn't know what to do. Thank goodness Noah has forgiven me.

Devon said I need to talk to Kennedy. A part of me wants to talk to her, but I'm scared to. I've never gotten over her. I've avoided dealing with what happened between us. It's not healthy. Even counselors have told me so, but I pretend it doesn't hurt. It hurts. It still rips my heart to pieces to think about it. Seeing her around town is really hard. Talking to her is going to bust open old wounds I've let fester for a decade. Devon also said we both were lied to. I'm not sure what he means, but I want to find out. Who lied to us?

"You okay, mister?"

I raise my head at the sound of the little girl's voice, but I don't sit up straight. It's kind of hard to worry about posture when you're defeated. One look at her, and I know she's Kennedy's daughter. She looks just like her mom.

"I'll be okay," I reply. I'm not sure if it's true or not.

"Would you like me to get you a blue balloon from Petals?" she asked.

Something about her captivates me. I sit up straight and grin. "You think I need a blue balloon?"

"Uh-huh." She nods. "They cheer my best friend up when he's sad. Well." She thinks for a moment. "He likes red balloons."

"You think I'm sad?" She's sweet to care about me.

"You are," she says matter-of-factly. Okay. She's blunt, too. That's not Kennedy's style. She must have gotten it from her dad.

"Thanks, Little Bit, but I don't think a balloon will cheer me up." I wish it were that simple.

"What's your name?" she asked.

"Aaron. What's yours?" I shouldn't ask. I don't know her. This is dangerous territory.

"Peyton."

I freeze. Peyton? That's impossible. I narrow my eyes and really look at the little girl, starting with her blue sneakers. From her shoes, shorts, t-shirt, and balloon choice, it's safe to say blue is her favorite color. It's mine, too. But why does Kennedy's daughter have my middle name? She's a mini version of her mother. Long legs and light brown hair. Her face is round, and her nose is tiny. My eyes finally lift to hers. All the oxygen is pulled from my lungs. Those are not her mom's eyes.

Blue. Blue eyes stare back at me. Not just any blue either, but sapphire blue eyes just like my dad's, like mine. It's impossible. My name and my eyes. If only she were a little older.

"How old are you?" I know how old she is.

"Nine," she replied.

By my calculations, her birthday should be in March. I left the first week in June. Kennedy got pregnant shortly after I left. June to March is nine months.

It's wrong to ask a child, but I have to know. "When's your birthday?"

"When's yours?" She narrows her eyes. Smart girl. She's finally getting suspicious of the stranger she just met.

"May tenth." I need to earn some brownie points with her.

"Really?" She smiles. "Mine is February tenth. That's so cool. We both have the tenth."

The world just stopped on its axis and came to a screeching halt. If her birthday is in February, she was conceived in May. I was here in May. I've gone over the math and possibilities a hundred times or more.

"Were you born early?" That would change things.

"No." Her hair swings from side to side when she shakes her head. "My best friend, Jeffrey, was a preemie. He was really sick for a while. He still has asthma."

"Your best friend is a boy?" I don't like the sound of that.

"Yeah." She nods. "He's the best."

"Where's your dad?" I've officially moved into creep mode. I should be asking her mother this question, not a nine-year-old child.

"I don't know." Peyton shrugs. The sadness on her precious little face makes me want to hurt people or destroy something. "Jeffrey got his dad. He's lucky."

More emotions than I can handle slam into me. Anger is one of them. I might actually need those anger management classes Megan mentioned. I should calm down before I do something drastic. I don't. My entire life just changed. I don't need anyone to confirm anything. I know beyond a shadow of a doubt Peyton is my daughter.

When Devon and Noah said I needed to talk with Kennedy, was this what they meant? Do they know Peyton is mine? Of course, they know. Everybody in this town knows this little girl has my eyes. Yeah, I know plenty of men around here with blue eyes, but none of them have this shade of blue. For years, people joked that Bailey's have their own personal shade of blue. Until this moment, I didn't believe it.

Did Mark know Kennedy's daughter was mine? If so, why did he lie? Maybe once he found out my girlfriend cheated on me, he assumed the child was the other man's. Still, I can't figure out why he told me Kennedy married Mick Calhoun. I need answers, and I'll get them. Right now, we'll start with confronting my daughter's mother.

"Come on, Little Bit. Let's go talk to your mom." I stand and hold my hand out. I want to tell her I'm her father, but her mother needs to be present for this announcement.

Peyton takes my hand. "You know my mom?"

"Oh, do I ever."

Chapter Thirteen

Aaron

I shove the door to Kenny's Kuts open with a little more force than necessary. I don't care if it does startle everyone in here. Kennedy jumps out of her brother's arms. Not sure what that's about. She and I have business to settle right now. Devon can comfort his sister later.

My eyes lock with Kennedy's. "Forget to tell me something?"

Her eyes drop to Peyton, who's holding my hand. "Aaron, you need to calm down." Calm down? Is she insane? "Pumpkin, you were supposed to go to Petals."

"I was going, but I saw the sad man on the swing and wanted to help," Peyton explained.

"Of course, you did," Kennedy mumbles. She looks at me. "We'll talk about this tomorrow night."

"No, Kennedy. We won't." I shake my head. "We'll talk about this right now."

"Aaron, that's not a good idea." Devon's eyes dart to Peyton and back to me.

I get what he's saying. I should think of Peyton first and not have this conversation in front of her. Sadly, I'm too overwhelmed to let this go.

"Sorry, man. You don't get to control this one." He has no power over this situation. I gave him what little he had up until now out of kindness. I turn my focus to Kennedy. "This is my daughter, and you kept her from me."

Peyton gasps loudly and steps away, but she doesn't let go of my hand. "You're my dad?"

"Yes, ma'am." I give her a sharp nod. I seriously need to learn how to talk to kids.

"Mom?" Peyton's voice shakes as she snaps her head toward her mother.

Kennedy looks at Devon for an answer. She wants to deny it, but she can't. Why, even now, does she want to keep my little girl from me?

"Mom?" Peyton asked again.

"I believe our daughter asked you a question. She deserves an answer," I snap. "It's more than you gave me."

"That's not true." Kennedy lifts her chin. Guess she's got a backbone after all.

"She has my eyes and my name," I point out.

Peyton looks up at me. "I have your name?"

"Yes, ma'am." I soften my voice for her. "Peyton is my middle name."

She smiles, and something inside my chest burns hot, but it's not anger. I know what love feels like. I've experienced it once before in my life. I glance at Peyton's mother. I loved her with everything I had in me.

"We'll talk about this over dinner at my place tomorrow night," Devon tries to take control of the situation again.

"This isn't waiting until tomorrow night." I step closer to Peyton. "I have a daughter no one told me about. This conversation is already ten years too late."

"I tried to tell you." Kennedy sniffles. "You sent all my letters back."

"You cheated on me and married someone else." I practically spit the words out. How could she marry someone else knowing she was carrying my child? It proves I loved her more than she loved me.

"That's not true." She swipes at the corner of her eye.

Zane Gallagher's phone dings with a text. "The station's order is ready."

"Look." Devon stands between Kennedy and me with his hands held out. "I know you three need answers. Lunch is almost over. The people in this room won't say anything. We all know if one customer walks in, the entire town will know everything by dinner time. Tomorrow night at my house, you'll have the privacy you need."

As much as I hate to admit it, he has a point. Peyton tugs on my hand. I haven't let go of her, and she hasn't pulled away. I give her my full attention.

"You really didn't know about me?" Her world sits in her eyes and hangs on the answer to this question.

I kneel in front of her and take a deep breath. "I knew your mother had a child, but I didn't know you were mine until I looked into your eyes out there." It's the truth. When she's older, I can explain why I didn't know.

She places her palm against my cheek. The warmth goes straight to my heart. "Tomorrow is fine with me."

I lightly chuckle. "Tomorrow, huh?"

"Yeah." She nods, and her expression turns serious. "You need a little time to process this."

I wholeheartedly laugh. So does everyone else. My daughter is very wise.

"Are you studying to be a therapist?" I tease.

"No." She laughs. It's the sweetest sound I've ever heard. "I'm taking dance classes, and I'm joining the band when school starts back."

"Wow. That sounds like fun." I'm already proud of her.

"I'm dancing on stage during the Memorial Day Festival. Will you watch?" She presses her little lips together.

"I wouldn't miss it. I'll be front and center." For the first time since being back in town, I won't even try to hide in the shadows.

"Thank you." She wraps her little arms around my neck.

I wrap my arms around her and hold her close. I'm already in love. I don't know what's going to happen with her mother, but I will forever love this little girl.

Devon clears his throat. "I hate to break this up."

Peyton steps back. "Tomorrow."

"Tomorrow," I confirm.

I stand and face Kennedy. "Put me off tomorrow night, come Wednesday morning, I'll stand in the middle of the square and tell everyone who I am." I don't have to say more. She understands the threat.

Kennedy says nothing yet nods. Devon doesn't look happy with me, but he doesn't say anything either. I want more, but it's enough for now.

"Bye, Little Bit." I kiss the top of her head and start for the door.

"Bye," Peyton says softly. She squeals and turns to her mom. "I can't wait to tell Jeffrey my Dad came back too."

I don't turn around. If I do, I'll push for more than any of us are ready for. I want all the answers now. They'll have to wait. It'll be a long night, but I'll wait. Peyton's right. We all need a little time to process this. Right now, my new job with Slone Security is looking pretty good. I now have two good reasons to stay in Montana. The job only became a good reason because I found out I have a daughter.

As excited as I am to get to know Peyton, my nerves are shot. If I'm going to make it through the night, I need to talk to someone. This is too much to hold in. I pull out my phone and search through my contacts. I bring up the number and hit the call button. A text just won't do.

"Hey, man," Noah answers.

"I have a daughter."

"Yeah, you do."

"I need…" I blow out a breath. I haven't done this in a long time.

"Friends?" Noah finishes for me.

"Yeah," I admit.

"I'll text Tucker and send you my home address. This is too serious to talk about at the bar." Noah says.

"Thanks." I end the call and head to my truck.

For the first time in years, I'm going to have a heart-to-heart conversation with my best friend and cousin. I'm sure Tucker and his entire family know Peyton is mine. I would be mad at them for not telling me, but I'm the one who pushed them all away. I was rude to Aunt Susie when I told her I never wanted to talk about Kennedy. It's my own fault. Everything changed today, though. A nine-year-old little girl just stole my heart.

Chapter Fourteen

Kennedy

Aaron didn't know Peyton existed. I'm stunned. Well, he knew she existed. He just didn't know she was his. How's that possible? I've been trying to wrap my mind around it for over twenty-four hours. I can't make sense of it. Tara couldn't piece it together, either. We talked for hours on the phone last night after the kids went to bed.

My situation sounds similar to Tara and Phillip's story. Phillip didn't know Jeffrey existed, either. However, that's where the similarities end. Phillip's parents interfered in their relationship. My parents and Aaron's father approved of our relationship. Devon said Aaron and I were lied to. Tara and I agree it means someone interfered ten years ago. There's only one person I can think of who would have talked to Aaron and me that summer—Mark Bevins.

Mark Bevins is the one person I wished I'd never met. He wasn't born and raised in Montana. I should have never listened to him. He was nice at first. Just before Peyton was born, he started showing his true colors. He left Montana when Peyton was two months old. Noah had always been leery of Mark. I should have been, too.

My last appointment left at 4:30. I don't schedule appointments after four. I usually spend the last hour or two helping the girls if they need it. I fell behind today because my mind's been focused on tonight's dinner with Devon and Aaron. I'm worried this won't end well. At least my brother will be there to keep the peace. This conversation won't be easy. A couple of my girls fell behind today, too, and will be at the salon until six. Savannah practically pushed me out the back door minutes after my last appointment left. She's going to help the others and close up tonight. I don't know what I'd do without her.

I pull into my brother's driveway a few minutes before six. He lives less than two miles from our parent's house. A blue truck I don't know is parked in the drive next to Devon's. I wanted to arrive at least thirty minutes early so I could talk to Devon for a bit. Unfortunately, I had a hard time getting out of my apartment. Peyton isn't happy with me. She went hysterical when my mom showed up to sit with her. She thought she was coming with me tonight. She wants to get to know her Dad. I want that for her, too. Aaron and I need to talk first.

I park behind my brother's truck and take a moment to settle my nerves before getting out. This is going to be so hard, but there's no getting out of it. Aaron knows about Peyton now. He's not going to let me bail on this. I sigh and grab the sweet potato pie from the passenger seat. Mom makes these all summer long for Devon and our Dad. Aaron likes pumpkin pie, but this is close enough.

I walk up onto the porch, grab the doorknob, and walk inside without knocking. The only time anyone in my family knocks is when the door is locked. I hear voices coming from the kitchen, so I head that way. Devon and Aaron are sitting at the table, laughing like they're old friends. Well, they actually are, but this is a little awkward. The laughter dies when they notice me.

"Hey, Sissi." Devon jumps up. "Let me get that." He takes the pie and sniffs it. "Ah. Sweet potato."

“Naturally.” I laugh. He knows Mom isn’t going to send him anything else. Devon is the baby of the family. Mom pets him as much as she does Peyton.

Aaron stands and rubs his palms on his jeans. “Kennedy.” His eyes meet mine and quickly dart away.

“Aaron.” I offer him no more as I look over the table. It’s already set with everything. From the looks of it, Devon stopped by Davis’s Diner. I take the chair across from Aaron and smile at my brother. “You thought of everything.”

“Actually, Aaron brought all of this.” Devon sits at the head of the table. He grins and rubs his hands together. “I’m not turning down Miss Cora’s fried chicken.”

Davis’s Diner does have the best fried chicken within a hundred miles. Well, unless you count Mrs. Hayes, but she doesn’t sell hers to the public. The chicken at the diner might be Miss Cora’s recipe, but I don’t think she cooks anything in the restaurant. Her husband is the main grill cook. I like this chicken, too. I’m not turning it down, either.

“Thank you.” I look up to find Aaron watching me. This is the longest he’s looked at me.

“Where’s Peyton?” Aaron asked.

“Mom is sitting with her.”

“I want to see her.”

“You can. She doesn’t need to be here tonight, though. I thought we should get the first conversation out of the way without her present.” I’m not trying to keep her from him.

“Okay. Let’s eat.” Devon reaches for the platter of chicken and helps himself before passing it to me.

The meal is extremely awkward. Aaron and I don’t know how to talk to each other. Devon does most of the talking. My brother could literally talk a toddler out of a lollipop. Aaron loosens up and starts talking a little more with my brother toward the end of the meal. He doesn’t speak to me. He’s getting braver, though, and watches me. When it’s time for dessert, Devon slices the pie while I make coffee. Mine and Devon’s phones ding with a text at the same time. Mom has us in a group chat.

Mom: *She's throwing a tantrum. I've called your father to come help me.*

"Oh no," I whisper. This is not like Peyton at all.

Aaron points at me. "I don't know what's going on, but you're not putting me off, Kennedy."

"I'm not. I promise." I sigh. I might as well be honest with him. "Peyton is upset. She wanted to be here."

"Well, let's get this over with so I can stop by and see her for a few minutes." Aaron taps his fingers on the table.

"You can't just invite yourself to my home," I snap.

Aaron shrugs. Devon sets three slices of pie on the table and pretends not to be in the room. Uh! As much as I hate it, it's time to get to the reason we're here.

"You don't even know where I live." Yeah, I'm being childish.

"The single-story apartments outside of town. Two doors down from Beth Murphy." Aaron casually takes a bite of his pie.

I glare at him. "You've been following me?"

Aaron shrugs again like it's no big deal. Is it a big deal? If it were anyone else, I'd say so.

"Great." I set the cups of coffee on the table and sit. "Let's do this. My daughter needs me."

"Our daughter needs us," Aaron corrects.

"Whatever," I grumble. Apparently, I'm a smart-mouthed teenager tonight.

Aaron ignores me. "Where should we start?"

That's a good question and one I've thought about all night. I have so many questions.

"The beginning," Devon suggested without looking up from his pie.

"Why do you think I cheated on you?" This completely baffles me.

"I got a letter from a friend." His voice lowers as he looks down at his pie.

"Mark?" He doesn't have to answer. I've already figured this much out. "I know it wasn't Noah. His letters got returned like mine did.

"Yeah, Mark," Aaron confirms.

When neither of us looks up or speaks after a few minutes, Devon taps the table between us to get our attention. He looks between us. "This is your common factor. Mark Bevins lied to both of you."

Aaron narrows his eyes at me. "Mark lied to you?"

"That depends," I reply.

"On what?"

"On the reason why you cut us all off and didn't come back," I snap.

"I got a letter from my friend telling me my girlfriend cheated on me, got pregnant, and was getting married." Aaron's breathing becomes hard and fast.

"I never cheated on you, Aaron," I tell him again. "Yes, I was naïve to believe anything Mark said, and I was stupid to get married. But it was supposed to protect Peyton and me. We were supposed to have been taken care of for life."

"I would have taken care of you both for life," he struggles to say the words.

"How could you?" I push a finger into the corner of my eye. "You got married two weeks after leaving here."

"What?" Aaron almost chokes.

My eyes slowly lift to his as the realization hits me. "You didn't get married to one of your Army buddies' sisters?"

"No, Kennedy. I was coming back for you. I told you before I left that I was doing this to give us a better start." He shakes his head.

"Oh my gosh," I cry and cover my mouth with my hand. It takes me a moment to speak again. "Mark said you fell in love with a skinny little blonde and married her right away."

"I was in boot camp. I didn't see anyone's sister," he says.

"Are you married now?" My eyes drop to his left hand. There's no ring.

"No." He swallows hard. "I never tried to get close to anyone again."

"Why would Mark lie to you two like this?" Devon asked. None of us are concerned with the pie anymore.

"I don't know." Aaron shrugs. "I thought he was my friend." He locks eyes with me. "I know now you didn't marry Mick Calhoun."

My mouth drops open. "Four? You thought I married Four?"

"Yeah. Mark said you did," he replies.

I drop my head back and laugh. "You should have known that was a lie. Is that why you beat Four up?"

Aaron nods. "Who did you marry?"

I glance at Devon. I don't want to answer this question. It proves how stupid I was. Mick Calhoun would have been a better choice. What am I thinking? Mick would have been a disaster, too. I have no courage, and my heart drops. He's going to hate me now, for sure.

Still, I left my eyes and brace myself. "Mark."

Chapter Fifteen

Aaron

"You did what?" I roar. My hands slam down on the table, and I bolt from my chair.

Devon is out of his chair just as fast and grabs my upper arm. "Aaron, calm down. You're here to talk this out, not lose your temper."

He's right. If I keep this up, Kennedy and I will be arguing. Arguing won't help me see Peyton tonight or any time soon. I force my emotions to settle a bit and sit back down. The last thing I want to do is get a lawyer involved to see my daughter, but I will if I have to.

One look at Kennedy's fearful eyes shifts something within me. Darn it. I didn't mean to scare her. For a moment, I'm reminded of the teenage girl I fell in love with. It has me wanting to shove this table aside and wrap my arms around her. Nope. That's not happening tonight. I close my eyes and rub them with my thumb and index finger. Devon will kill me for destroying his table, and I'm not ready to touch her. Kennedy wouldn't let me right now, anyway.

Too much has happened for us to go back to the life we knew ten years ago. We can't just forget what happened and sweep it under the rug, even though it would be the best thing for Peyton's sake. It wouldn't be healthy for Kennedy and me. Sooner or later, all the bad stuff would work its way to the surface and destroy us again. First, we need to figure out exactly what happened all those years ago.

I look her in the eye and hold my hands up. "I'm sorry."

She nods and relaxes a little. She's still on edge. I can't say I blame her. I really need to control my temper around her. I never want to lose it in front of Peyton, either. Devon is cleaning up coffee with a dish towel. I didn't realize I knocked my cup over. This is not going well.

"Why did you marry him?" My girlfriend married one of my best friends. I can't wrap my head around any of it.

"He said since you weren't coming back, it would save my family from embarrassment and protect the baby and me for life." She wrings her hands together but doesn't look up.

"How did Mark know you were pregnant?" Devon asked. "We didn't until after you married him."

"About a week after Aaron left, we had a big party and camped out at the lake. I just found out I was pregnant, so I wasn't drinking. Morning sickness can actually be an all-day sickness. I tried to slip away to hide it, but Mark saw me," she explains.

The high schoolers have that party every year. We do it early in the summer because some graduates leave before August for college. I was supposed to be at that party but had to leave early for boot camp.

"You were only seventeen. You shouldn't have been drinking anyway," Devon scolds.

"Yeah." Kennedy fakes a laugh. "We all know the teens sneak alcohol out there anyway."

They do. We did. Devon probably did, too. He's not the good, sweet son his mother believes he is. He's a few years younger than Kennedy, but he looks older. Surprisingly, Kennedy looks as though she's hardly aged at all. At first glance, you'd swear she just got out of college. When I take a closer look, I can see a few worry lines. Being a single mom isn't easy. She's probably had some sleepless nights. She shouldn't have been a single mom at all. I was coming back to marry her and live here for the rest of my life. I would have married her before boot camp if I had known she was pregnant.

"Neither of you knows why Mark would do this to you?" Devon asked.

"No." I shake my head. "I have no clue." I should have listened to Noah in high school. He could see Mark wasn't trustworthy when I couldn't.

"I can't make sense of it, either," Kennedy replies.

"Does she have his name?" I press my lips together to keep from snapping off something hateful.

"No." Kennedy shakes her head. "She did for a few weeks, but Mark made sure it was changed in the annulment."

"Annulment?" Devon's eyebrows draw together. "You didn't get a regular divorce?"

"No." Kennedy looks away.

"How's that possible?" I'm even more confused now. "Are you actually legally divorced if you just got an annulment?"

"We didn't consummate the marriage," Kennedy replies softly.

I can't explain how relieved I am to hear those words. I'm still confused, though.

"Just what kind of marriage did you have?" I snap. It's good to know she didn't sleep with my traitorous friend, but this has stepped into bizarre.

Devon holds his hand out to settle me down. He focuses on his sister. "Maybe you should explain *exactly* what happened between you and Mark Bevins."

Something is seriously wrong here. Devon should already know everything. Why would Kennedy hide her life from her family? The Reeds were close. They might not share everything about their lives with the public, but they do with each other. They accepted me with ease. My dad was even invited over for holidays and get-togethers. I enjoyed spending time at their place.

Kennedy keeps her head down. "I wrote to Aaron once a week for a month. They were all returned without being opened. In all of them, I told him I was pregnant. In the last one, I was begging him to talk to me. Mark showed up with a letter from Aaron. It said he fell in love and got married two weeks after leaving. He didn't want to hear from me, and he was never coming back to Hayden Falls. Mark even had a picture of the wedding."

"That's not true." I point at her. "I have no idea whose wedding that was, but it wasn't me."

Devon holds a hand toward me again but keeps his eyes on his sister. This is all new to him, too. "Keep going."

"He offered to marry me and give my baby his name so we wouldn't be looked down upon. He said he wanted to help me and ensure my baby had a good future." She swipes at the corner of her eye. "We had separate bedrooms, which was fine with me. He said we didn't love each other, and he wasn't going to force anything on me until I was ready."

"There's more," Devon pushes.

I want to say so much right now. Well, I want to shout and break something, but Devon is making progress here. I'll let him continue. He's right. There's more. I feel it as well. At first, I thought it was a bad idea to meet here. I would have never been able to get all the information from her as Devon can.

"About a month before Peyton was born, Mark said since he wasn't her father, I should put her real father on the birth certificate. The nurse thought it was odd, but I put Aaron's name on it at the hospital. Two weeks after she was born, Mark said he couldn't raise another man's child like he thought he could. He said I should be free to find love because it wasn't going to happen between us. He offered me twenty-five thousand dollars to agree to the annulment." She shrugs. "I took it. It's how I bought the salon. He used the birth certificate as proof Peyton wasn't his. He insisted on both of our names being changed to Reed. The Judge easily granted everything."

I lean back in my chair and start biting on my thumbnail. It's the only way I won't explode and say something to hurt Kennedy and piss Devon off. Mark Bevins best hope I never see him again. He destroyed three lives ten years ago. Well, he destroyed us for ten years. Our future will be different. I glance at Kennedy without raising my head. Devon hands her some tissues. She can cry it out now. Hopefully, after tonight, we can start fixing this mess.

Devon slides a chair next to her and pulls her into his arms. "I'm sorry, Sissi. We didn't know. We'd have never let you do it if we had known."

"It's my fault," I admit.

"How's it your fault that piece of crap lied?" From the sound of Devon's voice, Mark best hope Kennedy's brother doesn't find him either.

"If I had just opened the letters sent to me, I would have known the truth. I could have stopped all of this." It guts me, but it's true.

"No. It's not your fault," Devon insists. "Mark twisted the story to you so you wouldn't want anything to do with Kennedy or Montana again. He knew exactly what to say to play you both."

Yeah, he sure did. But why? What was the purpose? It makes no sense. The friend I knew would have never done something like this. Obviously, I didn't know the man at all. Was I that blind to who Mark Bevins really was?

Kennedy wipes her eyes and finally looks up at me. I hate seeing her cry. "I'm sorry."

I reach across the table and cover her hand with mine. "I'm sorry, too."

Our apologies don't fix things. Hopefully, it's a start so we can heal. I'll do whatever it takes to mend things and make them right. Do I hope Kennedy and I can have a relationship again? I'd be lying if I said I didn't still love her. But we're so broken, I don't know if it's possible to be anything more than friends.

Hers and Devon's phones ding with another text. Devon reaches for his.

Devon reads the message and glances between us. "Uh. Mom and Dad couldn't settle Peyton down. Jeffrey's trying, but the little guy isn't having much luck."

"Oh my. That's bad." Kennedy's quickly on her feet.

"Real bad," Devon adds.

I'm out of my chair and heading for the door. "Let's go."

We hurry to our vehicles and head to Kennedy's apartment. Apparently, my daughter has a temper—no idea where she got that from. I roll my eyes at myself. I might need to look into those anger management classes. From the sound of it, my little girl will be sitting on the sofa next to me.

Chapter Sixteen

Kennedy

I'm the first to arrive at my apartment. Aaron and Devon know where I live, so I don't bother to see if they're behind me. All I can think of is getting to Peyton. Thank goodness I don't pass anyone from the Sheriff's Office. They would lock me up for how fast I'm driving.

By the time I get my car into park, I'm already opening the door. If Jeffrey can't calm Peyton down, it's beyond bad. Tara's car is here. So are both of my parents. I hear cars pulling in behind me. I'm sure it's Aaron and Devon. My thoughts are only on Peyton as I bolt for the front door. I shove it open and freeze in the doorway.

"I want my dad!" Peyton screams.

Our living room looks like a tornado went through it. I think I'm in shock. My daughter is standing in the middle of the room with a throw pillow in her hand. Her little body heaves with each breath she takes. My heart shatters. She's never been this upset.

Jeffrey stands in front of her with his arms out—brave little guy. "Your dad's here, Pey. They just need to talk."

"They can talk here!" Peyton yells. She's never yelled at Jeffrey.

Jeffrey isn't fazed. He shakes his head. "You know we don't get to listen in on grown-up talk."

"I want to see him!" Peyton throws the pillow on the couch and clinches her little hands into fists at her side. What has happened to my little girl?

"Peyton." I walk further into the room. Her head snaps in my direction. "Pumpkin, calm down."

"No, Mom!"

I'm taken aback a little. She's never yelled at me like this, either. "Peyton Rose Reed, you're really upset, and you're scaring everybody."

"You can't keep him from me! It's not fair! I just got him! You can't take him away from me," Peyton cries. She doesn't bother to wipe her tears away.

I have no idea what to do right now. Before I can speak, I'm pushed aside.

"I'm right here, Little Bit." Aaron falls to his knees in front of Peyton.

"Dad," she cries and throws her arms around his neck.

"I got you." He gently rubs her back while she cries on his shoulder.

"You can't leave." Peyton sniffles.

"I'm not."

"You don't live here." She tightens her hold on him.

"I have a house here and a job now," Aaron says softly.

Peyton leans back enough to look at Aaron but doesn't release her tight hold on him. "But you don't live here," she repeats.

"I do now," Aaron says.

"Really?" Her little voice is full of hope.

"Yeah." Aaron nods. "My dad's house is being remodeled, and I just got a job."

"In town?" She bites her bottom lip.

"The house is outside of town, and the job is in Missoula." Aaron smiles, hoping she will too.

I want to interrupt and tell him not to make her promises he can't keep. After seeing the condition of the living room and the emotional state of my parents and Tara, I stay quiet. If Aaron leaves again, he'll completely destroy our daughter.

"Oh." Peyton drops her head.

"Hey." Aaron gently lifts her chin with his fingers. "Missoula is only an hour away."

"But you'll come home every day?" Peyton blinks back tears.

"I just got this job with a security company. I don't know exactly what I'll be doing yet, but I'll come home to Hayden Falls every day I can," Aaron answers her as honestly as he can.

"But…" Peyton's breathing becomes erratic.

Jeffrey puts his hand on her upper arm. "Slow down, Pey. Slow, deep breaths. Like this." Peyton nods and mimics Jeffrey's breathing.

Aaron glances at the little boy and back at Peyton once she's settled down again. "I take it this is your best friend."

"Yeah. This is Jeffrey." She looks at her best friend and smiles a genuine smile. She leans into Aaron. "This is my dad."

"Hi." Jeffrey holds his hand out to Aaron. "I'm Jeffrey Carlton Crawford. It's a pleasure to meet you."

Aaron shifts Peyton to his left arm and takes Jeffrey's hand with his right. "Hello, Jeffrey. I'm Aaron Peyton Bailey. Nice to meet you."

Aaron looks at Tara and smiles. Jeffrey is a little guy, but he's big on manners. Tara has done a great job raising him. Phillip has been a great influence on his son over the past few months, too.

Jeffrey smiles at Peyton. "You really have his name."

Peyton giggles. The sound is music to my ears.

"Her middle name is my grandmother's," Aaron's eyes meet mine for a moment. I nod. I gave her as much of him as I could.

"Your Grandmother's name was Rose?" Peyton asked.

"It was," Aaron confirms. Peyton looks so proud.

Jeffrey places his hand on Aaron's shoulder and looks him dead in the eye. "I'm glad you're here," he says with a firm nod.

"Me too, Buddy." Aaron's trying not to laugh. Peyton giggles again. Aaron playfully narrows his eyes at her. "What?"

"His mom calls him Buddy." She snuggles closer to her dad.

"Is it okay to call you Buddy?" Aaron asked.

"It's fine," Jeffrey assures him. Tara nods her approval.

I take a chance and step closer. "Do you feel better now?"

Peyton nods again and drops her head. My parents sigh with relief.

Aaron looks around the destroyed living room. "Well, Little Bit. We made quite the mess here."

As far as I know, Aaron hasn't had any experience with children. I'm left speechless, watching him with Peyton and Jeffrey. I like how he used the word *we* instead of outright scolding Peyton for what she did. I take a chance and get closer. I kneel next to her and place my hand on her back.

"I'm sorry," Peyton whispers.

"You had some big emotions today. Some you've never had before." I don't want Aaron to think she acts like this all the time. Peyton nods. "Don't worry, Pumpkin. We'll find a way through this. For now, we need to clean this up."

"Why don't you start helping your mom clean this up? I'll go to the market and get ice cream for everyone," Aaron suggests.

"No." Peyton wildly shakes her head and tightens her arms around Aaron. "You can't leave."

"Okay." Aaron takes a deep breath and tries again. "Why don't you and I help Mom clean up the aftermath of Hurricane Peyton while Uncle Devon goes to the market for ice cream?"

"With all the toppings?" Peyton blinks and pouts. Oh, she's playing on her dad's emotions already. She and I will have to talk about this later.

"Absolutely." Aaron pulls out his wallet and hands Devon some cash. "Get enough for everybody and whatever toppings we need. Is that enough?"

Devon doesn't bother to count the money. "If it's not, I'll cover the rest."

"I'll go with you." Dad follows Devon out.

We're in big trouble now. My dad is the one who started Peyton and Jeffrey on ice cream parties. Devon loves them, too. Dad uses all the toppings he can get his hands on. I'm not sure how much money Aaron gave him, but Devon will need more with Dad along.

Mom hurries to the kitchen and comes back with a couple of trash bags. She hands me one. "I don't think all of it is salvageable."

"I don't either." I look around and sigh.

"I'm sorry, Mom."

I look at Peyton, but I don't smile. I don't want to upset her again, but she needs to know this behavior is wrong. "We'll figure this out as we go, but this can't happen again."

"Yes, ma'am." She leans against Aaron.

"We'll take it day by day. Okay?" Aaron keeps his voice calm and even. "This is new territory for us all." His eyes lift to mine. "We're going to have to learn how to work together."

"We will," I agree.

I catch his meaning. He's talking about our entire family. Somehow, someway, we'll figure this out. If we don't, our daughter is going to need professional help.

Chapter Seventeen

Aaron

The ice cream party was a huge success. It's now one of my favorite things to do. We will be having more of these in the future. Peyton stayed in the chair next to me the whole time. Of course, she slid her chair over until it touched mine. Trust me. I'm not complaining. She's a precious little girl. I'm the luckiest man alive to be her father.

She and Jeffrey laughed through the entire party. The adults laughed, too, but there was a look of uncertainty in their eyes when the kids weren't watching them.

Devon's no longer angry with me. His attitude toward me changed the night I was arrested. I guess since the charges from that have been swept under the rug by Slone Security, I should say it was the night I beat up Four. Mick took the settlement Jude offered. I don't know the amount of money Jude handed over on my behalf yet. He'll be back on Friday to inform me of everything my new mystery job entails.

Mr. and Mrs. Reed won't be easily won over to liking me again. Their smiles fade every time our eyes meet. Unless Devon shared what he learned at the Sheriff's Office last week, the Reeds believe I'm the problem. The way Mr. Reed's eyes cut through me, I'm sure Devon hasn't told them anything yet. At one point, I thought the man was going to say something to me. Devon quickly shook his head. His father settled back against his chair and remained quiet.

Phillip Crawford won't easily be swayed to my side, either. He arrived toward the end of our little party. Unlike Kennedy's father, Phillip has no problem popping off a smart comment every now and then. I'd pop something back to him if there weren't kids in the room. I didn't witness my daughter's tantrum, but the aftermath was enough to know how bad it was. The last thing she needs to see is me losing my temper.

Finally, everyone leaves, and it's just the three of us. Peyton loses her smile and goes quiet. Kennedy talks to us while she cleans up the kitchen. I'd help her, but Peyton hasn't moved from my lap. She glances between the front door and me a few times. She knows I'm the next to leave.

"Pumpkin, we need to get your bath and get ready for bed." Kennedy puts the last dish in the dishwasher and presses the start button.

"I don't want to." She looks up at me. "You'll leave."

"He has to go home, Peyton," Kennedy says softly.

"But his house isn't ready."

"He's staying at the Inn and with his aunt until it's ready." Kennedy holds her hand out to Peyton.

I meet her eyes over Peyton's head. I didn't tell her where I was staying. It looks as though I'm not the only one checking up on the other. She rolls her eyes when I grin.

"I don't want him to go," Peyton pouts and leans back against my chest.

"Hey, Little Bit." I turn her to face me. "Why don't you get your bath, and I'll stay until you fall asleep?"

Kennedy narrows her eyes. I ignore her. I want more time with Peyton. I have no problem with inviting myself to stay longer.

"Okay." Peyton gives in and goes with her mother down the hall.

Once they're out of sight, I grab my glass of sweet tea and go to the living room. I sit on the couch and look the place over. The two-bedroom apartment is small, but it's the right size for the two of them. They deserve so much more than this. They would have had more if I had known I had a family. Peyton broke a lot of trinkets today. Thankfully, she didn't get hurt or bust the tv. If I play my cards right, maybe Kennedy will let me watch a movie with Peyton before I have to leave.

In less than twenty minutes, Peyton runs into the living room and jumps on the couch next to me. Kennedy's standing in the hall with a towel and a hairbrush in her hands.

"Are you sure you're clean?" I tickle her side.

"Yeah. Smell me." She leans her head close so I can smell her hair. She smells like strawberries.

"She was afraid you'd leave and rushed through everything." Kennedy waves the hairbrush. "I'm surprised her pajamas aren't on backward."

"I promised to be here when you got out." I hold my hand out. "I'll brush her hair."

"Really?" Peyton's eyes widen.

"Really?" Kennedy doesn't sound so sure.

"Really." I wiggle my fingers for the brush.

"Okay." She reluctantly hands me the hairbrush.

"Why don't you go get a shower?" I suggest to Kennedy and motion for Peyton to turn around.

"I had a shower earlier." Kennedy heads toward the kitchen.

"Then take a bubble bath and relax," I call out.

"Yeah, Mom. You love those." Peyton climbs onto her knees and looks toward the kitchen over the back of the couch. "Dad and I can watch a movie while you relax."

Best daughter ever. She's finding us more time without my interference. Is it wrong to let her play her mom like this? Probably, but I'm not going to say anything.

"Grab the remote, Little Bit, and find us a movie," I say before Kennedy can object.

Peyton reaches for the remote on the coffee table. She settles back on my lap, and I start brushing her hair. She flips through several channels. A few, I hope, are her Mom's choice for after she's asleep.

"Fine." Kennedy tosses her hands in the air. "But don't let her watch anything scary. The last one gave her and Jeffrey nightmares."

I turn Peyton to face me. "You watch horror movies?" I should scold her mom for allowing it.

"She and Jeffrey snuck and watched one in her room one night," Kennedy said.

Peyton sighs and drops her head. "We were grounded for a long time. But don't worry. I never want to see another one. I don't like being scared."

I motion for her to turn back around. "I don't like being scared either. So, pick something non-scary, but please, no *Disney Princess* movie."

Peyton giggles. "I like *Brave*."

"The little redheaded girl with the bow?" I've seen that one.

"Yeah. It's my favorite."

"I can watch *Brave*." I smile and nod. It's not as girly as the others are.

"Good." She finds the movie and finally sits still long enough for me to brush her hair. It's still wet, but hopefully, it'll dry before she goes to bed.

I settle into the corner of the couch. Peyton lays her head against my chest, and I wrap my arms around her. Kennedy refills my tea and sets Peyton a cup of milk on the end table next to me.

"You sure about this?" She slowly walks toward the hall.

"Yeah, Peaches. I've got her." I kiss the top of Peyton's head.

Kennedy stops and looks over her shoulder. I snap my head in her direction when I realize what I said. I used to call her Peaches in high school. She loved peach pie, peach cobbler, peach ice cream, and milkshakes. We stare at each other for a moment, but I don't apologize. Yeah, it was a slip of the tongue, but I'm not taking it back. She presses her lips together and disappears down the hall.

I mentally kick myself after she's in her room. Being here with her and Peyton made it easy to forget all the bad stuff for a little while. Somehow, we have to find a way to fix things.

Somewhere before the end of the movie, Peyton falls asleep against my chest. I don't know how long this movie is, but I'm dozing off myself. My eyes pop open when I hear Kennedy in the kitchen. She walks in, takes our empty glasses away, and leaves a bottle of water on the end table. My eyes follow her every move.

My daughter is wearing a blue pajama set with flowers all over them. The pants are long, and the top has short sleeves. They're cute and modest, exactly what a little girl needs. Her mother's pajamas are another story. I'm glad Kennedy enjoyed her bubble bath and feels comfortable around me, but I'm in so much trouble here. I can't watch her walk around in blue plaid pajama shorts and a dark blue tank top. Well, that's a lie. I have no trouble watching her. It's not wise, though, with our daughter here. Peyton being here does stop me from getting up and doing something stupid.

I shift to lift Peyton so I can carry her to bed. Her eyes pop open. The fear I see in her eyes guts me. I can't move her just yet.

"It's okay. Go back to sleep." I gently nudge her head back toward my chest. She settles against me without saying a word.

Kennedy disappears down the hall again. She comes back with a pillow and a blanket. She fluffs the pillow and puts it behind my head. She unfolds the blanket and drapes it over Peyton and me.

"What are you doing?" It's clear what she's doing, but I need to know I'm reading this right.

"She'll freak out if you leave," Kennedy whispers. "The couch is comfortable. We've fallen asleep on it many times. Tomorrow, we'll find a way to help her let you go home. For tonight, we do what's best for her."

She leans down and kisses Peyton on the cheek. I gently grab her wrist. It was a bad move on my part, but I couldn't help it. She doesn't pull away. Hope begins to build, and old memories flash in my mind.

"Thank you," I whisper.

"I'm doing this for her."

"Thank you for her." I release her wrist and watch as she locks up the apartment and hurries to her room.

I crossed a line by touching her. It was bound to happen, but it was too soon. After learning the truth, I can't get her out of my head. I couldn't understand why she'd cheat after the passionate relationship we had. She didn't cheat on me. It was the reason I tried to hate her. I don't hate her. I want her. I want both of them.

Chapter Eighteen

Kennedy

Last night's decision to let Aaron stay was a good thing and a problem at the same time. It was what Peyton needed, and her needs will always come first. However, it was a problem for me. I tossed and turned all night. Just knowing Aaron was in my apartment had my mind so messed up.

I woke around three with a terrible headache and slipped to the kitchen for some ibuprofen and water. My daughter was sound asleep in her dad's arms. I wasn't prepared for the sight. Yes, I've imagined them together many times. Seeing it pulled at my heartstrings. I may have gotten my phone and snapped a few pictures. Okay. I did get some pictures of them asleep together on the couch. Staring at those pictures kept me awake for over an hour.

A sound from the kitchen has me bolting upright in bed. It's not super loud, but I hear the music, singing, and laughter. Peyton isn't a grumpy morning person. She's not exactly bouncing off the walls first thing in the morning, either. Hearing her sing and giggle pulls at my heart a little more.

The clock by my bed says it's almost seven. Peyton rarely sleeps past eight, even on weekends and when school's out. I have about three hours before I have to be at the salon. I slide out of bed and tiptoe down the hall toward the kitchen. If I'm lucky, I'll get a video of them before they notice me.

The scene in the kitchen is priceless. Peyton is sitting on the counter with her feet gently swinging as she sings. Aaron's cooking breakfast. I smell bacon and eggs. He appears to be making pancakes now. Maybe Aaron staying over wasn't such a bad idea after all. At least now I don't have to cook breakfast.

As soon as the song ends, Peyton snatches the phone up and starts a new one. I watch and record as they sing along. I want to laugh, but I'm not ready to give myself away. The song they're singing is from the *Disney* movie *Frozen*. For somebody who doesn't want to watch Princess movies, Aaron sure knows all the words to the song. I freeze and stop recording.

Still unnoticed, I slip back into the hall and cover my mouth with my hand. He knows the words to *Disney* songs. He said he wasn't married, but it doesn't mean he doesn't have other kids. He wouldn't know the words to a girl movie song unless he knows a little girl. My heart breaks thinking of someone else having kids with him. But what did I expect? He's the sexiest man I've ever seen. A woman was bound to snatch him up sooner or later. It'll destroy Peyton if he has a family he's going back to.

"We're done," Aaron announces.

"I'll go get Mom." Peyton hops off the counter.

Oh no. I have to move. To keep from getting caught watching them, I rush toward the kitchen. Peyton and I collide in the doorway.

"Morning, Pumpkin." I try to sound a little sleepy. I'm not sure it worked.

"You're up." Peyton takes my hand and pulls me to the table.

"What's all this?" I pretend to be surprised. Well, I am surprised. I wasn't expecting Aaron to make breakfast.

"I was hungry, so Dad cooked breakfast." Peyton pulls a chair out for me.

It concerns me a little how easily she took to calling him dad. She was happy when Jeffrey's dad became a part of his life last year. She tried to hide it, but I saw the sad look she'd get sometimes. She wanted her dad, too. Phillip stepped up and became an uncle to her. Devon has always made her feel special. Still, there's nothing like your real dad. I've always had mine. I don't know what it's like not to have a loving father around. When I became a single mom, my dad was here, holding my hand.

"This looks amazing." Peyton leans in for a hug, and I kiss her cheek. My eyes meet Aaron's over the top of her head. "Thank you."

"It's not a problem." Aaron smiles and slides a cup of coffee across the table. "I hope you still take it with cream and sugar."

"I do." I take a sip and watch as Peyton hurries over to sit beside her dad. I feel a little left out over here by myself.

"So, what's the schedule for the day?" Aaron places a pancake on Peyton's plate and two on his. He acts like this is a normal domestic thing we've always done.

"Well, I open the salon at ten, like always. Peyton is spending the day with Aunt Tara and Jeffrey. I'll meet her and the kids at Enchanted Stitches around four. Today's their final fitting."

"If they fit, we get to take them home," Peyton adds.

"Mind if I'm there for the fitting?"

"Mom, can he come? Please?" Peyton practically begs.

"If he wants to. It's fine with me." I shrug.

"Good." Aaron takes a sip of coffee. "I'd like to introduce my daughter to my aunt."

"Your aunt?" Peyton's eyes widen.

"Peyton and Mrs. Wallace already know each other," I remind him. It's a small town. There's no way she wouldn't know his aunt.

"Mrs. Wallace is your aunt?" Peyton's mouth drops open.

"She is." Aaron taps Peyton on the nose. "You two may know each other, but I want to formally introduce you to your great-aunt."

"Mrs. Wallace is my aunt too?" Peyton is totally shocked.

"She is," I confirm.

Peyton's face scrunches up. "Does that make Tucker and Tristan my uncles? Those two are weird."

Aaron and I laugh. Tucker and Tristan are fun and outgoing. They're always acting up for a laugh during the town festivals.

"No, Little Bit. Tucker and Tristan are weird, but they're your cousins," Aaron replies. "So are Marley and Haven."

"Wow." Peyton just realized how much larger her family grew. Aaron's aunt has four children: two boys and two girls.

"If you're finished eating, why don't you wash up and get dressed?" I suggest.

Her head snaps toward Aaron. "Are you leaving?"

"I'll wait and walk you, ladies, to the car." He holds up a finger and slightly tilts his head. "But remember, I told you, I have some things to do today." Peyton pouts. "Don't be sad. I'll see you this afternoon at your fitting."

"Okay." Peyton slides out of her chair and gives Aaron a hug. When their little moment is over, she hurries to her room.

I busy myself with cleaning up. "Thank you for talking to her."

Aaron starts loading the dishwasher. "I wasn't trying to overstep. I just didn't want her to freak out today. I explained the best I could that I couldn't spend every minute with her."

"It's fine, and I appreciate it. I want you to know she's never freaked out like that before." Just thinking about it makes me want to cry. My usually bouncy, happy little girl couldn't handle her emotions yesterday.

"Hey." Aaron covers one of my hands on the counter with his. I focus on them for a moment before looking up at him. "This was a lot for her. Honestly, it's a lot for you and me too. I'm not sure how to handle things. We can't expect our nine-year-old daughter to be able to either."

"You're right." I hold his gaze. His blue eyes were always hard to look away from. "You're good with her."

"She makes it easy." He shrugs. "Being around her calms me. It feels natural."

"You obviously calm her, too," I say softly.

Aaron's eyes drop to my lips and back to my eyes. Oh. My. Gosh. I swear the temperature went up twenty degrees in here. Maybe it was just my blood. Oh, how I wish he were still mine.

"You and I need to have a private conversation soon." His voice lowers as he leans a little closer. "Unless you feel the need to have another chaperone."

"I don't." I shake my head. Yeah, it was nice having Devon with us last night. He actually helped.

"Good," he whispers. "I'll arrange it."

"Mom!" Peyton calls out. "Where's my bag?"

Saved by our daughter. Or was I? "By the front door!"

"I got it." Aaron grins and slowly backs away. He finds the backpack and takes it to Peyton.

I start the dishwasher and head to my room to get dressed. Aaron is leaning against the doorframe to Peyton's room. She's packing her bag for the day with Jeffrey. The moment in the kitchen still has me hot and bothered. If there was a moment. Well, for me, there was.

I pause in the hallway and glance over my shoulder at him. Aaron's eyes slowly move up my legs and finally to my eyes. His lips turn up on one side in a sly grin. I glance down and gasp. I rush into my room and close the door. I'm still in my shorty pajamas. If there wasn't a moment in the kitchen, there definitely was one in the hallway. The way his eyes hungrily moved over me will have me messed up for the rest of the day.

Chapter Nineteen

Aaron

Peyton's costume fitting went well. She and Jeffrey got to take their costumes home afterward. My little girl is going to look amazing on stage during the Memorial Day Festival. My little girl. Wow. That statement alone is amazing. Peyton was beyond thrilled to officially meet her great-aunt. Miss Susie has become Aunt Susie to her. It was one of the proudest moments of my life. By the look on Aunt Susie's face, she already knew Peyton was my daughter.

I've been helping Wade and Sawyer work on my dad's house. I need the place remodeled and fast. Noah and Tucker don't have a lot of spare time, but they promise to help out when they can. Even Tucker's little brother, Tristan, has offered to help.

Today, I'm finally going to get to sit down with Jude and talk about my new job. He called last night to inform me we'd be having a late breakfast this morning. Breakfast is usually over at The Magnolia Inn at ten. The dining room closes for an hour before opening back up for lunch. It's a little off, but my breakfast with Jude is scheduled at ten.

Who in the world makes a breakfast business appointment when a place is closed? I didn't argue the fact with Jude. I just agreed. We can move our meeting to my room when he discovers the dining room is closed. Well, it's still technically Jude's room, but I've stayed here as he so nicely requested. It was a firm request, I might add.

I arrive in the dining room fifteen minutes early. I might as well grab a quick meal before the restaurant closes. A family and two elderly ladies from town look like they're finishing up. The family ignores me, except for the dad. He smiles and nods. I do the same and make my way to a small table in front of the windows. The two elderly ladies watch my every move. Great. Hayden Falls gossipers lurk around every corner in this town. These two old biddies don't even try to hide their whispering.

"Good morning, Aaron." Riley sets a cup of coffee on my table with a small container of cream and sugar packets. She's been my server every morning.

"Good morning." I drop my eyes back to the menu.

"Your meal has already been ordered," Riley informs me with a smile.

I lightly laugh. I'm not that predictable. "How do you know what I want?"

"I don't." Riley shakes her head. "E said everything for you was taken care of, and your friend should be here soon."

"Ah." I nod and hand her the menu. There's no point in looking at it. My mysterious boss has, once again, handled everything.

Riley moves to her other guests and lets them know the dining room is closing in ten minutes. The family thanks her and quickly finishes up. They gather their two small children in their arms and leave. The two elderly ladies will use every second of their ten minutes. I casually sip my coffee and ignore them.

At ten o'clock on the dot, E Maxwell enters the dining room. She goes straight to the two women. "Ladies, the dining room is now closed. I hope you enjoyed your breakfast."

"We did." The lady in the purple flower pantsuit looks around E at me. I'm pretty sure she's Ms. Taylor.

"Lovely." E motions to the door with one hand. "If you don't mind, we have a lot to do to get ready for lunch."

The two ladies try to linger, but E ushers them to the dining room doors. Once they're in the hallway, one of the front desk clerks takes over and walks them out of the Inn. E quickly closes the double doors to the dining room and locks them.

If I weren't a man who could fight his way out of a tough situation, I'd be alarmed about now. I'm not locked in a room with no exit. There's a side entrance to the dining room. It leads to the hallway where the offices and restrooms are. I've mainly seen employees use it. E locks it, too. Still, I'm not sweating over it. There's another exit through the kitchen.

Approximately ten minutes later, Jude walks in through the kitchen door and sits down across from me. Riley has already cleared the dining room tables. E comes in with a serving cart with enough food to feed an army. She hurries away and returns with another cart with coffee and every drink you could imagine for breakfast.

"You, gentlemen, have about forty-five to fifty minutes before we open for lunch. You can have more time if no one is waiting in the hallway." E refills my coffee and pours Jude a cup.

"Don't you have to get ready for lunch?" I asked.

"Beverly and I have already prepped for lunch today. The kitchen door is locked. You two won't be disturbed." She smiles at Jude. "Text me if you need anything. I'll be in my office." E hurries out the side door and locks it behind her.

"Good morning." Jude takes a sip of his coffee. He doesn't smile.

"Why all the secrecy?" I ask.

"I don't like discussing business in the open, but the Inn is easy enough to secure." He sets his cup down. "I'd prefer to bring you to the office in Missoula for this. Since you have a new obligation here, and there's a big holiday festival starting tomorrow, I figured you wouldn't want to leave town just yet."

Somehow, he knows about my daughter. I'm not sure if it's a good thing or a bad one. I don't know this man. I'm not sure I can trust him.

What's your interest in me?"

"We can always use someone with your skill set, and you came highly recommended." Jude begins to fill his plate and passes the severing bowls to me.

"Why would a security company in Montana need my skill set?" I seem to have lost my appetite. I fill my plate anyway.

"We aren't just limited to Montana," Jude replies.

"What makes you think I'm a good fit for your company?" Why does it feel like I'm the one leading this conversation? Shouldn't he be the one asking all the questions here?

"You're a sharpshooter and a darn good one. Your family doesn't even know that. We've been looking for a sharpshooter for a while now." Jude pauses to take a few bites. At least one of us can eat.

"Why does a security company need a sharpshooter?"

"It's rare, but sometimes, we have special jobs and need the skill." Jude grins for the first time.

There are so many hidden meanings behind his statement. I'm not sure I like what he's implying. Then again, maybe the man just gives off a mysterious persona to throw people off.

"You know a lot about me." I pick up a piece of bacon and take a bite. As much as I love bacon, I don't really taste it. I've been waiting days to talk with this man, and he has me a bit on edge.

"We know more than we need to in order to offer you the job," he admits.

I have no doubts Slone Security has run a profile on me. Something tells me they've dug a lot deeper than the average company can. Even if I had something to hide, it would be pointless. The man sitting across from me already knows everything about me.

"I didn't realize I had a choice in this." I lean back and cross my arms.

"You can always say no if that's what you want." Jude pulls out a piece of paper and slides it across the table.

"What's this?" It's just a list of numbers.

"The top number is what we paid Mick Calhoun. The second number is a rough estimate of his medical expenses," Jude explains.

"You gave Mick Calhoun twenty-five thousand dollars for pain and suffering?" Now I wonder if Jude is as smart as I thought he was.

"He probably would have taken less. We would have paid more, but Mr. Calhoun agreed to our first offer." Jude props his elbow on the table and tosses his hand up as though it's no big deal. "Doctor Larson assures me that Mick will be fine. His cheek will take a few months to heal, but he doesn't need surgery. His medical expenses shouldn't break ten thousand."

"There's another twenty-five thousand on here," I point out.

"That will be your donation to the Hayden Falls Sheriff's Office," Jude explains.

"What? You're buying the Sheriff's Office?" I never in a million years imagined Sheriff Barnes was a dirty cop.

"Not at all." Jude shakes his head and ignores my outburst. "We don't work that way. It's a *thank you* for them handling things in a quiet and timely manner."

"Twenty-five grand is an awfully big *thank you*," I mumble.

"This is your hometown. Your family is here. After your little incident at Cowboys, this will help keep peace with the local authorities." Jude shows no signs of emotion. Maybe he's an honest man. At the moment, I don't rightly know.

"How long do I have to work with you to pay this debt off?" I ask.

"We take no one on for less than three years." Jude doesn't even twitch.

Three years? It sounds like I'm signing up for the Army again. "At the end of three years, I can leave?"

"If you wish." Jude refills his coffee cup.

"Has anyone ever left?"

"No," he replies. "Every member of our team becomes family the day they're hired. Look. I understand your concerns. It might take you a little while to warm up to us. But trust me. One day, you'll see how tight of a group we are. Slone Security has some of the best men and women on the planet."

There's an even larger number at the bottom of the page. I point to it. "And this?"

"That's your yearly salary." Jude doesn't bat an eye. "Plus, you get holiday pay with time off on them if possible. We even have an outstanding medical and dental package."

If I didn't know better, I'd swear he's teasing. One look at his face and it's perfectly clear, Jude Harrington doesn't joke when it comes to his business.

"Who recommended me?" Maybe knowing this will help calm my nerves.

"Two men I trust and highly respect." Jude looks over his shoulder. We're still alone and have plenty of time before the restaurant opens for lunch. He looks me in the eye. "Aiden Maxwell was the first."

Ah. It explains why Aiden was acting weird the night I hit Four. He seemed pretty friendly with Jude when he arrived at the Sheriff's Office.

"Aiden called you when I was arrested?" He doesn't have to answer. I'm sure of it.

Jude nods. "He knew the type of agent we were looking for. We ran your name in a quick search, and I made a phone call. Within twenty minutes, I was on my way to Hayden Falls."

"Who did you call?"

Jude sighs. He doesn't want to give up the person's name. I raise an eyebrow. If he wants me to work for him, he needs to be honest with me.

"Cage Cunningham," he finally replies.

"Okay." I trust both of these men as much as Jude does.

"Okay? Does that mean you're part of Slone's team?" Jude taps a finger on the table. His expression is hopeful.

"Do I have to live in Missoula?" This wouldn't go well for Peyton.

"No. Your father's house is fine. We'll contact a moving company and have your things from North Carolina brought here." Jude waits for a firm answer.

"Yeah. I'm part of your team," I reply. I'm still not a hundred percent sure of what I'm signing up for.

"Welcome to the Slone family." Jude holds his hand out. "I'll text you the office address. Be there Tuesday morning to sign your contract. Those never leave the office."

It explains why he doesn't have the contract with him today. I take his hand. A handshake between honest men is just as good as a signature. I wasn't planning on taking a job in security when I left the

Army. Sure, a lot of ex-soldiers do it. If Jude's right, this will probably be my lifelong career. We'll have to wait and see. If it doesn't work for my family life, I can quit in three years.

"Thanks, man." For now, the job helps to keep me here. I was going to have to find one anyway because I'm not leaving knowing I have a daughter here.

"We're also helping you with your other little problem." Jude leans back and picks up his fork.

"Problem?" Mick Calhoun was enough of a problem for me.

"You have a lot of resources available to you now. You need to find Mark Bevins." Jude grins. The twinkle in his eyes scares me. "He's still in Denver, by the way."

I nod. My grin matches Jude's. I definitely want to find that snake. One day soon, I'll look the man who destroyed my life in the eye. Mark Bevins will pay for what he's done to my family.

Chapter Twenty

Kennedy

My last appointment before lunch left around eleven thirty. I move around to each of my girls' stations and help out as much as I can so we can lock the doors at noon. Lindsey and Hope are finishing up when the bell above the door jingles. I close my eyes and groan. So close. Only ten minutes before we can close for lunch. It doesn't matter who the new customer is. We're all booked solid for the next three weeks.

"Hey, Aaron," Savannah calls out. She continues sweeping up the hair from her last cut.

"Hey, Vanna. Good to see you," Aaron says.

"This looks great." I praise Jade's work before turning to face Aaron.

He stands in front of the reception desk with three boxes of pizza from Antonio's. I wasn't expecting him to bring lunch. Well, I assume it's for all of us.

"What brings you by?" I ask.

"If that pizza isn't for us, he can leave and never come back," Hope teases. Well, I don't think she's really teasing. Hope loves pizza.

"Two are for you, ladies." Aaron sets them on the desk.

"Oh, thank goodness." Lindsey runs to the front door and locks it behind Jade's last customer.

Aaron laughs as she grabs the two boxes. Savannah hurries to the employee lounge for paper plates.

"Thank you." I walk toward him. "You didn't have to do this."

"I wanted to." He shrugs. "I hope you don't mind."

"Hope does not mind at all." Hope grabs the first slice from the top box.

"I don't mind." I lightly laugh. "The girls love pizza."

He laughs, too. "Yeah. I can tell. I thought Lindsey was going to tackle me for them."

I point to the last box on the desk. "Are you taking that one to Peyton? She's at Mom's house today."

He tilts his head slightly and grins. "No. I thought you and I could have lunch in the park."

I take a step back. "You want to have lunch with me?"

He nods. "If you have the time. If not, I can join you ladies here."

"Oh, she has time." Savannah sets two paper plates and a stack of napkins on Aaron's pizza box.

"And here." Jade shoves two sodas into my hands.

"Use the back door," Hope suggested.

"Okay." I motion for him to follow me through the salon. "I guess we're having lunch in the park."

We walk out the back door and cross the small street behind the salon. You can't call this an alley because no buildings are behind this row of shops. There are parking spaces on both sides of the one-way street for the shop owners and employees. Past the street is the park.

A few families are having lunch with small children running around. Starting tomorrow, the park will be packed for three days straight for the Memorial Day Festival.

The Fire Department is to the right of the park and below the diner. They have a lot of activity going on today. They aren't heading out for an emergency call at the moment. The Fire Department grills during the summer festivals. I see Devon and wave. He pauses and stands up straight. He sees the pizza box Aaron's carrying. He nods but gives me the fingers to his eyes. My dear little brother will be watching. I laugh and shake my head. Devon plays the Big Brother role to the fullest sometimes.

We walk to a picnic table next to the river. It's in view of the station but away from the other families. "Is this okay?"

"It's fine." Aaron sits on the bench next to me. He sets the pizza box on the table and opens the lid. "I hope you still like Supreme."

I set the plates out and eagerly reached for a slice. "Absolutely."

Aaron laughs and grabs a slice. "I take it you have to get pepperoni with Peyton."

I nod while taking a bite. Peyton refuses to try anything but pepperoni. I tried to do veggie pizza for a couple of months, but it failed big time. Aaron takes a napkin and wipes the sauce from the corner of my mouth. Embarrassed from being so eager, I drop the pizza on my plate and take the napkin from him.

"Thank you," I say softly.

He lets the moment drop. "So, has the Memorial Day Festival changed much?"

"No," I reply. "The party at the lake will be in full swing by dinner tonight. Some of the campers are probably already getting set up. A few tourists will start showing up tomorrow. It's mainly a day for the shops around the square. Several hold little events or drawings. Sunday, the park will be overflowing with families. Monday is the big day. The stage will be busy from nine in the morning until the fireworks at the end of the festival. Of course, the baseball game is in the middle of the afternoon. It's still a big hit."

"Do you know what time Peyton will be on stage?" Aaron pops the tops on our sodas.

"Around one. My shift at the salon ends at noon. I'll watch Peyton and Jeffrey perform, and we'll head to the game." I can't wait to watch my little girl perform.

We don't have regular appointments on festival days. It's a day of fun and games. We mainly do fingernail painting during events. It's first come, first served. We even hold a nail painting contest for prizes.

"Sounds about the same as I remember." Aaron notices Devon watching us and laughs. "Do you always watch the game?"

"Not always. The girls and I switch up who works the afternoon shift every year. If Devon is on duty, I'm at the salon." I wave to my nosy brother. He seems to be itching closer to the park. "Peyton and I wouldn't miss it this year."

"Devon must be playing this year." His expression turns sad. "I haven't played baseball since my Senior year."

Neither of us brings up when that was. It was a week before he left for boot camp. The high school team won every year he played in the town's charity game. The years they had Aiden as their pitcher, they couldn't lose. Sadly, Aiden never got the professional career he was destined to have. He seems happy right where he is, though. He has E and little Caleb now. His younger brother got an MLB career. Aiden shows no sign of resentment. He's Brady's biggest fan.

"Don't worry. You'll do great," I assure him.

"Huh?" Aaron's eyebrows pull together.

"I'm sure playing baseball is like riding a bike. You'll be fine." I grab another slice of pizza.

"I don't understand." He pulls one leg over the bench and turns to face me.

"You're on the team." I lightly laugh. Maybe he forgot.

He shakes his head. "No. I'm not."

That's weird. "Your name is on the list."

"Where did you see this list?"

"Hayden Happenings." I pull up the website on my phone and hand it to him.

His eyes lift to mine. "I didn't sign up."

His eyes are so blue, I swear I could swim in them. On many occasions, I did. They pull at me now just like they did years ago. I have to force myself to look away.

"You can call Aiden and tell him there's a mistake," I suggest.

"No. If Aiden signed me up, there's no mistake." Aaron exits the blog site and opens my contacts.

"What are you doing?" I reach for the phone.

He holds it away and quickly sends a text. His phone in his back pocket dings. "Now, you can have it back."

"You just got my number." I snatch my phone from his hand.

"Yes, ma'am. I sure did." He pulls out his phone and saves my number in his contacts.

"What if I didn't want you to have it?" I huff and shove my phone into my back pocket.

"We have a daughter. We need each other's number." He leans close and whispers, "Besides, I think you wanted my number."

Oh, the nerve of this man. I turn my head toward him and slowly lift my eyes to his. He's not wrong. I've asked every member of his family for his number several times over the years. His Aunt Susie flat refused to give it to me. The rest of his family said they didn't have it. Noah didn't have it either. He would have given it to me if he did. Even drunk, Tucker wouldn't give it to me. I finally gave up trying.

He's so close. It wouldn't take much to lean over and kiss him. I'd be lying if I said I didn't want to, but I can't. After all these years, being close to him still affects me deeply.

"Aaron," I whisper. Yeah, I just gave myself up here.

"Don't worry, Peaches." He drops his forehead against mine. Oh, how I've missed him. "We're gonna fix this."

I'm not sure what he means. He can definitely fix things with Peyton. It doesn't bother her in the least that he's been gone for ten years. I'm happy for Peyton. I really am. So much bad stuff has happened. I don't know if it's possible to fix things between him and me. If there was a way, would I take it? In a heartbeat.

Chapter Twenty-One

Aaron

The moment my eyes opened this morning, a buzz of excitement went through me. It's my first Memorial Day in Hayden Falls in ten years, and I get to spend it with my daughter. My daughter. That's so amazing. Oh, and let's not forget her mother. I'll definitely be seeing more of her. After stealing Kennedy's phone number on Friday, I texted and called her every day. Okay. I've used her number several times a day.

The Magnolia Inn is booked up for the holiday weekend. My wonderful new boss has included my room as part of my pay until my dad's house is ready. Apparently, I can be called in the middle of the night for emergencies. I'm a security guard, not a cop or firefighter. Still, I'm expected to move when I'm called. The room here keeps me from disturbing my aunt's family late at night. My new job has too many mysterious details. There's nothing I can do about it now, though.

Surprisingly, Jude is here. Somehow, he managed to secure his own room in a booked-out Inn. I'm not going to ask questions. He and I have had breakfast together every morning. After breakfast, I don't see Jude again until the next morning. He never tells me where he's going. The man just disappears all day and pops up at the strangest times.

I've wandered around town for a couple of hours. I've even played a few games. I haven't won anything, but it's been fun. I really wanted to win the six months of free ice cream for Peyton. Sadly, my churning skills weren't up to par. Some guy in Walsburg won. Mackenzie Hanson announced that another six-month prize would be up for grabs at the Fall Festival. Six months is usually Frozen Scoops' prize for every festival. This year, for the Fourth of July Celebration, the prize will be a year of ice cream. I'll be polishing up my skills for that one.

It's almost noon. Kennedy's shift is about to end. With only an hour until Peyton performs on stage, I'm guessing our little girl will be getting ready at the salon. I grab a couple of chocolate milkshakes for Peyton and Jeffrey. The two are inseparable. The little guy will be getting ready wherever Peyton is. Kennedy needs a treat, too. I head over to Beth's for coffee for her and her girls. I would be murdered on sight if I showed up with only one cup of coffee. I made sure to include Tara. She's bound to be at the salon too.

Beth was a little out of sorts today and a bit snappy. Thankfully, Hadley Lunsford helped me out and made everyone's favorite drinks for me. I didn't even question what she charged me. I happily paid the bill. Hadley gives me two to-go carrying trays with handles. I slide the kids' milkshakes into two of the slots and head out the door. Stepping outside, I come face-to-face with Jessie Calhoun.

"Aaron." Jessie dips his chin.

"Jessie." I do the same.

"See you at the game." Jessie opens the door to Beth's.

"Yep." I smile and walk away. Yeah. I'll see him at the game. We're on the same team.

The only member of the Calhoun family I've seen since the night I hit Four was Marcie. She's a front desk clerk at the Inn. The moment I looked across the counter into Marcie's green eyes, I knew she was a Calhoun. She's sweet and polite. She never mentioned the fight, so I didn't either.

I weave through the crowd to cross the street. I'm a little shocked when I step up onto the sidewalk outside Page Turners. I wouldn't have thought Hayden Falls needed a bookstore, but from the number of people I've seen go in there, I'm wrong. People are waiting to enter now.

"Hey, Aaron." Karlee Davis steps up onto the sidewalk beside me. She's carrying a couple of huge to-go bags from the diner.

"Hey, Karlee. Where you heading?" After what ended up in the gossip blog from buying her coffee, I shouldn't be talking to her. However, I'm not trying to be rude today.

"The salon," she replied. "Hope called the order in."

I groan inwardly. Just my luck. They're not locking the door today for lunch because of the festival, but I wanted to arrive before Kennedy's shift ended. I'm not sure if it's a good idea to walk in with Karlee. I have nothing against Karlee. I just don't want her to get the wrong idea.

"I didn't know the diner was delivering today." I keep the conversation light and casual as we weave through the customers outside the bookstore.

"We usually don't. Hope called back to say they'd be late picking it up. My grandmother wasn't having anybody getting cold food. So, here I am." Karlee lightly laughs.

Is her laugh genuine? Or is she flirting with me? I sure hope she's not. I don't flirt, so I don't know how to take this. It's Megan's fault. If she hadn't written the blog post, I wouldn't be concerned right now.

"I got it." Phillip Crawford holds his hand out for the to-go bags. "You can head back to the diner. Miss Cora is running ragged right now."

"Oh, thanks, Phillip." Karlee's eyes dart away as she hands the bags to Phillip.

"Wait, Karlee." I try to juggle the coffee to get my wallet. "Let me tip you." It was nice of her to bring the salon's order out.

"I got it." Phillip moves both bags to one hand and offers Karlee some cash.

"Uh." Karlee seems reluctant to take the money from him.

"Here. I'll tip her." Devon hands her ten dollars.

Karlee takes the money from Devon without hesitation. She turns and leaves so fast it has me scratching my head. Well, mentally, anyway. My hands are full.

"What was that about?" I look between Devon and Phillip.

"The last thing you need is for it to get back to Kennedy that you had anything to do with Karlee," Phillip says as we start moving through the crowd again.

Devon pokes Phillip on the shoulder. "The same thing goes for you. Tara will claw Karlee's eyes out."

"We're married." Phillip narrows his eyes. "Tara knows she has nothing to worry about."

"Doesn't matter." Devon shakes his head. "I admit Karlee has been quiet lately, but she's still Karlee."

"Do I want to know what you two are talking about?" Karlee isn't a problem for me. If they think my talking to her will affect Kennedy somehow, then I need to know what's going on.

"Let's just say Karlee and Brittney Douglas caused a lot of trouble after you left town," Phillip replied.

"They still try at times," Devon adds.

Okay. Good to know. I'll get them to tell me more later. For now, I'll watch what I say and do around both women.

"Hopefully, the little moment back there doesn't end up in Hayden Happenings," I mumble. Being in there once was enough for me.

"It probably will," Phillip said.

"Maybe not. Megan has her sights set on bigger stories right now." Devon reaches for the door of the salon.

Phillip stops him from opening it. "Such as?"

"Brady Maxwell and Levi Barnes," Devon replies.

"Levi?" Phillip sounds shocked.

"Yep." Devon laughs. "He's livid right now. Megan has a photo of him talking to Tabetha Sailors at the market. She twisted the moment so badly."

"Poor Levi." Better him than me, but I do feel bad for Levi.

"Okay. Let's go make our ladies happy." Phillip holds up the bags of food and nods toward the coffee I'm carrying. His eyes meet mine. "Then we'll help our kids get ready for their performance."

"Sounds good to me." I'm so ready for this.

Devon opens the door, and we follow him in. I'm going to have to get used to Phillip being around. His wife is Kennedy's best friend, and his son is my daughter's best friend. The talk around town is he's not the jerk he was in high school. It would be bad if we were enemies.

"Uncle Devon!" Peyton shouts and runs into his arms.

Jealousy will crush a man's spirit. Devon has been a constant figure in her life. I understand it, but it still hurts seeing her run to another man. My daughter hasn't seen me yet. A couple of tourists have stepped into the salon, blocking her view of the door.

"What about me?" Phillip asked.

"Hey, Uncle Phillip." Peyton waves to him.

"Dad!" Jeffrey rushes to Phillip as he sets the bags of food on the reception desk.

"Hey, little man." Phillip scoops his son up.

"What about me?" I step into Peyton's view.

"Daddy!" Peyton wiggles out of Devon's arms. I kneel, and she runs into mine. Devon glares at me. Now he knows how I felt a few minutes ago.

I hug my little girl the best I can with the trays of coffee in my hands. Devon hurries over to take them. I close my eyes and hug her tightly to my chest for a few minutes.

"I got you and Jeffrey chocolate milkshakes." I stand and point toward Devon.

"Thank you, Daddy." Peyton gets hers and hands Jeffrey his.

"Thank you, Uncle Aaron." Jeffrey takes a sip and follows Peyton to the back of the salon.

I freeze and look between the little boy and Phillip. He called me uncle. Philip laughs and nods. Guess I'm being accepted into their family.

"What's this?" Kennedy asked.

“I got coffee for you and your girls.” I take one of the trays from Devon and start handing the cups out. Thank goodness their names are on the cups.

“You didn’t have to do this,” she says.

“Hush up, girl.” Savannah grabs the other tray and passes those out.

Surprisingly, there’s a coffee for Andi Crawford. How Hadley knew I’d need it is beyond me. I’ll be sure to thank her for it later.

“Thank you for this.” She slightly lifts the cup and motions for me to follow her. “You know they’ll be expecting little treats like this from now on.”

“It’s not a problem,” I assure her.

We make our way to the employee lounge. It’s really just a fancy breakroom. Tara is already setting the kids’ food on one of the tables. Their costumes are hanging on hooks by the door. My excitement builds. I can’t wait to see Peyton on stage today.

“After Peyton eats and gets changed, do you want to walk to the stage with us?” Kennedy’s eyes drop and quickly come back to mine.

“I’d love to.” I grin at her and wink at Peyton. My little girl giggles and bounces in her chair.

I was going to be there anyway. It’s nice to be invited, though. I have no idea how to be a father. So far, I’m enjoying every minute of it.

Chapter Twenty-Two

Kennedy

Peyton and Jeffrey wave to us from their place in line next to the stage. Hannah leads her younger class down the steps on one side while the high school class takes the stage from the other side. Peyton and Jeffrey are next. I'm even more nervous than she is. The dance school's recital is two weeks away. It will mainly be family and friends at the recital. I can handle the recital. Today's audience is bigger and full of people we don't know.

Tara leans close, and we grab each other's hands. She's practically vibrating in her skin. She has more reasons to be nervous than I do. She has Jeffrey's inhaler in her purse in case he needs it. Hannah assures her he'll be fine.

The high school girls are amazing. Peyton watches from the steps in awe. She could be in a bigger class like this, but she refuses to leave Jeffrey out. I'm proud of how protective she is of him. I glance around the square. More than half of these people could take friendship lessons from her.

Chloe Hamilton is front and center. She's leading the others, but they move as a group. Still, it's hard to take your eyes off Chloe. The girl has moves I wish I had. She has a solo dance after Peyton and Jeffrey. Her brother, Miles, and his wife, Katie, watch from a few feet away. Like us, they're in the front of the crowd.

Miles beams with pride. He glances around the crowd at times and glares like he wants to poke a few teenage boys in the eye. I can understand why. The high school girl's costume is slightly more revealing than the younger girls. Someone is watching Chloe with stars in his eyes. I'm not about to point the boy out to Miles.

As Peyton and Jeffrey walk onto the stage, Phillip steps behind Tara and wraps his arms around her. She needs it. Her husband can comfort her in ways her best friend can't. Aaron gets closer to me and places his hands on my hips. I close my eyes for a moment and get lost in his touch.

"Breathe, Peaches," he whispers in my ear. "She's going to do great."

I simply nod and lean back a little. He doesn't wrap his arms around me like Phillip did Tara. I'm a little jealous of my friend. His hands stay on my hips, so I take comfort in that. I release a shaky breath when the music starts. The music has a catchy beat. It's not too lively of a tune. Still, Tara stiffens a little. Even though there's no singing in this number, the crowd is enjoying it and clapping along. True to Hannah's word, Jeffrey's part of the routine is kept at a steady pace so it won't tire him out. Tara has tears in her eyes. She never imagined her son could do something like this.

Peyton and Jeffrey hold hands and take a bow when the music stops. Shouts, cheers, and whistles come from around the square. Aaron, Phillip, and Devon whistle and shout at the top of their lungs. I'm not sure who's the loudest. Peyton and Jeffrey grin at each other before hurrying to exit the stage. Hannah is beaming with pride as she helps them down the steps. Jeffrey rushes to his parents. Peyton runs straight for Aaron.

"Daddy!" she yells as she leaps into his arms.

"Little Bit, you were amazing."

The shift in the air is so strong I feel it in my bones. The tourists smile at the loving father and daughter before turning to watch the next performance. Chloe will wow them with her solo dance. The locals stop and stare as Aaron spins around with Peyton in his arms. Several women automatically drift into little groups. They huddle close and whisper behind their hands. Why do people do that? It's a dead giveaway that they're gossiping. I stiffen my spine and hold my head high.

"What's wrong?" Aaron bumps my shoulder with his.

"Nothing." My eyes dart around the square.

Aaron does the same, except he looks our wonderful townsfolk in the eye. I can feel the moment happiness is sucked from him. He sets Peyton on her feet.

"Little Bit, why don't you go back to the salon with Aunt Tara and Jeffrey?" He places her hand into Tara's.

"Come on, kids. Let's go get changed for the ballgame." Tara hurries Peyton and Jeffrey across the street.

"Aaron?" I place my hand on his arm. He's still looking around at the crowd. The nosy heifers are still staring and whispering.

Aaron waits until the music for Chloe's dance stops and for the applause to die down. His expression is hard, and his jaw is set tight. He takes a deep breath. I've never seen him like this. This is not the sweet, fun-loving boy I fell in love with in high school.

"That's right, Hayden Falls." Aaron steps away from me and holds both arms out. "Peyton is my daughter. Of course, you all already knew that. I don't know why you're acting so shocked now."

"Aaron." Devon tries to get his attention.

"Since you old biddies are going to stand here and whisper like children, let's get this over with. I'm right here. So if you have questions, ask them now." He makes a full circle around the crowd. The tourists look confused.

"Aaron, please," I softly plead with him.

"Sorry, Peaches. I don't have time for their foolishness." He tosses his hands up, prompting our townsfolk to speak. No one does.

"Let this go," Devon warns.

Aaron doesn't let anything go. "Where's Megan Sanders?"

Oh no. This fool is about to stir up a whole mess of trouble. He's going to get arrested again. Lucas Barnes is watching from outside Beth's Morning Brew. Hopefully, he'll stay on the sidewalk.

"Right here." Surprisingly, Megan steps forward.

Aaron points at her. "My daughter's name best never show up in your little blog. These people may be scared to go after you, but I'm not. I swear, if I see one hint of this in Hayden Happenings, I'm coming for you."

Shocked gasps come from the crowd, myself included. No one has ever openly threatened her. I glance toward the coffee shop. Lucas drops his head and laughs.

"My blog is for entertainment." Megan lifts her chin. "Besides, I never use kids like that."

"See to it you never do." Aaron takes a step toward Megan. Lucas moves to the edge of the sidewalk. He's no longer laughing. "Just because you have the little entertainment clause on your site means nothing to me. You and I both know it can still be taken down."

All eyes drift to Megan. She nods. "Not a problem." Before Aaron could say more, she disappeared into the crowd.

"Since there are no questions, go about your business." Aaron flicks his wrist, waving the crowd away.

I grab his hand and pull him toward the salon before he starts up again. Phillip and Devon walk behind him as a security measure. It's ironic. They're securing the security guard. The moment we step into the salon, my girls cheer and clap. They each give Aaron a high-five or a fist bump.

"That was epic!" Andi Crawford claps as she bounces up and down.

"Relax, Priss." Devon places his hands on Andi's shoulders and guides her to one of the chairs in the waiting area.

I whirl around to face Aaron. "Are you insane?"

"What?" Aaron shrugs.

"You can't go off on the whole town like that," I snap.

"I didn't." He shakes his head. "I just confronted Megan and all the nosy old biddies."

"You threatened Megan," I correct him.

"Somebody needed to," Phillip mumbled.

"Look, Peaches." Aaron places his hands on my hips again. "I'm sorry you're upset, but I'm not sorry for what I did."

"You can't threaten people. You could get arrested." If he goes to jail, we lose him again.

"I won't." His eyes drop to my lips.

"You don't know that." My eyes drop to his lips.

The heat in the room just jumped fifty degrees. People move about the room. Fingernail painting is going on at several little stations. All I see is him.

"He won't," a man confirms.

We turn to find Jude Harrington standing in the doorway. Phillip uses this man's security company to monitor the bank. He's tried to talk me into getting one of Slone Security's systems. I've had no need for a stronger system. The one I have was purchased from the hardware store here in town. I monitor it through an app on my phone and computer.

"Jude, good to see you." Aaron looks at him over his shoulder. He doesn't let go of my hips. "We good here?"

"Yep." Jude nods. "We'll monitor the blog. If your daughter shows up in it, we got it covered."

"Thanks." Aaron nods, and Jude quietly leaves.

"We have a game to get ready for," Devon reminds everybody.

"Come on, Bailey." Phillip tosses an arm over Aaron's shoulder. "Our uniforms are in the back. We'll change after the kids finish up."

Aaron, Phillip, and Devon disappear into the back hallway. Phillip brought in a duffle bag earlier. I wasn't aware it was their uniforms for today.

"Girl," Savannah loudly whispers as she loops her arm around mine. "I thought he was going to kiss you." The others nod.

A slow smile crosses my lips. "I wish he would."

Savannah, Hope, and Lindsey wrap me in their arms. Jade and Andi giggle like teenagers. I feel like one right now.

Maybe, just maybe, there's a chance to fix things with Aaron. I leave the girls and hurry to my office to change. A great place to start will be cheering him on during the game today.

Chapter Twenty-Three

Aaron

I rode with Kennedy and Peyton to the baseball field. It's good to see that the town has added to this area. They've added another field for the younger players. The concession stand and restrooms are bigger and have a modern design. The bleachers are metal and not the wooden things we had to use. There are a couple of batting cages, too. I'm impressed.

Nearly every man I walk past from the parking lot to the field gives me a high-five. The ones too far away throw their hand up. Today wouldn't be a big deal if the rest of them would stand up for what's right. For goodness sakes. It's a freakin gossip blog for entertainment. Whatever that's supposed to mean. Megan knows it's more than entertainment. Still, it's not like she can physically hurt anybody. Yet, her words have a way of stirring up turmoil for innocent people.

Kennedy and Peyton set their chairs on the grass in the shaded area near third base. I put their cooler and beach bag of snacks behind their chairs. Naturally, Tara and Jeffrey set up next to them. Surprisingly, some of Kennedy's friends are also lined up along this spot. Several of these ladies have a husband or boyfriend on the team. I like that my girls are here instead of in the bleachers. It looks as though the men's team has the dugout on this side of the field.

"Okay, ladies. It's time to go score some runs." Hopefully, I can still play baseball.

"Good luck, Daddy." Peyton wraps her arms around my waist.

I lean down. "How about a kiss for luck, Little Bit?"

She giggles and kisses me on the cheek. Standing up, I glance at her mother and grin. Might as well go for broke.

I tap my other cheek. "What do you say, Mom." She cuts her eyes at me. "For luck?" I coax.

"You're impossible," she whispers.

Still, she lifts up on her toes and presses her lips to my cheek. Perfect, but I want more. Sadly, I can't take more from her yet. I never would without her permission.

"I can't lose now." I reach for Kennedy's hand and give it a light squeeze. This little bit of contact will have to be enough for now.

I ruffle Peyton's hair and walk away. Before I walk through the gate, I glance back at them. Peyton and Jeffrey are opening sodas while their mothers whisper to each other. The joy on Kennedy's face makes me smile. As happy as this moment is, my heart hurts. I should have been here with them like this all along.

"They're fine." Phillip pats me on the back as he walks by.

"Let's go show these teenagers how to play." Devon follows Phillip through the gate.

Aiden's waiting for us outside the dugout with a clipboard in his hand. He quickly assigns our positions. Thankfully, he gave me my old spot in left field. I'll be close to my girls.

Since both sides are home teams, we take turns on who bats first every year. The high school team is up first this year. That's good. I'll get to warm up a little before I have to bat. I slip my glove on, and Phillip tosses me a ball. He'll be in center field today.

"Take a few minutes to warm up, but play hard," Aiden calls out. He's our team captain. "My little brother cannot win this."

"I didn't know Brady was here." I look around but don't see him. He's not a teen anymore. Surely, they aren't letting a professional baseball player on the high school team.

"He's not." Aiden points to the kid on deck. "My parents adopted Chase a few months ago."

Wow. I didn't know that. Looking at the kid, you'd think he was a Maxwell by blood. Aiden's parents are on the other side of the field. His wife and son are near Kennedy. The biggest surprise of the day is Aiden's older brother, Colton. He's sitting in the bleachers next to his parents. The Maxwell family is divided today. It should be a great game.

"Is he any good?" Chase concerns me. If he's anything like Aiden and Brady, he's a force to be reckoned with. We might not stand a chance.

"He does okay." Aiden points to the kid standing at the edge of the dugout. "Elliott Matthews is the one we have to watch. Brady trained him."

I hear Peyton's laughter and snap my head in her direction. She sees me and waves. I'll give this game my all. There's no way I'm losing in front of my little girl.

"Aiden, we have to win this. I can't look bad in front of her." I may pass out from the heat, but I'm fighting to win today.

Aiden laughs. "I know how you feel. It's my son's first game. I can't lose either."

I glare at him. "Your son is nine months old. He won't remember this game."

"Not the point." Aiden presses his lips together and shakes his head. "It's still his first game."

Okay. I get it. Aiden wants bragging rights for when his son is older. Our eyes meet, and I nod. We have to win.

"And thanks for everything." It's not the time to talk about this. However, we never seem to have a private moment. "You signed me up for this game and got me the job with Jude."

"I did on both," he admits.

"Why the job?"

"When you showed up in town, I did a little digging. You're good. Jude needs that. When you got arrested, I knew he could help you." Aiden looks around nervously. I've never seen him nervous. We shouldn't be talking here.

I glance toward my girls. "Thanks again." I pat his arm and start toward left field. I make it two steps.

"I did it for them," Aiden says.

I pause. "You knew she was mine."

He nods. "Now, let's win this for our kids."

Aiden is almost as mysterious as Jude. Aiden's a little more talkative than my boss. I don't like people digging into my life. Since Aiden did me a huge favor, I won't be complaining this time. It concerns me knowing my information can be easily found. Perhaps Jude can help me secure it. I'll bring it up tomorrow when I go to the office.

Today, we're here to have fun. Well, that's what the town council says. This may be a charity baseball game, but every man on both teams is here to win. When I get in position in left field, Phillip and I toss the ball a few times. I'm surprised he's in center field. This is Phillip's first time playing in the charity baseball games. He was pretty good in high school. Let's hope he still is.

The first few innings go okay. Phillip and I seem to be playing like we never stopped. That might not be true. We are a little slower than we were in high school. So far, we're only down by one run. Not too bad for *old guys*. I swear these high school boys love heckling us. We're going to have to step up our game because losing by one run is still losing.

Aiden wasn't kidding when he said Elliott Matthews was the guy to watch. He just graduated and is going to college on a full scholarship. Brady did an outstanding job training the kid. He's only been playing for a couple of years. The boy will go pro without a doubt.

Aiden still has an arm on him. He strikes out half of these guys. I think Chase is their family clown. Whenever someone gets a hit, Chase heckles Aiden. Chase is who started these kids calling us old men. Chase isn't a bad player. He's gotten a couple of hits and scored one of their five runs. Aiden struck him out a couple of times, too. This time, he pops it to left field. I catch it easily for the out. Instead of throwing the ball back to Aiden, I jog to the chain link fence and toss it to Peyton. Aiden laughs and shakes his head. Chief Foster is our umpire today. He throws a new ball to the pitcher's mound.

We're still down by one run at the top of the ninth inning. Another pop fly comes to left field. I toss this one to Jeffrey. Phillip gives me a thumbs-up.

"Hey, Bailey! Stop giving the balls away!" Aiden shouts.

"I paid for a box of those!" I shout back.

When Miles came around yesterday to collect the fees to play in today's game, I gave him extra to help purchase the baseballs. During the years I played, we lost several during the day. Me giving away two balls shouldn't be a problem.

Aiden strikes out the last kid without giving up any more runs. After the Chief tosses the ball back to him, he jogs to the fence and gives the ball to his wife for his son. I laugh and shake my head. Now, it's okay to give the game balls away.

We have one inning and three outs to get two runs. The excitement around the field doubles. Peyton and Jeffrey are hanging on to the fence and shouting. We have water and *Gatorade* in the dugout, but the kids bring Phillip and me bottles of water to the fence. I've only known she's mine for a few days, and I already love being a Dad.

"You're doing great." Peyton holds her hand up for a high-five.

I reach over and grab it and lace our fingers together instead. "Thanks, Little Bit. I'll see you in a few minutes."

She waves as I hurry to get my helmet and bat. Phillip is at the plate. I'm on deck. Phillip hits a ground ball to left field and makes it to second base. He's in scoring position. We'll tie the game if I can get a hit and get him home. I do get a hit and make it to first base. Sadly, Phillip got stuck on third. We have one out, so we have a couple of chances left.

The crowd is on their feet and shouting as Miles walks up to the plate. He's played first base for most of the game. Miles isn't a big baseball fan. Still, he plays the game really well. If he strikes out, Lucas Barnes is up next. Just when I think it's over for Miles, a loud crack rings out. I start for second base and smile when the ball goes over the fence in center field. The crowd goes wild. Miles just won us the game by two runs.

As I round third base, my daughter and her best friend jump up and down. I swear they're the loudest people here. I cross home plate, where the rest of the team is waiting. Once Miles' foot touches the plate, we surround him. Aiden, Phillip, and I can forever boast to our kids about how we won today for them. Best Day Ever!

Chapter Twenty-Four

Kennedy

Rather than celebrating the win with our families, everyone met in the dayroom at the Fire Department. Chief Foster wasn't about to pass up a chance to celebrate his Assistant Fire Chief winning the game. Unsurprisingly, the Hayden Sisters showed up with enough food to feed an army.

"You two are getting close." Tara hands me an iced coffee. She sits down beside me on the sofa.

Beth and Hadley are making cold drinks in the kitchen area. Mrs. Barnes has started a couple of pots of brewed coffee as well. Some of these crazy people still want a hot coffee. You can tell who wasn't outside sweating at the game today.

"Yeah. A little bit." I look around the room. A few of the older ladies cut their eyes at me every once in a while. "Do you think it'll be a problem?"

"I think it's great. You and Aaron were cheated out of a life together like Phillip and I were."

Easy for her to say. This town thinks Phillip and Tara being together is great. Phillip stood up for Luke Barnes in a town meeting and lost everything. Well, he lost his hateful parents and brother. He ended up finding Tara and Jeffrey. He's one of the town's most loved citizens now. Our townsfolk won't be that way with me.

"These people are already talking about us. They think I lied about everything."

Technically, I did lie. For about ten months, I lied and pretended to be in a loving relationship with Mark. I let everyone believe he was Peyton's father. Anybody with half a brain would know it was a lie from the start. Those who believed me knew it was a lie the moment they looked into my daughter's eyes. I'll give the town gossips credit. None of them ever said anything to me or where it would come back to me if they did. They're talking now, though.

Aaron confronting everyone in the middle of the square today won't stop them from gossiping. If anything, he just fanned the flames and started a wildfire the HFFD can't put out. Peyton will never end up in Hayden Happenings. Everyone, especially Megan, knows Aaron will make good on his threat. He and I will probably be headline news several more times before this is over.

"Don't worry about them. You only have to worry about Peyton and Aaron."

"I don't think my parents like it." Mom and Dad haven't said anything yet. I've seen the secretive looks they give to each other, though.

"You should sit down and tell them everything," Tara suggests.

She's right. I should have done it years ago. Since Aaron and Mark were no longer in Hayden Falls, I avoided the subject entirely. It was out of sight, out of mind for me. My parents love Peyton. They've never asked what really happened. They were actually relieved when I told them Mark and I were divorced. I was thrilled when he told me he was leaving Montana and never coming back. His presence here would have confused Peyton. One of these nosy people would have said something in front of her, and she'd think Mark was her father.

Peyton has asked about her father several times, especially since Jeffrey met his dad. I didn't lie to her. I just couldn't tell her the truth.

All she knew was that her father didn't live in Montana anymore, and I hadn't heard from him since high school. Yeah, it was a coward's way out. It was easier than the truth. I wasn't going to keep it from her forever. When she was older and could understand, I was going to tell her Aaron was her father. When she turned eighteen, she could hunt him down if she wanted to.

Peyton flops down next to me. "Mama, I'm hungry."

"Me too." Jeffrey leans against Tara's side.

"Did you two not eat enough at the field?" I know Peyton had two hotdogs plus the snacks we brought with us.

"That was hours ago," Peyton whines.

I'm not sure it was hours ago. We haven't been here that long. I swear my child should be twice her size with as much as she eats. Both kids have been eyeing the dessert table since we got here.

"Come on, bottomless pits. Let's feed you before you pass out." Tara leads the way to the kitchen area.

Aaron watches us from across the room. He's playing pool with the guys. Chief Foster finally agreed to let them have a pool table. I'm sure the full-time firefighters were bored with watching television and playing video games when they weren't on calls. It's good to see Aaron reconnecting with the guys he went to school with.

Tara and I insist the kids eat one sandwich or veggies and dip before they attack the sweets. They choose veggies and dip. It's not surprising. This is Jeffrey's favorite after-school snack. It's also not as filling as a sandwich would be. They aren't fooling us. It leaves them more room for dessert.

"Maybe you should go play pool," Sammie tells Levi.

"But I want a cupcake." Levi looks heartbroken.

"You can't have one today." Sammie holds the tray away from him.

Usually, Sammie Foster is happy and teasing. I don't think she's happy or teasing today. I glance between Levi and Sammie. I'm not the only one. Several people are watching. Mrs. Barnes wants to step in and help her son. With what, I'm not sure.

"What if I said please?" Levi gives Sammie his big puppy dog eyes.

"Why don't you ask Tabetha for a cupcake?" Beth practically slams an iced coffee on the table in front of Levi. Some of the contents splash over the sides. She doesn't wait for a reply. Beth goes back to the counter to make another drink. There's no love lost between her and Tabetha.

Levi drops his head back and shouts, "I don't like Tabetha Sailors!"

"Fine." Sammie pushes the tray across the table to Levi. "But you can get it yourself."

Everyone in town has seen the article in Hayden Happenings. Megan is already predicting wedding bells for Levi and Tabetha. I see Tabetha around town all the time. She even comes to the salon. Lindsey is the stylist she usually requests. Other than what I hear in the gossip circles, I don't know much about Tabetha.

"I wish Tabetha and Karlee would find a guy and get married," Tara whispers.

More than half of the women in this town wish those two would settle down or leave town. It was a great day for us when Brittney Douglas married Roman Crawford. From the rumors going around our salon chairs, it's not going so great for Roman. Nobody is crying over it, though. He got what he deserved.

I do feel bad for Levi. He doesn't deserve this. Usually, Megan reports on sightings of Tabetha with Brady Maxwell. Brady hasn't been back to Hayden Falls since Christmas. It looks as though Levi's getting the spotlight in his place. Oh, Megan has an article up today with Brady and his supermodel girlfriend, Ariel Snow. It explains why Beth is so snappy today.

Beth shoves an iced coffee in front of me. "Here you go."

"Beth, I already have a drink." I hold mine up.

"This one is for your man."

"Oh. We're not together." I quickly shake my head.

"Oh, but you are." She hands me the drink and walks away.

I can't believe her. Beth is blunt and pushy most of the time. Usually, it's in a fun and teasing way. She's a bit on edge today. She's never been snappy with me before. I swear she gets stranger by the day.

Tara giggles. "Go on, *Peaches*. *Your man* looks as though he may pass out from dehydration."

I glare at my best friend. Only Aaron calls me Peaches, and she knows it. Haha. She's so funny today. With these two calling Aaron my man, there'll be a new gossip article about us tomorrow. Every woman in the kitchen area is smiling and watching me. One of these nosy women is reporting back to Megan. I just know it.

"Fine," I mumble so only Tara can hear me.

When I turn toward the pool table, I find Aaron watching me. Oh no. He heard Beth. She's not exactly quiet. His grin widens with each step I take. Yep. He heard her.

"Hey, Peaches." His blue eyes dance with laughter as he holds out a hand. "That for me?"

Oh. He's a little cocky today. Every man around the pool table snickers. Nope. We're not doing this.

"No." I lift my chin and shake my head. "This is mine."

I spin on my heels and start back toward the kitchen. He can pass out from dehydration. Good thing several EMTs are standing nearby. He won't be out for long. Laughter erupts behind me. It's not enough to make me turn around. Tara's wide eyes and open mouth should be, though.

I squeal when an arm goes around my back and under my knees. In a swift movement, I'm lifted off the floor. Oh, my goodness. I can't believe he did this. I weigh more than I did in high school, but he lifts me like it's nothing.

"Sorry, Peaches. That's mine." Aaron twirls me around in the middle of the room. When he stops, I'm holding his drink in front of us. "But I will share," he whispers. His head lowers, and he takes a sip through the straw.

Chapter Twenty-Five

Kennedy

A horrible beeping sound shrieks in the darkness, waking me from a peaceful sleep. I slap my hand against the nightstand several times in search of it. Finally, I make contact and kill the horrid beast. Alarm clocks are evil. I peek through one eye at the digital numbers. Six a.m. flashes at me. It's really laughing at me. I only get up this early on school days. School is out. This shouldn't be happening. My body knows it and insists I go back to sleep. Too bad I can't.

No amount of grumbling will change things. I sit and swing my legs over the side of the bed. I'd feel better if I'd gotten a peaceful night's sleep. It's hard to sleep when your ex-boyfriend is sleeping on your couch.

Peyton was so excited yesterday. It was probably from all the sugar she ate at the Fire Department. Whatever it was, it had her inviting her father to have dinner with us. Aaron wasn't about to say no. Naturally, dinner meant they got to watch a movie, and a movie led to those two falling asleep on the couch again.

Peyton is taking advantage of the situation. I know it. She knows it. Aaron knows it. Aaron and I can't keep walking on eggshells around her. The tantrum Peyton threw a few days ago freaked my entire family out. None of us want to see it happen again. However, coddling her isn't healthy either.

As I walk through the edge of the living room on my way to the kitchen, I pause to watch them sleeping for a few minutes. I've dreamed of this scene so many times over the years. She deserved to have her father in her life. After these visions, I'd go back to hating him for not being here. The reason he wasn't with us was a lie. He's here now. Nothing would ever cause me to completely hate him, not even when I tried all those years.

Aaron has to be at his new job at nine. It's why I set my alarm so early. Missoula is about an hour away from here. Peyton is using her father's chest as a pillow. They look so natural together. I smile at them and snap a quick photo. As peaceful as they're sleeping, I won't wake them just yet. The least I can do is start the coffee before I wake Aaron up. Maybe Peyton will sleep for another hour or so.

I don't turn the kitchen light on. We've always used the light above the stove as a nightlight. It's enough light for me to start the coffee maker. I lean against the counter while I wait for the coffee to brew and check my messages. Social media is the same old drama. My text messages are utterly ridiculous. Tara created a group chat with my girls from the salon.

Tara: *Definitely do something I'd do.*

Savannah: *Tell me he's not really sleeping on the couch.*

Hope: *There's your first mistake.*

Lindsey: *No. She has a long list of many mistakes.*

The row of laughing emojis she added is not necessary.

Jade: *Girl! Do you need some pointers? You don't put a man that fine on the couch.*

Tara: *Surely, it hasn't been THAT long.*

Andi: *Oh! I have lots of tips.*

Andi? How did she get into this chat? Jade and Andi are younger than the rest of us. The last thing I need is tips from them.

Andi: *I can find you some videos.*

Videos? Is this girl insane? The last thing I need is videos. She's lost her sweet little girl reputation with me. Andi and I should have a serious talk. What is she watching? No. Never mind. I don't want to know.

Me: *NO!*

I sigh and toss my phone on the counter. Nothing is happening between Aaron and me. My friends need to stop.

I gasp and cover my mouth with both hands when the cabinet next to me opens.

"Sorry." Aaron pulls out two coffee mugs.

"I didn't mean to wake you."

"You didn't. I think it was the coffee." He nods toward my phone on the counter. "It's a little early for Hayden Happenings."

I laugh to play it off and flip my hand. "Oh. It's just the girls being crazy."

"Ah." He moves to get the cream from the fridge.

"We should talk." I pour the coffee into our mugs.

"We should." He adds the sugar and cream. "What would you like to talk about?"

That's a loaded question. The answer is everything. Our first talk was interrupted by Peyton's tantrum. Since then, I've been putting off serious conversations with him. With as friendly as he's been getting lately, we need to set some boundaries.

"First and foremost, we need to talk about Peyton and what exactly you plan on being for her." I reach for one of the coffee mugs.

Aaron's hand quickly covers mine and holds it down on the counter. I can practically feel his eyes staring into the side of my head. From how tense his hand feels, I may have struck a nerve. Looking up at him will undo me. Since I crossed this line, I can't turn back now. Slowly, I turn my head and look up at him. He's fighting to remain calm.

"She's my daughter. I'll be everything a father is supposed to be for her and more." His voice is calm yet stern, and his eyes never leave mine. His eyes are so intense that I have to look away.

"You can't just show up after ten years and jump in here like nothing happened."

He steps closer, crowding my space. The coward in me refuses to look up at him.

"Yeah, Kennedy. That's exactly what I'm doing."

Being close to him makes my brain foggy. How, after all this time, does he still affect me this way? I push away to try and clear my thoughts. If I don't have a level head around him, I'll do something stupid. Would that be so bad? No. I can't think that way.

"But…" Guess I'm not level-headed yet.

He grabs my wrist and pulls me to him. His deep blue eyes bounce between mine and cloud over with something I can't read. Once again, I'm lost within those orbs, causing my protest to disappear.

"I've lost ten years. I'm not losing another day."

"She's only nine."

He releases my wrist and drops his hands to my waist. I love the feel of his touch. I'm so messed up in the head. This is a serious subject, yet here I am, fantasizing about being with him. It feels as though I've pushed him across a line. Is this the boy I fell in love with? Or is he the hardened military man the Army trained him to be?

"I should have been here with you through your pregnancy." He closes his eyes and drops his forehead against mine. His voice softens. "I was cheated out of my life. You were cheated. More importantly, Peyton was cheated out of the family she was supposed to have."

"You can't start a relationship with her and take it away."

"I won't."

"You don't live here," I remind him.

"I do now."

I lean back to look him in the eye. "You'd move here for Peyton?"

"The only reason I never came back was because I thought the woman I loved cheated on me, got pregnant from it, and married the guy."

Loved. Past tense, not present. I press my lips together and take a deep breath through my nose. What was I expecting? Nothing. I shouldn't have allowed myself to dream.

"Jude's having my things in North Carolina packed up. Once my dad's house is remodeled, I'm moving in there."

Wow. I didn't know where he ended up. North Carolina is on the other side of the country. He really did put as much distance between us as he could. He must really hate me.

His hands come up to cup my face. "I'm sorry I wasn't here." He shakes his head. "I can never make up for that. But I will be here for you and Peyton from now on."

I swallow hard. Dreams are trying to filter back in. "Your job."

"Is the only thing that will take me away, but it won't be forever." He leans closer. "I will not lose you two again."

"Aaron," I whisper.

He gently presses his lips to my forehead and wraps his arms around me. I go to him without protest. Only a fool would deny herself from being in his arms.

"I don't know how it's all going to work out." His arms tighten. "But I'll warn you now. You'll never be able to run me off."

The last thing I want to do is run him off. Being in his arms again is magical. I want to savor every minute of it. He's here, and he's staying. My heart does a little happy dance. It falls a little, too. I still haven't asked him how he knows the words to girlie princess songs. He's not married. His things are being packed up and brought to Montana. Does his things include a little girl and her mother? Can Peyton and I share him with them if it does? Will they be willing to share him with us? I should ask him.

The messed up me stays quiet and soaks up the minutes I have with him. We'll wake Peyton up soon. He can't leave for work without telling her good morning and that he'll see her tonight. Soon, I'll need to pull up my big girl pants and ask the hard questions.

Chapter Twenty-Six

Aaron

Slone Security is nothing like I expected. Maybe I'm at the wrong place. I again type the address on the back of the business card Jude gave me into my GPS app. Nope. I'm not wrong. It says I've arrived at my destination.

The old brick warehouse is on a side street near the interstate. With the way Jude throws money around, I was expecting something a lot fancier than this and in a wealthier part of town. Nothing about this place is flashy. The only thing that makes me believe I'm in the right place besides the GPS is the small sign above the front door. It's just the initials S. S.

Every building on this street has a chain-link fence around them with keypad entries. I flip the business card over. It only has the address and phone number. Jude didn't give me a code or tell me I needed one. I glance at the keypad box outside my window. There's no call button either. How does this fool expect me to get inside? I glance back at the building.

"You gonna sit out there all day?"

I jump and accidentally hit the horn. Laughter from more than one person erupts through the speaker. They're watching me sit here. A quick glance at the keypad box again doesn't reveal the camera or speaker. It's well hidden because Jude's voice is close, and the laughter still hasn't died.

"The speaker is hidden under the box," another man says.

"There's no call button, and I don't have a code. How was I supposed to get in?" I snap.

"You have my number."

I can practically see Jude rolling his eyes and shaking his head. His voice is calm and even. He's not the jerk laughing at me. I'm not so sure I like my new fellow employees, teammates, or whatever we're supposed to call each other.

"I gotcha, Bull," the other man says. Within seconds, a peep is heard, and the gate rolls open.

The moment I clear the gate, it quickly closes. There's no way another vehicle could enter behind me. I scan the area closer as I drive to the front of the faded brick building. For a rundown warehouse and lot, there's some high-tech security installed here. Jude opens the front door before my truck is in park and waits for me.

"Glad to finally have you here." Jude shakes my hand and leads the way inside.

The reception area looks like a typical waiting room for a business or doctor's office. A woman with short blonde hair sits behind a sliding window with a *'sign in'* sign on this side of the counter. Jude walks to the window. Surely, we're not children and need to sign in every day.

"This is Jasmine. She's worked for us for about six years." Jude gives the woman a fist bump through the open window. He steps aside so I have a clear view of the receptionist again. "Jaz, this Aaron." His eyes meet mine. "If she's at this desk, you say hello upon entering."

There's no room for defiance about this in his tone. I nod. Got it. Always speak to the pretty lady at the front desk.

"Nice to meet you, Jasmine." I extend my hand through the window.

"Glad to finally meet you, Bull." Jasmine holds up her fist. I easily transition to a fist bump. Guess she doesn't like shaking hands.

Slone Security has run a deep profile on me for them to know my code name. My drill sergeant bestowed the name on me in boot camp after our first day of target practice. I hit the bullseye every time. Jasmine is more than a secretary if she knows the information in my profile.

"Let's make you an official member of the team." Jude crosses the room to a door with an electronic pad on the wall. He places his palm on the pad, and the lock disengages.

We enter a huge room with a large breakroom on one side and the office where Jasmine works on the other. Straight ahead is a long hallway with several doors on each side. The first room on the right is a conference room. The blinds are up, revealing several men sitting around a large round table. We enter and join the five men.

I sit to Jude's right and take in every man here. They're all ex-military or ex-law enforcement. By the look on their faces, they're all tight-lipped, too. They won't be sharing their stories with the new guy today. I'll have to earn their trust. The man across from us slides a file to Jude.

"This is our main team." Jude motions around the table.

"Main?"

"We have smaller teams and individuals out on assignments," the man who pushed the file across the tables replies.

"The six of us started this company." Jude pushes the folder to me. "This is your contract. You'll sit here and read this over. We'll give you a little history of Slone Security throughout the day. After you sign the contract, you'll get a code for the gate and have your hand scanned to open the special access doors in the building."

Reading. Great. I groan when I open the folder, and not inwardly, by the way. This is a thick contract. No business requires paperwork this thick. Maybe I should get a lawyer to look at this first. Quinn was cool. He might help me out.

"I know it looks overwhelming, but it breaks down into three parts," Jude explains.

"I thought y'all said this guy was smart." The tallest man in the room laughs and pushes to his feet.

I could recognize his laughter in the dark. He's the jerk who was laughing at me through the speaker. With his deep southern drawl, he has to be from Texas. His size alone is intimidating. I'd pity any man who had to go one-on-one with this dude in a fistfight. Until I know him better, I won't be pushing his buttons.

"Sharpshooters don't have to be smart. They just gotta know how to aim." The man who first had my file laughs. He was at the speaker too. He's officially jerk number two.

Two others stand and snicker. Since they stay quiet, I won't put them in the jerk category just yet.

"This is Tex, Smoke, and Scotch. They'll drop in when they can and give you a few insights on what we do here." Jude motions toward the door.

The three men give me a single nod and leave the room. Well, except for Tex. See? I knew he was from Texas. He pauses at the door.

"Hopefully, we won't have to hold your hand too long." Tex wholeheartedly laughs before leaving. Closing the door behind him does nothing to muffle the sound. We can still hear his laughter as he walks down the long hallway.

"Sorry about that." Jude sighs. He motions across the table to jerk number two. "This is Sherlock. He's our computer genius and hardly ever leaves this building."

"Got any questions?" Sherlock asks.

Oh, only a million. I turn to Jude and start with one of my top questions. "Why's your company so secretive?"

I get privacy is important nowadays. These guys are a little over-the-top for a security company in Montana. Missoula is bigger than Hayden Falls, but surely, it doesn't need this much security.

"For starters, I helped start this company, but it's not technically mine." Jude's eyes flick to the man on my right.

This guy is tall, muscular, and has dark, piercing eyes. None of these guys are small by any means. Sherlock might be the smallest, but even he works out. The company owner looks nothing like any business owner I know. This man doesn't wear a suit or stand out like most owners. Black T-shirts and jeans seem to be the company's attire. At first glance, I thought this man was part of the field team.

"This is Sabastian Slone. Better known around here as Boss." Jude introduces the owner.

"Bull." Boss holds his hand out. "Glad to have you aboard."

"Thanks." I take his hand and don't point out that I didn't have a choice in the matter.

Jude taps the open file in front of me. "Read and fill this out. The last part is your employee handbook. You can take that home with you."

I gape at him. "Handbook? As secretive as you are, you have an employee handbook?" This is getting crazier by the minute.

"You work for a legitimate company. You get an employee handbook," Jude states with a firm nod.

Sherlock points to the folder. "The first part is your paperwork for Slone Security." He grins wickedly. "We gotta pay those taxes correctly. The second part is a privacy form for the Elite Team."

"Elite Team? What *exactly* is my job with this company?" I glance at the three men around me.

"You're a security guard." Boss taps his fingers on the table. "For the most part," he says with a chuckle.

"We give you three months to decide if you want to work for us. If you decide to leave, you simply pay us back what we've paid out on your behalf." Jude doesn't bat an eye. "Once you fill these forms out, we'll give you your first assignment."

"You can have a lawyer look the contract over. Those forms never leave this office. He or she will have to come here and sign a privacy form before seeing our paperwork. That's on your dime, though," Boss adds.

"While you're filling these out, I'll be working more on your little problem." Sherlock stands.

"My problem?"

"Yeah. Mark Bevins. By the time I'm finished, you'll have more than you need to confront him."

"Any idea why he destroyed my life?" I can't figure this out.

"Yep." Sherlock nods. "Money."

I narrow my eyes. "Money?" I don't understand. How does money play into this? "You care to explain?"

"After you sign the paperwork, I'll tell you what I know. I'm still digging for the details, though." Sherlock tosses up two fingers and walks out.

"I've already told you when you become one of us, you have access to our resources. Sherlock is the best I've ever seen. You won't be disappointed." Jude stands. "Jaz will bring you a cup of coffee and some type of pastry. It's not her job. She just likes doing it."

"Don't worry, Bull." Boss slaps me on the shoulder. "We'll explain it all to you." He follows Jude out and closes the door.

Within minutes, Jasmine enters with a box of apple fritters. They aren't from Sweet Treats, but they don't taste bad. I can never mention this to Sophie. Jaz starts the coffee maker on the counter and shows me where everything is in the cabinets. Apparently, I'm expected to keep this pot full and fresh while I'm stuck in here with paperwork. Jaz informs me that all the guys will be in throughout the day for coffee, a treat, and to talk about the company with me.

I can leave after three months if I want. However, paying back the money they've paid out for me isn't possible. I'm not broke. I would be if I had to hand over that amount of cash, and my dad's house would never get remodeled. If I stay with them, I'll have this job for at least three years. As mysterious as this job is, I am curious about it. What exactly does their Elite Team do? Is it illegal? It doesn't matter. I'm stuck here for now. My main reason for keeping this job is because of Peyton and Kennedy. It allows me to be with them. They're all I see when I close my eyes.

Chapter Twenty-Seven

Kennedy

"Where is he?" Peyton walks into the kitchen with her hands on her hips.

I turn from the stove to face her. "You know he started his new job today. He'll be here for dinner."

Inviting Aaron to dinner tonight wasn't part of my plans for the day. Peyton and I got home around four this afternoon. Within thirty minutes, I had to text him the invite. He replied, saying he would be here around seven tonight. The closer it gets to seven, the more upset Peyton gets. He still has forty-five minutes. If my daughter will relax, I have time to finish prepping this chicken casserole and have dinner on the table by seven.

"Missoula's an hour away. He hasn't called." Peyton crosses her arms and huffs.

Aaron never said he'd call before he left work. Like Peyton, I was expecting him to do so.

"Why don't you set the table? I'm sure we'll hear from him soon." Hopefully, giving her a task will settle her down.

"Fine." Peyton stomps over to the cabinet and pulls out three plates. "But call him again."

Wow. My child has a severe attitude problem tonight. After dinner, Aaron and I can sit down with her and hopefully work this issue out. As I slide the casserole dish into the oven, Peyton sets the plates on the table so hard it's a wonder one of them didn't break. Okay. This conversation isn't going to wait.

I turn to face her. Hopefully, I can defuse this ticking time bomb. Her face is red, and she's taking fast, hard breaths. That concerns me. She jerks open the silverware drawer, grabs the utensils, and slams the drawer shut.

"Peyton, you need to calm down. Your attitude and I aren't going to live in the same house. Guess which one is leaving?" I should have chosen better words.

"It's not right, Mama!" She grabs onto the back of one of the chairs. Her little body shakes, breaking my heart even more. "He's supposed to be here!"

"Pumpkin, he has to work just like I do. You know he's coming for dinner."

"He should call. He shouldn't keep us wondering." She sniffles hard as the first tears fall. Her voice softens. "You always call."

She's right. I do let whoever is watching her know if I'm running late and when I'm on my way. I even call her during breaks if she's not in school. Aaron doesn't know our routine. Working for a security company won't allow him to be as free with his time as I can be.

"I'm sure we'll hear from him soon."

"What if he went back home?" She's back to shouting. "He hates Montana! He could have left!" Her breathing becomes erratic. "What if I'm not enough for him?"

"Peyton, no." I rush to her. She moves around the table to avoid me.

"I want him! He can't leave me!" She dashes into the living room.

Thank goodness there's nothing in here she can break. Well, unless she goes for something expensive or huge like the TV or furniture. Those could hurt her.

She's standing in the middle of the room by the time I reach her. Her shoulders rise and fall with each sob. Her little hands are balled into fists. The TV is only a few feet away. I kneel next to her. I'm relieved when she lets me touch her arms and turn her away from the TV. My relief is short-lived, though.

"He can't, Mama. He can't." Her words are broken by sobs.

"He loves you, Peyton," I say as calmly as possible. Her behavior has me freaking out. "He's not leaving you."

"He can't." Her breathing becomes more erratic. She's sweating and shaking. I don't believe she can hear me.

"Peyton?"

She shakes even more and begins to gasp for breath.

"Peyton!" I shake her, but she doesn't respond.

A cry that pierces my soul escapes from my little girl. On another gasp, her eyes roll and close. I scream as she goes limp in my arms.

"Peyton!" I scream her name again. She still doesn't respond.

I have enough sense about me to know I need help. My phone is on the kitchen counter. As gently as possible, I lay Peyton on the floor and rush to the kitchen to make an emergency phone call I never imagined I'd ever have to make.

Before I have 911 dialed, the front door bursts open. Beth Murphy rushes into the apartment. She sees me on the phone and Peyton on the floor. She runs to my daughter's side and pulls out her phone as I tell the 911 operator what's happening.

"Spence, Peyton's unconscious." Beth's quiet for a moment. "I don't know. She's breathing, but hurry."

She tosses her phone on the floor and rechecks Peyton's airways. I toss my phone on the couch and drop to my knees beside them.

"I think she hyperventilated and passed out," I tell Beth.

She looks at me, a little confused, before turning her attention back to Peyton. Yeah, I know. A nine-year-old shouldn't be passing out like this. Go ahead and give me the Worst Mother of the Year Award.

"You're probably right, but they'll be here soon to check her out." Thankfully, Beth doesn't call me out for being a bad mom.

One of the perks of living in a small town is that you don't have to wait too long when you call for help. Sirens can already be heard in the distance. Within minutes, my brother and Zane burst through the door. Spencer is on their heels.

Zane and Spencer go straight to Peyton. Devon pulls me across the room.

"What happened?"

"I think she hyperventilated and passed out."

Devon snaps his head toward Peyton. Zane waves something under Peyton's nose, and she starts to stir. Spencer nods to my brother, confirming I was right.

"Why?" Devon demands. He's not going to go easy on me as Beth did.

"She wanted Aaron." Tears of relief flow down my face as Zane helps Peyton sit up.

Devon jabs his finger toward my face. "This is getting out of hand."

I agree with him, but what does he think I should do? We should have already talked to her about how things would work with Aaron in our lives now. I haven't pushed the subject because I'm not sure he's here to stay. I know he loves her and wants to get to know her. He hasn't told us about his life in North Carolina. Does he have family across the country he'll return to one day?

"You want me to get the stretcher, or do you think you can walk?" Zane asked Peyton.

"Is that necessary? She should be fine now. Right?" I don't think we need to go to the hospital.

"No. I got her." Devon ignores me and scoops Peyton up. He pauses at the door. "She's probably fine, but since she's so young, we'll let Matt check her out."

He carries Peyton to the ambulance and climbs into the back with her. Zane gets into the driver's seat. I watch from the doorway as they pull out of the parking lot with flashing lights but no siren.

"Do you need me to drive you?" Beth asked, bringing me out of my haze.

"No, but thank you for helping." I grab my purse and phone.

"I was getting out of the car when I heard you scream."

I'm glad she came home early. Having her here kept me focused. Spencer tells his sister bye and walks with me to my car. "Matt is already at the hospital." He puts his hand on my arm. "I'm sure she'll be fine."

"Thank you for helping." There's nothing else I can say. I get into my car and hurry to catch up with the ambulance.

Chapter Twenty-Eight

Aaron

My heart pounds as I clench my hands around the steering wheel. It takes all of my military training to keep my mind and emotions calm enough to drive. The call with the business owner of my first assignment with Slone Security was interrupted and cut short. How Sherlock does the things he does with computers is beyond me.

My mind spun out of control for a moment, hearing he got an alert of a 911 call with an ambulance and cops on their way to Kennedy's apartment. The next words out of his mouth almost gutted me on the spot. The victim was nine years old. Peyton. Something's wrong with my little girl.

Without a second thought, I take the turn to avoid Hayden Falls and head toward Walsburg as fast as I can. Sherlock promised to call me back when he had more information. So far, nothing. Minutes feel like hours.

My eyes flick to the rearview mirror for a minute. An SUV is closing in fast on me. Great. One of Hayden Falls' finest is about to pull me over. It's probably a Barnes. I get the feeling I'm not Lucas' favorite person. He can give me my ticket when we get to the hospital. We're less than fifteen minutes from Walsburg. I'm not stopping when I'm this close.

My phone rings. A number I don't recognize flashes on the screen. It's local, so I hit the Bluetooth to answer the call. It could be about Peyton. My eyes flick to the rearview mirror again. No lights. No siren. This might be my lucky day.

"Yeah?"

"It's me. I'll follow you in. No one will stop you or give you a ticket," Aiden says.

Whew. That's a relief. I swear, Aiden has a private line to Jude. Can't complain. It works in my favor today and on a few other occasions.

"Thanks, man." I give him a thumbs-up. He probably can't see it. "Any word on Peyton?"

"Yeah. She's going to be fine."

More relief washes over me. Still, nobody is telling me what happened to her. This is one time I believe privacy laws are ridiculous.

I glance into the mirror again at the cop behind me and chuckle. "But you're not slowing me down or giving me a ticket?"

"Nope. If it was E or Caleb, I'd be breaking laws to get to them, even if it wasn't serious."

Aiden's a family man. Of course, he understands. I give a silent thanks that I didn't get Lucas behind me today. If it were him, I'd be in cuffs and on my way back to Hayden Falls.

I slow down when I hit the city limits, and the hospital comes into view. Aiden parks next to me and follows me to the Emergency Room. The ambulance from Hayden Falls is parked off to the side. Devon must have been on duty today, or the EMTs would have already left.

I was expecting to see Devon waiting for me. Instead, I find Mr. Reed in the waiting room. The man still hasn't warmed to me. He looks frazzled but relieved. Hopefully, it's a good sign. He quickly crosses the room to meet me.

"How is she?"

He grabs my arm and pulls me to the side to allow a couple of nurses to push a bed down the hall. Surprisingly, Aiden is still behind me.

"She seems fine to me, but Matt's running some tests to be sure."

"What happened?" I still don't know.

"She passed out." Mr. Reed presses his lips together and looks away.

If we weren't in a hospital, I believe I'd yell at this man. It would come back to haunt me later, so I don't. Kennedy and her parents have always been close. Peyton adores her grandparents and her uncle. I should say uncles. Phillip Crawford weaseled his way into my daughter's life. Mr. Reed is hiding something from me, and I don't like it. This is my daughter. Nobody has a right to hide anything from me, not even her grandfather. If tests are being run, I deserve to know why.

We arrive at ER6. Mr. Reed motions to the door. "They're in here."

Without knocking, I open the door and step inside. Mrs. Reed and Devon are sitting in chairs at the window. Kennedy's on the bed, holding our daughter. My heart breaks seeing them like this.

Peyton sees me and springs up onto her knees. Her smile breaks through the darkness surrounding me. "Daddy!"

"Hey, Little Bit." I quickly close the distance and take her into my arms.

"You're here." She snuggles into me.

"Of course I am. I got here as fast as I could." I tighten my arms around her.

"You didn't call." Her voice saddens as she swipes at her cheek.

What? I lean back enough to look at her. I wipe away her tears with my thumb. She's serious, but I don't understand. I look at her mother.

"She thought you were going to call when you left work," Kennedy explains. It doesn't explain why we're here, though.

I turn my attention back to Peyton. "I left work late. I had to call the business owner of the first assignment. I sent a message saying I'd be there for dinner."

"You're supposed to call." She lays her head against my chest and sniffles. Mrs. Reed hands her a tissue.

A quick glance around the room tells me that every adult here is hiding something. They don't want to talk in front of Peyton. Sadly, I don't always stay quiet when I should.

"What's going on? Why did she pass out?"

It doesn't escape me when Peyton trembles in my arms. I rub her back to offer her comfort. Kennedy looks at her parents and brother. Oh, no. That's not how we're going to do things. Peyton is my daughter. She doesn't need permission from anyone to tell me what's going on with Peyton.

"Kennedy." My voice is a little sharper than I intended. I hate being stern with her, but I need answers. "What happened?"

"Why don't you two step into the hall and talk?" Mrs. Reed reaches for Peyton.

"No!" Peyton screams. She springs onto her knees again and wraps her arms tightly around my neck.

"Whoa, Little Bit." I rub my hand up and down her back. "It's okay. Your mom and I will just be outside the door."

"You can't leave." Her arms tighten even more.

"I'm not leaving. I promise. We'll be on the other side of the door," I assure her.

"That's leaving." She doesn't loosen her hold.

"Peyton, sweetheart." Kennedy leans around to look her in the eye. "Daddy and I are just going to talk about what happened. It'll only take a few minutes."

Peyton shakes her head. If she won't let go, we'll have to talk in front of her.

I soften my voice. "I need to know what happened so I know how to help you."

She loosens her hold and drops her head against my chest. "You didn't call."

"I'm sorry about that." I would have called her before leaving Missoula if I'd known she expected me to do so. "But I really need to know why you passed out."

"I couldn't breathe," she says softly as the tears start again.

Does she have a medical condition no one told me about? Or is she saying what I think she's saying? Did my daughter panic and pass out because I didn't call her? I'll lose my mind if this is my fault.

"Come on, Pumpkin." Devon holds his hands out. "I'll hold you while they talk. I promise nobody is leaving you."

"But." She looks unsure.

"I could handcuff him to the door knob if you'd like," Aiden offers.

Peyton looks over my shoulder. The hopeful expression on her face concerns me. I glance over my shoulder at the deputy smiling at my daughter. This fool is supposed to be my friend. Right now, I want to tackle him. He can't be serious.

"Do it, Mr. Aiden." Peyton gives him a firm nod, sealing my fate.

Wait. What? My daughter actually agreed to this? What in the world? How did this even happen? Peyton is dead serious. Aiden is utterly ridiculous. How's this man even a cop? He pulls out a pair of handcuffs and dangles them at me. I want so badly to smack the stupid grin off his face. This fool is entirely too happy about this.

"Seriously?" I ask my sweet little daughter.

"Mmhmm." She nods.

She's sweet, and I love her with all my heart. It looks like I'm about to be handcuffed to a door. Devon snickers when I hand Peyton to him. Yep. I'll be paying him back later, too. Aiden is first on my list. For now, Kennedy and I follow Aiden to the door.

I poke the Deputy in the chest. "Mr. Aiden, you and I will be talking about this later."

"Sure, man. We can do that. Right now, you're getting handcuffed to this door. Hold your hand out." He clamps one cuff around my left wrist and looks at Peyton. "You sure, Little Lady?"

My dear, wonderful, sweet daughter firmly nods again. Without hesitation, Aiden closes the other cuff around the door knob. I'll be making a formal request to the hospital administration that they need to upgrade from old traditional door knobs to push doors.

The moment we step into the hallway and close the door behind us, phones are held up, and cameras flash. Great. I'm about to be front page news in Hayden Happenings again.

Chapter Twenty-Nine

Kennedy

This man amazes me. Who would allow themselves to be handcuffed to a door to make a child happy? Well, he's not doing this for just any child but his daughter. Something tells me he'll do anything for Peyton. I will have to come to terms with how much they mean to each other. Yet, I'm not sure I can. Having my parents and brother in our lives has been great. Without them, I wouldn't have made it on my own as a single mother. Letting Aaron into our lives will change everything.

"Move along, ladies." Aiden walks toward the nurse's station and waiting area. He motions with his hands for them to get back to work.

The wonderful citizens of Walsburg mingle with our town gossip from time to time. From what I hear, they have their own little gossip circles. At least they don't have an online blog to display their lives to the world. Okay. Maybe Megan only reaches half of Montana. Who knows? I have no idea how many followers she has for her blog.

"Okay, Peaches." Aaron brings me back to our situation. "I'm tied to a door. Now, tell me why our daughter passed out. Is she sick, and you haven't told me?"

"No. She's not sick." I should slap him. It's not a good idea. I'd have to run if I did. "I wouldn't keep a medical condition from you."

"Okay. Then what happened? What brought us here?"

"Peyton thought you would call before you left Missoula. She panicked when you didn't. She was scared you left Montana and went back home." This part is going to be hard for me to say, but he needs to know the truth. "She was worried she wasn't enough for you to stay."

"What?" Aaron goes pale and slumps back against the door. Everyone in Peyton's room no doubt heard him. "This is my fault?" He closes his eyes and drops his head.

"It's both our faults." His eyes meet mine. "We should have already sat down and explained to her how things would go with you working."

"Yeah," he agrees. "We'll talk to her when we get home and work out a system or something."

I'd suggest we wait a day or two so Peyton could get over everything that happened today. Waiting will only make things worse. I hold up a finger when my phone dings with a text. Automatically, I pull it from my pocket.

Tara: *We're on our way.*

Aaron sees the text. "You should answer her. Let Jeffrey know Peyton's going to be okay."

He's got a point there. The last thing we need is for Jeffrey to have an asthma attack because he's worried about Peyton. It's sweet of him to be worried about his best friend.

Movement at the nurse's station catches my eye. Matt is walking toward us with Aiden. I pray the test results in his hand say my little girl is truly okay. I have time to send Tara a quick text before he gets here. I step to the side as Aaron lets a nurse into Peyton's room.

Me: *Tell Jeffrey she's going to be okay. Don't rush, and drive safe.*

"What do we need to do for a DNA test?" Aaron asks Matt.

I suck in a breath. What? He wants a DNA test? Now, I should definitely slap him. One minute, she's his world. The next, he wants proof she's his. Unbelievable. Aaron Bailey should have never come back to Montana. We were doing fine without him.

"If Kennedy agrees to do the test, it's a simple process. We can take a blood sample, swab your mouth, or have you spit into a tube," Matt answers without giving it a second thought.

"Thanks, man. We'll talk about it. I think a swab or spit test would be the easiest on Peyton." Aaron doesn't even look my way.

I stomp right up into his face. "Seriously?"

"What?" Oh, he can drop the confused look.

"You want a DNA test? You want proof she's yours?" I toss my hands in the air. The teenage me lets herself be known. "Fine. Take your blasted test. She's yours, you idiot, but whatever."

He grabs my wrist and fills the doorway with his body, blocking me from entering my daughter's room. I try to jerk away. He only tightens his grip.

Aaron holds his left hand up as far as the handcuffs allow. "Aiden, get these off now."

Aiden quickly unlocks the handcuffs without saying a word. Since moving back to Hayden Falls, I've never seen Aiden Maxwell give in to anyone's demands so easily. Maybe he's not the respectable man I thought he was.

Aaron moves us away from the door and presses my back to the wall. With eyes still glued to mine, he motions for Aiden and Matt to enter Peyton's room. Matt hurries inside. Aiden leans his shoulder against the wall on the other side of the door. He crosses his arms and waits. The cop is not leaving. At least the cop is doing his job. The question is, will he protect me or back Aaron? I'm being ridiculous. Aiden isn't a bad guy. I'm just mad.

"No. I don't need a DNA test to know Peyton is my daughter. I knew it the moment I looked into her eyes." He pauses and takes a deep breath. "But not everyone will take my word on it."

"Who cares what other people think?"

"Legally, it matters."

"Does it? You're on her birth certificate."

"Thank you for doing that. But since we weren't married or living together when she was born, insurance companies need proof," he explains.

"Insurance?" Now I'm confused.

"Yes. Insurance. I asked Jude to add you and Peyton to my insurance. We're not married. If we were common law, Sherlock might be able to slide Peyton in as my stepdaughter." His eyes narrow, and his voice hardens. "She will *never* be listed as my stepdaughter."

His explanation makes sense. Sadly for both of us, I'm still mad and not listening.

"How many dependents did you list on your insurance?"

"What?"

A part of me doesn't care if he's confused. For some reason, a bigger part of me feels like my little jab at him is wrong. I immediately regret saying it. This is a private matter and not something we should talk about in a hospital hallway. We seem to have a knack for having serious conversations in public places. Why change now?

"Never mind," I mumble and look away.

Aaron takes my chin and turns me to face him. "You and Peyton are the only dependents I have."

"We're not you're dependents," I snap.

"But you are," he insists.

"But." I clamp my mouth shut. Now's my chance to get the answers to questions nagging at me. All of a sudden, my thoughts and questions feel petty and childish.

"Why did you say that?" He's tense, yet somehow, his voice remains calm.

"You know the words to girly princess songs," I whisper and drop my head.

"So?"

He doesn't get it. Devon and my dad wouldn't know princess songs if it wasn't for Peyton.

"You have another little girl to know those songs." Just saying those words hurt me deeply. He's not mine. I have no right to want him for myself.

He slightly lifts my chin until our eyes meet again. “Peyton is my *only* child. My Army buddy in North Carolina has a little girl. I rent the house next door to them.”

Now I feel like an idiot. I’ve also given myself away. It’s been hard hiding my true emotions where he’s concerned. I haven’t even been honest with Tara about my feelings for Aaron.

His lips turn up into a knowing grin as he leans close. “But your jealousy thrills me.”

“I’m not jealous.” It’s a lie.

I stiffen when he leans even closer. It’s a fight I’m losing with my own body. I really want to wrap my arms around his waist and pull him closer.

His nose slightly touches my cheek and slides until his lips are at my ear. My body breaks out into goosebumps. “Oh, but you are. We’ll explore this later.” He lightly presses his lips next to my ear before stepping away.

Explore? Oh, how I’d love to explore this more with him.

Chapter Thirty

Aaron

Thankfully, all of Peyton's tests came back normal. After hearing why she passed out, Matt suggested Kennedy and I come to his office tomorrow to talk more. With her heightened emotional state, Matt didn't want to talk in front of Peyton. Stepping out into the hall again was an issue, too. I have a lot of respect for Matt for putting Peyton's needs first.

Our family and friends were also concerned about Peyton's emotional state. Once she and Jeffrey were their usual happy selves, everyone said their goodbyes at the hospital. Mr. and Mrs. Reed wanted to follow us home. Kennedy convinced them to go home and rest since they were watching Peyton and Jeffrey tomorrow. Devon and Zane had to leave the hospital before we did. A car accident in Willow's Bend needed assistance. Devon wouldn't be so easily put off if he wasn't on duty. Kennedy texted him the test results as soon as Matt walked out of the room.

Relief washes over me as I follow Kennedy to her apartment. Loneliness sets in, too. They're in front of me. I have them in my sights. Yet, I miss them. The need to have them with me is strong. I love them, but I'm afraid to say the words out loud. If I voice my feelings, the universe will latch onto them and take my family from me again. Well, it's how my life has felt so far. Every time I thought I could be happy, it was snatched from me.

I've dated a few times. I was my own worst enemy when it came to relationships. When things appeared to be moving past casual, I was reminded of losing my high school sweetheart. Either I ended things abruptly, or the woman caught onto my cold attitude and stopped talking to me. Not once did I fight against their decision. I wanted them gone and never felt the loss of their company. Yeah. I know. I was a jerk.

I park next to Kennedy and get Peyton out of the back seat while she unlocks the door. I noticed when her little head disappeared about halfway home. The trauma and excitement of the day finally wore her out. I carry her to the couch and settle in the corner with her in my arms.

A light knock comes on the front door. Peyton stirs in my arms but doesn't wake up. Kennedy pauses in the kitchen doorway and looks at me questionably. I shake my head and shrug. I'm not expecting anyone. She hurries to the door before they knock again.

"Oh, hey, Beth." Kennedy keeps her voice low.

"Hey," Beth says softly. She glances over to Peyton and smiles before turning back to Kennedy. "You forgot to lock up and turn the oven off."

Kennedy gasps. "Oh, my gosh."

Beth grabs her wrist before she runs to the kitchen. "I watched it. After the casserole had finished baking, I set it on the counter. I gave it time to cool and came back to put it in the fridge. I locked the door when I left."

"Thank you for everything today." Kennedy steps back and motions for Beth to step inside.

"No," Beth declines. "You had a long day. I didn't want you to freak out when you realized you didn't put the casserole in the fridge." She gives Peyton another small smile. "And I wanted to see how our girl was doing."

"All of her tests were fine."

"Good. If you need me, just knock." Beth sighs with relief. She gives me a little wave.

"We will. Thanks again, Beth." I smile and nod. I can't return her wave with Peyton in my arms. Devon told me how Beth helped this afternoon. I'm glad she was here.

Kennedy gives Beth a hug before she walks away. She closes the door and comes over to the couch. For a moment, she stands there, watching Peyton sleep. Today scared her, too. I want so badly to comfort her. She reaches down and gently moves Peyton's hair from her face. It must be a mother's thing to check for a temperature. Peyton isn't sick. Still, Kennedy lays her hand against her forehead.

"I didn't know you and Beth were such good friends."

Kennedy's eyebrows pull together as she shakes her head. "We're not really. I mean. We talk and help each other sometimes. We've never had a problem with each other. But we're not close like I am with Tara or the girls at the salon."

"Beth's a good person. I'm glad she was here for you today." I've heard the rumors around town. Beth isn't as bad as what people say.

"She is a good person. I just wish she and Brady would work things out. They belong together." Sadness clouds her face for a moment. I have to agree. Beth's story is sad. Kennedy takes a deep breath and smiles. "If you're hungry, I can warm the chicken casserole up."

"Chicken and rice?" The thought of it has me licking my lips. She knows it's one of my favorite dishes.

She nods as her eyes drop to my lips. Her tongue slides across her bottom lip before pulling it between her teeth. Talking about a casserole shouldn't stir up these types of feelings. There's no denying that I want her. I'd pull Kennedy onto my lap if our daughter weren't asleep in my arms. My mind's so messed up. Peyton should be my main thought. My thoughts are of Peyton, but I want to pursue more with her mother. From Kennedy's reaction, she wants more, too.

After learning Kennedy didn't cheat on me, I can't force myself to have an ounce of hate for her. Just remembering the times I hated her over the past ten years guts me now. At first, it was easy to hate her. I thought she betrayed me in the worst way possible. Over time, the good memories with her haunted me. Sadly, I didn't handle those nights well. I'd wake up the next morning on my buddy's couch or floor with an empty bottle of alcohol next to me. I never had a preference for what I drank as long as it numbed the pain in my chest and made me forget.

Memories of us fill my mind tonight. Some memories and deep emotions are running through Kennedy, too. She can't hide the wanting look in her eyes. I've missed her sweet brown eyes looking at me like I'm the only man in the world.

I wrap my hand around her wrist when she starts to pull away. "Yeah, Peaches, I'd like that."

We both want more than dinner, and we'll definitely be pursuing these feelings later. First, I have to figure out how to get some alone time with her.

Kennedy starts to speak but snaps her mouth shut. I don't trust myself to say the right thing either right now. She rushes to the kitchen the moment I release her wrist. For a moment, I stare at the doorway, hoping she'll come back. She won't. She's running from what she's feeling.

Peyton seems to be out for the night. It encourages me to try something different. Very slowly, I ease off the couch and carry her to her room. It's a struggle to get the covers turned back with one arm. Somehow, I managed it. She's still asleep. My hope rises. If I'm lucky, she'll sleep in her bed tonight. The moment I pull off the first shoe, my hope is lost. She bolts upright in bed.

"Daddy?" Her little arms automatically reach for me.

"Hey, Little Bit. I'm right here." I hold her by her upper arms and rest my forehead against hers.

"Are you leaving?" The fear in her voice breaks me.

"No, sweet girl. I'm not going anywhere." I sit back slightly and pull off her other shoe. "You don't have to worry about me ever leaving you. I have to work, though. You have to go to school and have other things to do, but I'll always be here for you."

"I don't mean to be scared."

"I know you don't. Mom and I are going to find a way to help you get past that," I assure her.

She nods and yawns at the same time. Her fear is understandable. I'm scared of losing her too. She's not clinging to me at the moment. I'll take that as a good sign.

"You had a big day with all the tests at the hospital. You're exhausted. I think you'll rest better in your own bed tonight."

"Will you be on the couch?"

"Yeah. I promise I won't leave until after breakfast. You have a play date with Jeffrey tomorrow." Jeffrey is a good kid, but it rubs on me having to say those words to my daughter. "Do you need anything before I tuck you in?"

"Pajamas, please." She points to the dresser across the room.

I open the second drawer and pull out the top set. Naturally, they're blue. I step into the hallway so she can change. When she's ready, I tuck my little girl in and sit on the side of the bed until she falls back asleep. She's out in less than ten minutes. With a gentle kiss on her forehead, I silently vow to give her the world she should have had the moment she was born.

Chapter Thirty-One

Kennedy

The moment with Aaron in the living room was so intense. I couldn't even look through the door to check on them. I know he's taking excellent care of Peyton, so warming up dinner becomes my focus.

I'm not sure if Peyton will wake up and eat with us. Devon slipped down to the hospital cafeteria to get her a cheeseburger and fries. I think my brother or Zane sweet-talked the cook because Peyton really enjoyed the burger. I've only eaten in a hospital cafeteria a couple of times. The food was nothing to brag about.

I grab three plates from the cabinet and set them on the counter. My mind betrays me and replays the moment with Aaron. My body's betrayal is deeper. I close my eyes and get lost in the memory of his touch. A small gasp escapes my lips when Aaron's hands land on my hips, and his body pushes mine against the counter. This is no memory or fantasy. Oh yes, I have lots of fantasies about him. This is really happening.

His nose slides across my hair above my ear, sending cold chills followed by heat down my spine. He inhales deeply as his lips brush against my ear. The chills and heat now run all the way down to my toes. Oh, this man.

"I hope those memories are about me," he whispers low and deep next to my ear. I swear I feel that in my toes too. I should push him away.

"We can't do this." My voice trembles as he kisses my neck just below my ear.

His lips work their way back to my ear. "Of course we can."

"But…"

His hands slide around my waist and lock me in his muscular arms. His lips pepper light kisses from my ear down my cheek. He's waking up every part of my body.

"I want this." Another kiss next to my ear. "You want this."

"People…"

"Who cares what people think?" He uses the words I threw at him at the hospital.

"We can't just pick up where we left off." My brain finally kicks in. Darn it.

He steps back just enough to turn me around to face him. Once again, he pushes me against the counter. There's no escaping him. It's not like I want to anyway.

"We're not." His blue eyes pull me in even more. "We're starting over."

"This isn't starting over. This is diving in." I lift my chin. Yeah, I need to fire my brain right now. She's being too defiant.

His lips turn up into a wicked grin. "No, Peaches. Diving in would be throwing you over my shoulder, carrying you down the hall, and tossing you on the bed."

I gasp loudly and unladylike. Oh yes, please. I want that. If I hadn't given myself away at any point before, I just did.

He leans close. His eyes practically dance. "Good to know." Yep. He knows without a doubt that I want him. "We'll definitely do that soon."

"Aaron." I swat his chest.

He laughs as he releases me. Coldness surrounds me. Darn it. Why did my brain have to get involved? He may have kissed me if I had given in to the moment. Aaron Bailey's kisses would definitely light a fire all the way to my toes.

Aaron grabs the plates and puts one back in the cabinet. He carries the others to the table. While he sets the table, I pop a bag of steamable green beans and another of corn in the microwave. These aren't straight from the garden like my mom does during the summer, but they're quick and easy. Hey, a single working mom needs shortcuts sometimes. Okay. A lot of times.

Through our meal, we talked about what happened today, all the tests at the hospital, and the appointment at Doctor Larson's office in the morning. After we finish eating, he helps me put everything away and loads the dishwasher.

"You don't have to help me with the dishes." I offer him a glass of sweet tea.

"You deserve to have some help."

"I'm perfectly capable of cleaning the kitchen." I huff. "I've been handling things for years."

"You are, and you have." He takes my hand in his and steps into my personal space. Trust me. I'm not complaining. "But you deserve to have some help. Just because you can do things by yourself doesn't mean you should have to. Besides, I'm not one to sit idly by and not pitch in."

No, he's not. Even when he was a teenager, he wasn't lazy, nor did he let someone wait on him hand and foot. When he came to my parents' house for family dinners, he helped out in the kitchen or around the house with my Dad.

For a long moment, we silently stand in the middle of the kitchen, staring into each other's eyes. I swear, his blue eyes have a way of wrapping me in their own special kind of hug. My deep sigh causes the corner of his mouth to turn up. Still holding my hand, he leads me to the living room. My eyes drop to the couch. It's empty.

Frantically, I look around the room and try to pull away. "Peyton. Where's Peyton?"

Aaron's grip on my hand tightens, refusing to release me. He calmly sets his glass of tea on the end table next to the couch and turns to face me. He's once again in my personal space.

"Shh, Peaches." He releases my hand and places both of his on my hips. "Peyton's fine. She's asleep in her room."

"Really?" I glance over my shoulder to her bedroom door. She refuses to sleep in her room when he's here.

"Really." One of his hands slides around to my back.

My eyes lift to meet his again. We're alone. Our daughter isn't between us tonight. This is dangerous. I now realize how much of a safety barrier Peyton's presence has been. Without her here, I'm going to do something stupid. From the look in his eyes, he's about to do something dangerous and stupid too.

"What are we doing?" I'm no fool. I know where this is headed.

He ignores me. "Go on a date with me."

Okay. Not what I expected him to say. "You want to go on a date?"

A part of me wants to laugh. Seeing the sweet boy I fell in love with in his eyes keeps my laughter at bay. He's serious. He wants us to start over. Can we do it?

"But Peyton." I try to look over my shoulder toward her room again. His other hand cups my cheek and keeps my focus on him.

"We'll talk to her and work out some kind of system to keep her from panicking." He rests his forehead against mine. "But have lunch with me tomorrow."

Lunch? We could do lunch. Our appointment with Doctor Larson is at eleven. We can go to the Davis's Diner afterward. Peyton and Jeffrey are spending the day with my parents. After lunch, I can go to work. Work? He has to work, too.

"Your job?"

"I won't have to go to Missoula every day. My first two assignments are close by."

That's a relief. Peyton will be thrilled to hear this. I don't know what security jobs are around here, but I'm glad he'll be close by.

"Come on, Peaches. Have lunch with me tomorrow." His thumb lightly moves across my bottom lip.

My lips slightly parted with a sigh. His eyes and the feel of his hands on my body almost drop me to the floor. How could I say no to him?

"Yeah. I'd like that," I say softly.

His thumb slides under my chin and tilts my face upward. I open my mouth to speak. My words are lost when his lips cover mine. Finally! After ten years, the only man I've ever wanted to kiss is kissing me again. If he ever leaves Montana again, Peyton won't be the only one who'll be crushed.

Chapter Thirty-Two

Kennedy

Aaron and I crossed a line last night. Not *the* line, but a line I'm not sure we're ready for. It was one kiss. One hot, steamy kiss at that. Yes, I wanted it, and more than I'm willing to admit. I want more hot, steamy kisses with him. We're not carefree teenagers anymore. We have some major responsibilities now. We can't go crazy and lose ourselves to our lustful emotions. It has to be lust. It's too soon for anything more. A single mom can't give herself over to silly emotions. But are they truly silly? Is it more than lust? Uh! This is getting too complicated.

After our kiss ended, Aaron calmly asked for a pillow and blanket. Calmly with a sly grin, I might add. I quickly got both from the linen closet and tossed them on the couch. The coward I was retreated to my room. It frustrates me even more because Aaron knows he's getting to me.

The imaginary walls I've built around my heart have already crumbled. I'm like a crazy person now, trying to gather and restack those broken pieces of brick. It's not happening. Those walls will never protect me again. Well, if he leaves again, I could rebuild them over time. I don't think he's going anywhere, though. He means every word he's promised to our daughter.

Tara dropped Jeffrey off at my apartment this morning. She thought Peyton would have an easier time letting Aaron go today if her best friend was with her. Plus, Jeffrey insisted on being with her. Peyton was nervous when Aaron and I dropped them off at my parents' house. Some of her fears eased when Aaron kneeled in front of her and explained how his day would go. He didn't give her the details of his new job. He did promise to call or text when he could. She relaxed even more as she watched him exchange phone numbers with my parents. Jeffrey was there holding her hand when we left.

Aaron follows behind me to Doctor Larson's office. He'll be heading to his first security job after we have lunch. He still hasn't told me what his assignments are. Are they dangerous? Maybe this job isn't a good fit for him.

My nerves shatter when I pull into the parking lot. The reality of the situation hits me in full force. Something is wrong with Peyton. Matt wouldn't have asked for this meeting if everything was all right. Did he lie about her tests at the hospital last night? If he did, it's very unprofessional of him.

Before I can open my door, Aaron is there, offering me his hand. After getting out of the car, I take several deep breaths and slowly release them. It's not helping to settle my nerves.

"Relax, Peaches." Aaron puts an arm around me and leads me inside.

"Something is wrong with our daughter," I whisper. There are too many nosy people in this waiting room to speak freely.

"Whatever is wrong, we'll handle it together," he whispers back.

Thankfully, Melanie Hansen takes us straight into the back and escorts us to Matt's office. The last thing I want to do is sit in the waiting room with everyone staring at us. The people in this town really need to get a life and stay out of everybody else's business.

We sit in the two chairs in front of the desk and wait for Matt. Aaron firmly presses his hand down on my knee to stop my leg from bouncing. I can't help being nervous. This is my baby. Tara must have been completely out of her mind when Jeffrey was born prematurely.

"Relax." He leans close and winks at me.

I give him a weak smile and stare into his eyes. It's the one place I can't help getting lost in. He grins and holds my gaze. He knows his eyes do me in.

Yeah, Bailey. This is exactly what I needed.

Matt finally walks into the office, causing me to jump. I have no idea how long it took him to join us. Calm is a thing of the past when another doctor walks in behind Matt. He closes the door and leans back against it while Matt takes a seat behind the desk.

"I'm glad you two could make it." Matt opens up what I assume is Peyton's file on his computer.

"What's going on, Matt?" Aaron eyes the new doctor up and down. His voice isn't calm anymore.

The new doctor is handsome, very handsome. He'll stir up a lot of gossip in our little town. I saw him with Matt at the diner a few months ago, but I never heard anyone mention his name. If he lives in one of our neighboring towns, he doesn't come to Hayden Falls often.

"This is Doctor Dylan Bennett. He's a good friend from college and helps out here from time to time. I'm trying to convince him to come on as my partner," Matt explains. "Dylan, this is Aaron Bailey and Kennedy Reed. They're Peyton's parents."

"Nice to meet you." Doctor Bennett offers Aaron his hand. Aaron accepts it but doesn't say anything.

Doctor Bennett gives off a strange vibe to me. His stance and attitude says he's cocky. He's pulling Matt along. I don't think he wants to settle down in Hayden Falls and be Matt's partner.

Aaron turns his attention to Matt. "What's this about? What's wrong with our daughter that requires another Doctor?"

Matt rests his forearms on the desk, clasps his hands together, and looks us in the eye. "Peyton's tests were fine. There's nothing medically wrong with your daughter—yet."

Yet? My entire world hangs on that one word. Just what did he see in those tests last night?

"What does that mean exactly?" Aaron never did like someone beating around a bush.

"For now, she's fine." Matt's voice stays calm and even. I don't know how he does his job sometimes. "But a nine-year-old child hyperventilating and passing out is serious to me."

It's serious to me, too. It also makes me feel like I'm a bad mom. My heart falls, and I sink back into my chair. Aaron's hand on my knee tightens. His eyes, however, remain on Matt. His body's ridged. I can feel the tension radiating from him. He needs comfort, too. I cover his hand on my knee with mine and give in a hard squeeze.

Matt continues, "Stress and anxiety, if not taken care of, will cause serious medical problems down the road, and that's at any age. Small children and the elderly with anxiety greatly concern me."

He's not wrong. I've read several medical reports about stress and anxiety. The effect they have on the body is shocking. As a single mom, I've had my own issue with it. I never told anyone, but I visited a doctor in Missoula for it a few years ago. I even took medication for about six months before I found a better way to deal with my problems.

"Spit it out, Doc. Just what are you trying to say?" Aaron jabs his thumb over his shoulder at Doctor Bennett without looking at the man. "And why do we need him?"

"Doctor Bennett is shadowing me. I hoped the citizens of Hayden Falls would make him feel welcomed so he'd join my practice." Matt holds a straight face. Doctor Bennett snickers. Aaron isn't amused.

I squeeze Aaron's hand harder and get the subject back on to why we're here. "Matt, how can we help Peyton?"

Just hearing our daughter's name changes Aaron's attitude. Well, he's still got attitude. He glances at me and sighs, but his body is still tense. Hopefully, now he won't snap at Matt anymore.

"Peyton's life was upended rather quickly." Matt focuses on me. "She's dealing with more emotions than she can handle."

I nod. There's nothing I can say. I agree with him. All our lives were changed drastically last week when Aaron discovered Peyton was his daughter.

"With Peyton's heightened emotional state and her inability to calm herself down, I thought it was best to speak with you two here. I want to suggest that you consider letting her see a therapist." Matt glances at Aaron. Aaron glares at our town doctor but doesn't speak. Matt continues, "You can try talking with her and see if it's enough. If it's not, I hope you will take my advice. I can recommend someone."

"That's not necessary," I tell Matt.

"You don't have to take my advice. But if Peyton has another episode, I hope you reconsider."

"Oh, no. That's not what I meant," I say quickly. "I already have a therapist in mind."

"You do?" Aaron narrows his eyes at me. We haven't had a chance to discuss this yet.

"Yes. Rachel Montgomery in Missoula."

Tara was considering taking Jeffrey to see Rachel last year. I was impressed with how she handled Phillip and Tara's appointment with the Judge for Phillip to get his parental rights back. She was there for Jeffrey since he was a minor. She stopped the proceedings when Jeffrey got upset.

"That's excellent." Matt perks up. "I was going to suggest Miss Montgomery. She comes highly recommended for her work with women and children."

"So, your professional medical opinion is for us to take our daughter to see a therapist?" Aaron sits up taller.

"It is." Matt doesn't let Aaron intimidate him.

"Thank you, Doctor Larson." Aaron stands and pulls me up with him. "We'll do what's best for Peyton."

Without another word, Aaron turns toward the door. Doctor Bennett opens it and steps aside. The Doctor grins and gives me a single nod as Aaron pulls me through the door behind him. Something has ticked Aaron off. He doesn't speak to anyone, me included, until we get to our cars.

"Why are you angry?" I ask as he opens my door. I bravely but gently place my hand on his arm.

Aaron closes his eyes and takes a deep breath. I can't prove it, but I swear he's silently counting. After releasing a few breaths, his shoulders drop. I can physically see most of his anger leave his body.

"I just found out she's mine. I want to do everything I can to help her and make up for the time we've lost." He takes another breath and looks away. "I feel so helpless."

Wow. It took a lot of courage for him to admit that. He's used to controlling his life. Right now, he doesn't have control of anything.

"Hey." I wrap my arms around his waist and step close to his body. His arms wrap around me. He looks down, and I almost drop to the ground from the pain in his eyes. "You're not helpless. We're going to find a way to help her."

"Yeah." He doesn't sound so sure.

"Why don't we go to the diner and talk about this over lunch?" I suggest.

"Only if we get a table in the back corner."

"Deal." I'm perfectly fine being away from all the nosy people with prickly ears in this town.

Chapter Thirty-Three

Aaron

Kennedy and I follow Miss Cora to the table in the far back corner of Davis's Diner. Miss Cora doesn't use the back dining room for lunch throughout the week unless it's a holiday. A twenty-dollar tip and a hug got us the table today. A hug? The thought makes me laugh.

Miss Cora was always sweet to my dad and me whenever she saw us. It didn't matter if we saw her in the diner or around town. We got a hug. When I got older, I teased Dad about her often. He assured me Miss Cora was happily married and wasn't flirting with him. I knew she wasn't. It was just cool to my teenage self to see my dad turn red with embarrassment. Miss Cora has a soft spot for single parents. It doesn't matter to her if they are a man or woman.

"What can I get you two to drink?" Miss Cora lays two menus on the table. I don't need it. I already know what I want.

"Sweet tea," I reply. Kennedy nods.

"Great. If you two need a few minutes, I can come back."

"What's today's special?" I ask before she can walk away.

"Meatloaf."

I scrunch my face up and shake my head. I ate enough meatloaf growing up. "I'd rather have your fried chicken plate."

"Sides?" Miss Cora pulls an order pad from her apron pocket.

"Mashed potatoes with brown gravy and corn on the cob." This was my dad's favorite meal. After he died, I made sure to have this meal on his birthday every year. Today isn't his birthday. Since Davis's Diner was his favorite restaurant, ordering his favorite meal today seems fitting.

"Kenndy?"

"I'll have the same, Miss Cora."

"I'll be back with your drinks." Miss Cora disappears into the kitchen.

"Hey." Kennedy reaches across the table and covers my hand with hers. Well, my hand is bigger, but the feel of hers calms me a little. "Are you okay?"

"No. I'm not," I admit. "Matt shouldn't have brought another doctor to our meeting."

"I'm sure Doctor Bennett is trustworthy, or Matt wouldn't have done it." Her hand squeezes mine.

"Not the point," I grumble.

"Are you upset because he suggested counseling for Peyton?"

"Not really." I flip my hand over and wrap it around hers. I wait until Miss Cora sets our drinks on the table and goes back to the kitchen before speaking again. "With everything that's happened, I was wondering if all three of us should go to counseling."

"Really?" Her eyebrows nearly hit her hairline. "You would go to counseling for Peyton?"

"I'll do anything for her. Whatever it takes to help her, I'm in."

Karlee walks over and sets our plates on the table in front of us. "Can I get you anything else?" She glances nervously between Kennedy and me.

"No, we're good. Thanks, Karlee. This is great." I give her a tight smile and quickly look back at Kennedy. She's not even bothering to acknowledge Karlee's presence.

"Okay. Grandma will be by to check on you soon." Karlee hurries back to the kitchen.

Hopefully, I didn't come across as rude to her. My actions just now weren't intended that way. I don't want Karlee to believe something will ever happen between us. Phillip and Devon have filled me in on some of Karlee's stunts. The way Karlee has acted around me since I bought her the cup of coffee hasn't given me the vibe she expects anything more between us. It's better to be safe than sorry, though. One article about the two of us in Hayden Happenings was more than enough. I'm not dumb enough to let my guard down around her or any other woman in this town. Well, except for the one sitting across the table from me.

"Hey." I give Kennedy's hand a light squeeze. She lifts her eyes but not her head. This won't do. She has no reason to feel as though another woman is more important than her. "Nothing will *ever* happen between Karlee and me."

"I know," she says softly.

Now's not the time to talk about Karlee. We need to get back to what really matters—our daughter. A text pops up on my phone from Slone Security. I can read the message straight from the notification from where it's lying on the table.

Sherlock: *I need the information for your insurance forms.*

Yeah, that's what we need to talk about. This will be a slippery subject for sure. Here goes everything. If she goes off on me like she did at the hospital, I'll have to rush us out of here.

"We didn't get a chance to talk about the DNA test last night or with Matt this morning."

Kennedy lifts her head and leans back in her chair. Her folded arms say she's getting ready to argue. Maybe we should have gotten our food to go. Where's Miss Cora? We need a couple of take-out boxes.

"Is this really about insurance?" She narrows her eyes and huffs.

I still don't see Miss Cora. Hopefully, I can keep her calm enough to have this conversation here. I never did have the best timing.

"Yeah. I swear it is." I open up the text message and hand her my phone. "Their insurance company is privately owned, but there are some legal matters Sherlock can't get around."

She reads the text and slides my phone across the table. "I wouldn't deny you the test either way. And I thank you for adding Peyton to your insurance."

"I'm adding both of you."

"But how? We aren't married."

No, Peaches, we're not—yet.

"Sherlock is a mad whiz with computers. He has ways of finding loopholes. We've been listed as common-law married. Peyton could be listed as my stepdaughter, but I never want her to be called that."

"I don't understand how he can do that when we don't even live together." She bites her bottom lip. She's considering it.

Trust me, Peaches. We will be together soon.

"I don't understand it either." I shrug.

"You don't have to help me, but I will never stop you from helping Peyton."

"I'm helping you both." I won't let her talk me out of it.

"I'll call Matt and set the DNA test up." She lets the insurance matter drop for now. We'll be revisiting this subject again later.

"Do you really trust this Montgomery woman?"

"Yes, I do. Tara was considering taking Jeffrey to see her when he found out Phillip was his dad. Jeffrey always thought his dad didn't want him. Phillip didn't know he existed. Learning that Phillip was his dad was a huge shock for him. Jeffery didn't talk for days."

Wow. I like the little guy. It was a shot to my heart when he called me uncle. Guess I need to get over the fact my daughter's best friend is a boy. I don't know all of Tara and Phillip's story, but it sounds like Jeffrey's had a hard life. The little guy really loves Peyton. He deserves my respect and gratitude. I'll accept him into my life just like Phillip accepts Peyton into his.

"Plus, E Maxwell and Katie Hamilton see her," Kennedy adds.

Okay. Both of those ladies are well respected around this town. Their husbands are good men. Aiden has done a lot for me, not that he asked me if I needed his help. Both couples seem happy. If they weren't, it would be front-page gossip around here.

"Okay. Set up an appointment with Miss Montgomery." I'll give the woman a chance. I'll also have Sherlock look into her first.

"Are there days that work better for you because of your job?"

"No. Make an appointment that works best for you and Peyton. I can work my job around it. When you have the date and time, send it to me. Sherlock can send over my insurance and payment details." The sooner we get these appointments started, the sooner we can help Peyton relax.

"So this Sherlock is your secretary?" She finally picks up her fork and begins to eat.

"No. Jasmine is our secretary." I pick up my fork. "Sherlock is our computer genius. He gathers all the data we need for our cases, among other things."

She pauses and stares at me. "Like what?"

"Loopholes for paperwork and finding people," I mumbled the last part.

Kennedy calmly, too calmly, sets her fork down. "You're looking for Mark."

It's not a question, but I answer it anyway. "Already found him."

"You're going to confront him." She knows I will.

"I am."

"Aaron, can we just leave it be?"

"Nope. Not happening." I drop my fork and lean back against my chair. "My used-to-be *friend* is gonna look me in the eye and tell me why he lied to us and destroyed our lives."

Just thinking about Mark Bevins makes my blood boil. If he had a problem with me, he should have confronted me about it. Kennedy and Peyton should have never been part of his vendetta against me. I have no idea what I did to make him hate me. Hurting me is one thing. Hurting my girls is another. It's a line no man should ever cross.

"Can I talk you out of it?"

I lock eyes with her. "You got feelings for him?"

"None that are good."

"Then no, Peaches, you can't stop me."

"If I cared for him even a little, you wouldn't go after him?"

I think about it for a moment and shake my head. "I love you, Peaches. But I don't believe anything will stop me from going after him."

Kennedy sucks in a breath, and her mouth falls open. It takes me a moment to realize what I just said. I love her. I really do. The words are out there now, and I refuse to take them back. Hopefully, the universe won't use it against us somehow.

"We'll talk about it later." I press my lips together and reach for her hand.

"Yeah." She glances around the diner. "I think that would be wise."

I lift her hand and press my lips to her knuckles. We're going to have to talk about a lot of things later. Hopefully, our daughter won't stay up too late tonight.

Chapter Thirty-Four

Aaron

Peyton seems to be handling me going to work better. Of course, it's only been two days. I text whoever she stays with during the day, even if it's just for them to tell her I said hey. I call during lunch and on my breaks to talk with her. This is so weird. I've never had to check in with anyone before. I don't mind, though. I'd do anything for my little girl.

I used to have less than twenty contacts on my phone. As of last night, I probably added about fifty more because of Peyton. That's not even a joke. Not only do I have every member of the Reed family's phone numbers, but I now have several of their friends, school, doctors, and all of Peyton's favorite stores around town. You never know when you'll need to call in a fast order for something.

Last night, I got a crash course about what it means to be a Dad. Kennedy gave me a list of all my new parental responsibilities. Most of it was common sense. I hope and pray I can model my life as a dad after my father's life. He was the best Dad in the world, and I miss him terribly.

Peyton, however, gave me a list of the fun things she expects from me. Yeah, I like her list better. Kennedy scolded her a few times because some of her suggestions were silly. Let's say my daughter has quite the imagination. A lot of her suggestions will have me playing with her and Jeffrey. She refuses to leave him out. I don't think I can turn their playset into a spaceship, but I'll figure something out.

Tonight starts our weekend camping trip. Well, the trip is just the lake outside of town. Devon was on duty last weekend, so Peyton didn't get to camp out for Memorial Day Weekend. I'm not sure I like the thought of my daughter camping at the lake during town events. Families do it, and they keep the kids away from the party field. It's not enough for me. Those parties get wild sometimes. You can hear the partygoers from nearly every campsite around the lake, even the ones on the other side.

After lunch, I went to the lake and helped Devon and Phillip set up the campsite. Surprisingly, a few more families are joining us. Miles and Katie will be there, along with their families. Aiden, E, and their baby are joining us, too.

Kennedy showed up with Peyton just before I left. Since I explained to her last night I had to work for a few hours tonight, Peyton didn't cause a scene when I left. Of course, the new three-room tent I put up for us had her and Jeffrey occupied. Sam Foster at the sporting goods store ordered it for me. There are enough toys and games inside to keep the kids busy for hours.

I hated leaving, but my second security assignment needed me tonight. Tonight is basically me casing the place out. Jude knew about our camping trip and allowed me the rest of the weekend off. That is unless I get an emergency call from the business owner. Like a cop, I'll have to drop everything and go.

My first Slone Security assignment is comical. I get the privilege and honor of keeping an eye on Crawford Bank. Yep. My wonderful job has me keeping Phillip Crawford safe. Phillip shared his and Tara's story with me yesterday and how he took over running the bank. The Crawfords were never liked by most of the townsfolk. My dad couldn't stand Phillip's dad. If the man would hurt his son the way he did, I can understand why people feel the way they do. Edward Crawford is the type of man to retaliate. He's not going to let this go. Trust me. I'll be ready for him.

My job is at Pete's Saloon in Willow's Bend tonight. Willows Bend is about the same size as Hayden Falls. Its bars are a lot rougher than ours. Pete's having more trouble than usual this year. A biker gang has moved into the area and seems to have made Pete's place their regular bar. Sherlock sent me a data packet on the Iron Rebels. They're a nasty bunch.

It's eight o'clock when I arrive at the bar. The parking lot is about half full of cars, trucks, and one tractor. Small towns are crazy. There aren't any motorcycles here. If I'm lucky, maybe this will be a quiet night for Pete, and I can get back to my family at a reasonable hour.

The first thing I notice is the cheap cameras on the corners of the building and at the front door. They probably don't even work. One I know doesn't because it's dangling from the cord.

The second thing I noticed is there's no bouncer at the door. Usually, little country bars don't need one, but as rough as Pete's can get, he needs a couple of big, strong men working for him.

Pete's Saloon is a little smaller than Cowboys. It's nowhere near as nice. A glance around the bar doesn't reveal Pete. He was supposed to meet me here at eight. That's a strike on his character. A man should always be on time for an appointment. No business owner insight, so I head to the bar. Pete's third issue is standing behind the bar, passing a beer to an elderly gentleman.

The bar is U-shaped. Typical. I take the stool on the far right. From this point, except for the hallway leading to the restrooms, I have a clear view of the entire bar.

"What can I get you?" The petite bartender asks.

What in the world was Pete thinking when he hired this little thing? She's probably about five-four and weighs less than a hundred and twenty pounds, way less. She has short blonde hair. It's called a bob cut, if I remember correctly. My friend in North Carolina has a sister with the same hairstyle. The little bartender's big blue eyes pop and pull you in. She's cute and reminds me of a fairy.

"Just a soda." I never drink alcohol when I'm working.

The little fairy shrugs and sets a can of *Coke* on the bar in front of me. "I would assume a tough guy like yourself would want something stronger."

"Not tonight." I slide five bucks across the bar. "Thanks, Tink." Another wrong choice of words on my part. Never mind that they're completely accurate.

The little fairy's big eyes widen even more, and her face turns red. With her hands on her hips, she tries to kill me with her big eyes. I will firmly stand on my assumption on this one.

"If I hear one more reference to that pixie, I'm going to hurt somebody."

The only thing she'll hurt is a fly if she has a swatter. The old man hunches over to try and hide his laughter. Something tells me he's seen this little tantrum a few times.

"You got a problem with pixies?"

"Just *that* one." She huffs.

"You do look like her." I really should shut up. My obituary will read *Death by Pixie* if I keep this up.

"I do not." She says each word slowly and with emphasis. It's a lie, and she knows it. She's a live version of *Tinkerbell*.

"You have seen yourself, right?" I point to the mirror behind the bar.

"Whatever." She rolls her eyes like a teenager but refuses to look in the mirror.

"Other than looks, do you have a reason for hating on the little pixie?"

"Yeah. She tried to kill Wendy."

"She was protecting her man." I've had to sit through that movie at least fifty times.

Tink taps her finger against her chin and glances toward the ceiling. She nods. "Never thought of it that way."

Good. Now, perhaps we can put this pixie issue behind us and get to work. Well, she is working. I'm trying to, but I couldn't pass up this little bit of fun.

"Well, Tink. When you get a moment, I need to see Pete."

"My name is Fayette, but everybody calls me Faye." She's still glaring at me, but her voice has softened a little.

I can't help but chuckle and shake my head. Her eyes throw more daggers at me. If I don't stop, my death will be attributed to a fairy. Pointing out that her name means *little fairy* in French would get me stabbed—literally. I have no doubts the little pixie has a knife hidden on her. She now eyes me up and down. It's extremely uncomfortable. She needs to stop.

"What do you want with my uncle?" Tink demands.

Ah. She's Pete Holland's niece. It explains why he hired her. He's an even bigger fool than I thought. He should have never put his niece in the middle of this riff-raff alone. Half the men in here look rough and ready to fight. The least he could do is be out here with her. The old man sitting halfway down the bar couldn't save her if something happened.

"Jude sent me."

She stands up straight, and all anger leaves her tiny little frame. "You work for Slone Security?" I nod. "I'm glad you're here."

"So am I," the old man mumbles.

"What time do they usually arrive?" I flick my eyes to the crowd and back to her. She knows I mean the bikers.

Tink steps closer to the bar and lowers her voice. "Usually, any time after nine, but rumor has it they're out of town for a couple of weeks."

"Left a couple of behind," the old man adds.

"George," Tink scolds.

She looks around nervously. I follow her gaze around the room. She relaxes, not seeing who she's looking for in the crowd. The little pixie is scared of these guys. I might need Jude to send more help if they're this much trouble.

George taps the bar with his finger. "Can I get a cup of coffee now, Tink?"

"Sure thing." She cuts her eyes at the old man but goes to the kitchen. She returns with a mug and pot of freshly brewed coffee.

I take a moment to look around at the customers. For the most part, they're a typical country bar crowd. The band consists of three guys. They're not terrible, but they're nothing to brag about.

I nod toward the crowd. "What about these guys?"

"Rough. Don't worry, though. I have the police department on speed dial for when they get out of hand."

When, not if. I'm going to have my work cut out for me. This will be more than just watching over the place. Things will get physical here. I rub the back of my neck. Guarding Crawford Bank will be a piece of cake compared to Pete's.

"We need some changes around here, Tink."

"Amen." George raises his coffee mug.

"That's why you're here." She sets another *Coke* in front of me. "And you're the only one who can call me Tink." She narrows her eyes and points at George. Oh, she'll be letting him call her Tink.

"What?" George plays dumb. "It's a cute name."

The old man is now in the same boat with me. I really like George. He and I are going to be good friends. He'll be a good source of information, too. He's pretty fond of the fairy. Maybe he knows why she's scared of the bikers.

"I'll get my uncle." Tink disappears down the hall to Pete's office.

Pete and I have a lot to talk about. The safety of his niece will be the first issue on our agenda. Tink is young. Leaving her alone out here is throwing her to the wolves. Being the father of a little girl sure makes me see things differently.

The next thing Pete's going to do is install one of Slone Security's systems. Third, he's going to hire some bouncers. If Pete won't listen to my advice, I'll get Jude and Boss on him. If he wants our help, he'll do things my way.

Chapter Thirty-Five

Kennedy

"Relax, Pumpkin. He's on his way." I hand her a bottle of strawberry-flavored water.

"I know." Peyton's pacing behind mine and Tara's camping chairs. Her eyes have been glued on the path leading to the restrooms at the party field for the last fifteen minutes.

Aaron called when he finished up in Willows Bend. It takes less than twenty minutes to get to Hayden Falls. He should be here any minute now. It was great he called her. His assignment at Pete's Saloon isn't so great. Fights happen at that bar nearly every weekend.

"You wanna play *Clue* or watch a movie?" Jeffrey covers a yawn with his hand.

Both kids are fighting sleep. It's nearly eleven and way past their bedtime. Peyton refuses to go to bed until her dad gets here. Naturally, Jeffrey is staying up with her.

"I can't believe they like that game," Tara whispers.

"I can't either."

Tara and I were never fond of board games. Our kids love *Clue* the most. We didn't introduce the mystery game to them. Devon was the culprit there. We weren't expecting Aaron to supply them with board games this weekend. By the boxes of games stacked inside the tent, I guess Devon told him which ones to buy. I never thought to bring games on a camping trip before. It was a great idea. They've kept the kids busy and laughing all afternoon.

I also didn't expect Aaron to get us such a large tent. Three rooms seem a bit much to me. The tent has one large room in the middle with two smaller rooms on each side. Aaron is set up to sleep in the middle room. He said one of the smaller rooms was for Peyton. Jeffrey could have the other if Tara and Phillip were okay with it. I guess he thinks I'm supposed to share the larger room with him. One of the small rooms was big enough for Peyton and Jeffrey's cots, so the kids insisted on sharing a room. Aaron will lose his mind when he finds out. He has a hard time with our daughter's best friend being a boy.

"No. It's late." Peyton places her hand on Jeffrey's shoulder. "You're tired. You can go to bed if you want."

"No, Pey. I'll wait for you." Jeffrey takes the bottle of water Tara offers him and goes to sit with his dad. These two really do look out for each other.

"Daddy!"

Everyone's heads snap in Peyton's direction as she runs toward the path leading to the party field. Someone carrying a flashlight is coming down the path, but I can't see who it is. Several of the guys stand at the same time as I jump to my feet. They can't tell who this is, either. Everything in me says it's Aaron, but it's better to be safe than sorry.

"Peyton, wait!" If she hears me calling out, she doesn't stop.

"Hey, Little Bit." We hear Aaron's voice before we see him.

My hand flies to my chest, and I sigh with relief. The guys nod to each other and sit back down. Aaron scoops Peyton up as he steps off the path and into the light of the battery-operated lanterns around our campsite. He looks tired but happy. He comes over and sits down in the chair next to me with Peyton on his lap.

"How did it go?"

"It wasn't too bad." He shrugs and kisses Peyton on top of her head.

That's good to hear. Of course, he can't really talk about his job in front of the kids. Jeffrey is about to fall asleep on Phillip's lap, but he's still within hearing range. I'm not even sure if he can tell me everything about his job. Are security guards held to the same standards as cops? I highly doubt Aiden tells E everything.

Surprisingly, Aiden and E are here tonight. One thing is for sure. E Maxwell does not like camping. It about broke my heart watching her tonight. She was okay, not great but okay, until the sun went down. The light from the fire and the lanterns weren't enough for E. She jumped at every little noise around us. Aiden and Katie had to calm her down a few times. Aiden offered to take her home, but she refused. She's bound and determined to spend one night camping with her husband. One night will be all she makes it. Aiden will be taking her and little Caleb home first thing in the morning.

"Are you hungry? I can fix you a plate," I offer.

Peyton perks up and sits up straight. "We had burgers. I helped Mama and Aunt Tara grill them."

Tara and I did grill burgers tonight. We had to swat Aiden and Miles away a few times. Both men tried to take over. Katie finally shooed them away and made them go fishing with Devon and our Dad. Phillip joined them when he got here. They didn't get to fish long before the sun went down. Four fish weren't enough for a fish fry tonight. Those four are in a huge container of water, waiting to see if enough are caught tomorrow for dinner. If not, the guys will toss them back into the lake.

Aaron taps Peyton on the nose. "Well, if you helped cook, I definitely need a burger."

Since I have to use the grate over the fire to warm up the burger, I don't let Peyton help. She has no problem staying with her dad and filling him on her day. Aaron gives her his full attention and laughs at her stories. He's falling easily into his role as a father. My heart swells and sinks, watching them together. Anger builds under the surface. Peyton and Aaron should have never spent a day without each other. If I could find Mark Bevins, I'd punch him in the throat for what he's done to us.

"This little guy has had enough." Phillip stands with Jeffrey cradled in his arms. The way he holds Jeffrey sometimes, you'd swear the little guy was a newborn.

Peyton sits on my lap while Aaron eats. She continues to talk about everything that's happened at the lake today. Naturally, Aaron makes a fuss over her cooking skills. Her *skills* consisted of helping put the patties on the grill with tongs and shaking the seasoning salt on them. By the time Aaron finishes eating, Peyton is sound asleep. I'm surprised she's lasted this long.

"I got her." Aaron tosses his plate in the trash can and takes Peyton from me.

I hold the tent flap open and show him which room the kids picked. He pauses in the doorway when he notices Jeffrey asleep on the other cot. After we get our little girl settled for the night, I zip up the door to their room and turn to face Aaron. His eyes glance at the kids' room and back to me. His issue with Peyton's best friend being a boy has to be something only a father of a little girl would understand.

"They're just kids. It's okay for them to share a room," I whisper.

"They won't be kids forever."

"We'll set some boundaries when the time comes."

He nods, but I'm not sure he believes boundaries are enough. "At least they have cots and not sleeping bags."

"Jeffrey is very sensitive. He couldn't handle sleeping on the ground, even with an extra sleeping bag under him. Devon bought them cots last summer." I smile and don't tell him they've had sleepovers plenty of times where they shared a mattress on the living room floor.

He glances around the room and notices only his sleeping bag is in the corner. "Where's your sleeping bag?"

His hands grab my hips for a moment before slowly moving around to my back. He doesn't have to pull me to him. My body has a mind of its own and steps closer to his.

"In there." I nod to the room Jeffrey was supposed to sleep in.

"I was hoping you'd sleep in here next to me." His arms tighten, pulling our bodies together. I remember this.

"Aaron, this is…"

"Starting over," he finishes.

"Diving in," I correct.

He lowers his head. "Oh, Peaches, that's definitely happening soon."

Oh yes, please. Throw me over your shoulder and drop me on the bed.

It's not happening tonight, though. We're in the middle of the forest, surrounded by our friends. I don't get a chance to say anything more. The moment the gasp leaves my lips at his words, his mouth covers mine. My body kicks my brain out and clings to him. Diving in can't happen soon enough.

Chapter Thirty-Six

Aaron

Fishing is one of my favorite hobbies. When Cade and I got out of the Army, we went fishing almost every weekend. It was a great way to unwind and forget the rest of the world existed for a while. It didn't matter to us if it was raining or not. We grabbed our raincoats and hit the lake. Only thunderstorms could stop us. Sadly, he and I haven't gone fishing at all this year. Today, I'm fishing with my daughter. Of course, Phillip and Jeffrey are sitting next to us.

"We've got enough for dinner tonight." Aiden reels in his fourth fish of the day.

"More than enough." Miles is sitting next to him. He caught six today and the four from yesterday.

Miles and Aiden were the first ones out here this morning. They've been best friends since they were kids, along with Spencer Murphy. Spencer stopped by early this morning with coffee from Beth's and donuts from Sweet Treats. He's on duty at the Sheriff's Office and can only join us at night.

Aiden was up before six. He had to take E and Caleb home. A noise in the woods, probably an animal, startled E awake. Her freakout this morning was worse than all the ones from last night combined. It took Katie and Aiden a while to calm her down. He immediately took her home. No one knows why she's so scared to go camping. I'm no expert, but there's a story there. Nobody freaks out like that without a good reason. Whatever E's trauma with camping is, I hope Aiden can help her through it. If he can't, camping trips in the future will be a dad-and-son thing. Mom will be staying home.

Their son is only ten months old. The little guy did surprisingly well last night. I, for one, would have never brought a baby camping for fear of them crying the entire night. E took Caleb inside their tent around eight o'clock last night. The little guy didn't make a sound until his mother screamed this morning. Her piercing scream woke our entire camp up. Aiden has apologized several times today. He doesn't need to. Everybody loves E and understands. Most of us fell back asleep for a couple of hours. Miles, however, had their fishing gear set up by the time Aiden got back.

"Oh my gosh!" Peyton jumps to her feet, clapping.

"That's it Little Man. You're doing great," Phillip encourages. He's squatting behind Jeffrey with his hands held out, ready to help his son.

"I finally got one!" Jeffrey shouts as he reels the fish in.

When the fish flops near the edge of the water, Phillip grabs the fighting net and scoops it up. The bass looks to be about fifteen inches long and weighs around eight pounds. Jeffrey probably wouldn't have been able to get it out of the water by himself if the fish put up a good fight. I'm surprised he got it as close to the bank as he did.

"Now, I know we have enough for dinner." Miles gives Jeffrey a thumbs-up. "Aiden and I'll start cleaning these. You two bring that one down to us." He wiggles Peyton's hat on her head as he walks by.

Our campsite is set up in the woods where there's a bend in the lake. We're mostly surrounded by water. The forest is behind the campsite. To the left is the path to the restrooms at the party field. We have a spot on the other side of the camp to clean the fish. Aiden helps Miles gather up the fish we caught today and heads to the cleaning area.

"Great job." Peyton pats Jeffrey on the back.

"I only caught one. You caught three." Jeffrey's face drops.

Peyton looks over his head at Phillip. They grin and nod to each other. I've seen them do this before. Phillip Crawford is going to explain to me what this little private conversation he has with my daughter is about.

"Yeah, but yours is bigger than mine." Peyton smiles sweetly at Jeffrey, too sweetly. That needs to stop right now. "The size and weight of yours is probably equal to my three." Peyton grins and bounces on her toes. "That's awesome!"

"You think?" Jeffrey scrunches up his face.

"Absolutely." Peyton gives him a firm nod. She's still smiling sweetly at him.

"Yeah. That is awesome." Jeffrey holds up his hand, and Peyton gives him a high-five.

Peyton and Phillip look at each other again. He gives her a little nod. Both are trying to suppress a knowing giggle. Jeffrey is once again a happy little boy. Ah. Even I can see what's going on. Peyton is lifting up and encouraging Jeffrey when he's down and sad. Phillip must have given her some pointers on how to help his son. My little sudden urge of anger totally dissipates. My daughter is amazing.

Phillip has Peyton snap some pictures of Jeffrey and him holding up the fish. Naturally, Peyton has to have one with Jeffrey, too. They're giggling so much it takes both of them to hold up the fish still on the line. Yeah, I snapped some pictures, too.

Phillip puts the fish back into the fishing net and removes the hook from its mouth. The kids are still laughing. It takes both of them to carry the net to Aiden and Miles. Phillip and I grin with pride, watching them walk away.

"They really are best friends." I sigh and let my shoulders drop as I continue watching the kids walk away.

"They are." Phillip gives me a playful shove. "And you need to get over this issue you have because my son is a boy."

That was a playful shove. Right? Surely, he's joking and not challenging me somehow. A close look at his expression tells me he's being as playful as he can. He'll also go toe-to-toe with me if I ever do anything to upset his son and the friendship he has with my daughter.

"I'm working on it." I hate admitting I have an issue with this. "When you have a daughter, you'll understand."

"You're probably right." There's a gleam in Phillip's eyes and a silly grin on his face.

"Wait." I grab his arm. "Is Tara pregnant?"

"Not yet, but we're trying." Phillip blushes a little. He's totally smitten with his wife.

"That's awesome. I'm happy for you."

"Took me nearly six months to convince her to try for another baby."

"Really?" I thought women were all for having a couple of kids when they were happily married.

"Yeah. It takes a little time to convince a woman who's been hurt and let down in the past to try again." Pain flashes in his eyes for a moment. "But I can't wait to experience everything with her from the moment she takes the pregnancy test until I'm holding our little one in my arms."

A sobering moment hits me. Both of us were cheated out of being there when our kids were born. I want to experience that, too. First, I have to get my girl back. If I'm reading Kennedy right, I'm already halfway there.

While we pack up our fishing gear, Phillip jokes about the things he's expecting from Tara once she's pregnant. Some of the food craving combinations he suggests turn my stomach. Naturally, he stops joking when we're within hearing distance of the campsite. If he gets caught joking about his wife being pregnant, it might take him another six months to get her to try for another baby.

"I hear we're having a fish fry tonight." Tara wraps her arms around Phillip's waist.

"Yep. You ladies get a break from cooking tonight." Phillip presses his lips to hers for a quick kiss. "Did you see his fish?" He's beaming with pride again.

"I sure did. I got a few pictures." She smiles up at him sweetly. "You can send me the ones you took later."

Kennedy's standing off to the side, wringing her hands together. Did something happen? Why's she so nervous? She glances from me to the loving couple standing between us before dropping her eyes to the ground. My lips turn up in a slow grin. She wants what Tara and Phillip have. I do believe I'm more than halfway to claiming my woman. Well, who am I to deny her? I drop the fishing rods into the barrel outside Phillip's tent and make my way to her. She looks around nervously.

Oh, no, Peaches. You have nowhere to run.

Reaching her, I grab her hand and pull her to me. Her gasp of surprise is lost when I crash my lips to hers.

Chapter Thirty-Seven

Kennedy

Peyton and Jeffrey's terrified screams jerk Aaron and me apart. For a moment, Tara and Phillip are as stunned as we are.

"Daddy!" Peyton screams as she runs up the path from the lake. She's alone.

Tara gasps. "Jeffrey!"

Phillip and Aaron are already running toward Peyton.

"Daddy!" Jeffrey yells as he comes into view. He's only a few feet behind Peyton. Phillip makes a mad dash to him.

Aiden and Miles come running up the path behind them. Devon, Zane, my parents, and everyone else camping with us come running up from the lake. Aaron and Phillip quickly move the kids to the middle of the campsite.

"What happened, Little Bit?" Aaron's frantically looking her over for injuries.

"Pumpkin, what's wrong?" I put my arm around her.

Tara and Phillip are checking Jeffrey over. His breathing is erratic. Tara rushes into their tent for his inhaler. Zane calls the station to let them know he's monitoring Jeffrey. If the inhaler doesn't work, Chief Foster will send an ambulance.

"Peyton." Aaron cups her face in his hands. "Come on, baby. I need to know what happened."

"He…" She takes several fast breaths and points toward the path. "He…"

"He? He who? Who's out there?" Aaron's about to come unglued.

I'm about to lose my mind, too. Is a strange man stalking our campsite and chasing our children? This is Hayden Falls. Stuff like that doesn't happen around here.

"That animal," Peyton says between sobs.

Jeffrey pushes his inhaler away. "We saw him. He growled at us."

"Oh, no," I cry.

"What animal?" Aaron checks Peyton for injuries again. "Did it hurt you?"

Peyton shakes her head. "Not today."

"We ran," Jeffrey adds.

Peyton turns her tear-filled eyes to Jeffrey. "You let go of my hand."

"You're faster. You could get help quicker." Jeffrey looks heartbroken. "It's why I let go and shoved you ahead."

"You made me let go." Peyton swipes at her eyes. "Don't ever do that again."

"I'm sorry, Pey."

"You wouldn't want me letting go," Peyton mumbles.

Jeffrey pushes away from Phillip and walks over to Peyton. He places a hand on her back. "Don't be mad at me, Pey. I'm little. I can't do much. It was all I could think of to save you."

Peyton squeezes her eyes shut. It doesn't stop the tears rushing from the corners of her eyes. Letting go of Aaron, she throws her arms around Jeffrey.

"I love you, Jeffrey."

"I love you too, Pey."

"You don't have to save me." She sniffles.

Jeffrey leans back and looks her in the eye. "I'll always save you, Pey."

They wrap their arms around each other again. Tara and I wipe tears from our eyes. Oh, the feeling of loving as openly and honestly as a child. My mom, Katie, and a few guys are pressing a finger to the corner of their eyes.

Aiden's already on the phone. "Lucas, round up as many men as you can. Peyton and Jeffrey just spotted Buck outside our campsite. Get Leo and Levi. They're the best trackers we have." He goes quiet for a moment. "We'll start tracking from here. Maybe we can catch this thing before he disappears on us again." He ends the call and pulls a couple of shotguns from his tent. He hands one to Miles.

"What's going on? Who's Buck?" Aaron looks around, waiting for someone to explain.

Phillip looks at me. "You didn't tell him?"

I shake my head. "The subject never came up."

"Well, the subject is up now, so somebody explain it," Aaron demands.

"On Thanksgiving Day, Jeffrey and Peyton were attacked by a wild animal," Tara says.

"What?" Aaron frantically searches Peyton over again. "Were you hurt?"

She holds up her left arm to review the scar. "Just scratches, but they did hurt. This one was deep." Thankfully, only one of the scratches left a scar.

Jeffrey holds up his arm to show Aaron his almost identical scar. "Doctor Matt took care of us."

Aaron stands and turns to me. "You didn't tell me this."

"I'm sorry. I wasn't keeping it from you." My apology is lame. Aaron says nothing to me. He looks around at everyone. "And y'all named a wild animal?"

"No, Mags did," Dad replies.

"That old loon thinks it's a dog," Phillip adds.

Zane runs into the camp. "I've found his trail. We should go."

Every man in camp pulls rifles and shotguns from their tents. Phillip hands Jeffrey to Tara. Aaron brings Peyton to me. His eyes are full of anger and pain.

"Buttercup, you stay in the tent until we get back." Miles gives Katie a kiss.

"No." Aaron looks over his shoulder to Miles. "Have everyone who's staying behind to go to our tent. It's big enough, so they all will be in one place."

Miles nods in agreement. He helps Katie grab a few things she might need from their tent. Mom hurries to get a few things as well.

Devon offers our dad a shotgun. "Will you stay here and guard the camp?"

My brother really wants to say *guard the women and children*. He doesn't, though. I'm not sure about Katie, but Mom, Tara, and I know how to use a gun.

Dad takes the gun. "Not a problem."

"Lucas is sending some men to search the forest on both sides of the party field. A couple will help you guard the camp." Aiden gives a nod of authority before turning to those staying behind. "No one leaves the camp without an armed escort until we return. If you ladies want to go home, a deputy will escort you to your cars."

"We understand." Katie leans into Miles.

"We'll leave if you call and say it's necessary." Oh, how I wish they had already caught this animal. Knowing it's close by scares me.

"I don't think any of us could leave knowing you're out there after this thing," Tara adds.

"Come on, kids." I hurry them inside to their room.

Aaron follows us in. He kneels and gives Peyton a hug.

"We'll get this thing," he promises.

Peyton cups his face in her hands. "Don't let it bite you."

He gives her a tight smile. "If we get to that point and I can't shoot it, I'm sure Uncle Phillip will."

"Dad won't stop until he gets it," Jeffrey said.

"No, he won't." Tara sits down on the floor in the middle of their room and pulls both kids into her arms.

Aaron turns to me. "Please don't leave this tent without an armed escort."

The hurt in his eyes has me dropping mine to the floor. "I really wasn't keeping it from you. So much has happened lately. It didn't cross my mind."

He steps forward and wraps me in his arms. "Don't worry, Peaches. I'm not mad at you. I'm mad at the situation."

I lift my head and softly kiss his cheek. "Stay safe."

Phillip sticks his head through the door. "You ready?"

"Yep," Aaron replies. His eyes stare into mine for a long moment after Phillip leaves. "We'll be fine. I want this animal found and killed for hurting Peyton and Jeffrey."

"Everyone in town does. Lucas has been taking hunting parties out since January." The hunting parties go out at least twice a month. I thought they would have found it by now, but no luck.

Mom enters our tent. "Hopefully, no one gets shot this time."

"Someone got shot?" Aaron raises an eyebrow.

"Yeah. Hadley Lunsford and her grandmother shot Four a few months ago." Katie pulls out a chair at the table. She opens the container of ice cream Miles got from Frozen Scoops this morning for Baby Hamilton. If they know the gender of their baby, Katie and Miles haven't revealed it yet.

"Hadley and Nancy Lunsford shot Four?" Aaron's eyes widen. We all nod. "He was shot twice?"

"Yep. Hadley shot him in the arm. Her grandmother shot him in the back." Katie scoops up another bite of ice cream.

"Wow, and I missed it? And he lived?" Aaron huffs. "Darn."

"Be nice." I swat his chest.

"Sorry, Peaches. He was a nuisance before I thought you married him."

Peyton pops her head through the door. "Why did you think Mama married Four?"

The room goes quiet. Aaron and I look at each other. How do we explain this?

Aaron shrugs. "It was something I heard."

"Daddy," Peyton scolds. "You know better than to listen to rumors around here. Half of these people are crazy." Everyone laughs.

"You're right, Little Bit. I should have known better." His eyes meet mine. He's beating himself up for believing Mark's lies.

"We all make mistakes." I was as much of a part of the situation as he was. Neither of us questioned Mark's lies.

"It'll never happen again." He gives me a quick kiss. "Stay inside." With that, he turns and leaves.

No, it'll never happen again. If anyone tries to come between us again, I won't believe them until I talk with Aaron face-to-face. Listen to me. He's not even mine, and I'm vowing to fight for him. It's what I should have done ten years ago. Will fate give us another chance? I have a feeling it will.

Chapter Thirty-Eight

Kennedy

Sitting in this waiting room is driving all three of us insane. Peyton has her legs pulled up in the chair with her arms around her knees. She won't let Aaron hold her today. That thought alone is scary. She went quiet and started closing in on herself the moment we got into the car this morning. She wanted Jeffrey to come with us, but this was one time I didn't think he should tag along.

Aaron sits next to me, strumming his fingers on his right thigh. His left hand is holding my leg down to keep it from bouncing. His eyes remain on Peyton sitting across the room from us. She wouldn't sit next to either of us. Thankfully, there's no one else in the waiting room to witness my little family falling apart.

When I called Rachel's office last week to make an appointment for Peyton, she didn't have one available until after the Fourth of July. Next month was fine with me. It would give me time to prepare Peyton for the visit. Rachel's secretary called two days ago and asked to move Peyton's appointment to today. Rachel has an unexpected family event next month, and she had a cancellation for today. It all sounds fishy to me. All this came about after Aaron gave our appointment information to whomever this Sherlock guy is.

"It's going to be fine, Peaches." Aaron leans over and kisses my cheek.

Our camping trip was two weeks ago. The guys didn't find Buck. It wasn't a surprise to anyone when Leo Barnes tracked the wild animal to Mag's cabin on the mountain. The old man burst out the door with a rifle and demanded the hunting party get off his property. Leo immediately called his dad. Sheriff Barnes ordered everyone back because they didn't have a warrant. By the time they got the warrant and Lucas pulled Mags out of the way, the animal was gone.

Everyone is disappointed and frustrated, especially Lucas. He feels as though he's letting everybody down because he can't catch this thing. Sheriff Barnes asked for Buck to be captured. The forest rangers would like to study the animal to learn more about it. The men around town and a few of the women have vowed to shoot to kill if they see it. I hate seeing an animal killed, but this one attacked my daughter. I couldn't care less what happens to it.

After seeing the animal again at the lake, Peyton and Jeffrey won't play on their playset unless an adult goes outside with them. We can't even sit on the back porch and watch them play. They only feel safe if we sit under the shade tree next to the playset. Aaron and Phillip got a covered swing and side tables, so Tara and I were comfortable out there. Tara's dad added a picnic table and chairs. It's now become mine and Tara's favorite spot outdoors. Her Granddad wants a grill added next. I expect one to show up any day now.

A door down the hallway opens. Rachel and a young woman steps out. The woman is tiny with short blonde hair. She's smiling. Hopefully, it's a good sign. Matt said Rachel was great with women and children.

The woman comes to an abrupt halt when they enter the waiting room. Unlike other doctor's offices, this one has no door between the waiting room and the hallway. The woman's smile fades as she looks around the waiting room at my family. Her gaze lingers on Aaron and me, mainly on Aaron. He gives her a small smile and a slight nod. She doesn't respond.

Rachel places her hand on the woman's arm. "See you next month. Call if you need me before."

"Yeah." The woman drops her head and rushes out the door.

Aaron takes a deep breath through his nose and releases it. His expression is unreadable. He's looking across the room, but I don't think he's seeing Peyton. Does he know that woman? Even though he didn't marry a skinny blonde like Mark said, does he prefer blondes? Maybe he likes women who have a perfect figure. I've never been able to lose all the weight after having Peyton.

"Hi, Peyton. I'm Rachel."

I snap my head in their direction. If I don't chicken out, I'll ask Aaron about the blonde later. Peyton is why we're here. Rachel is sitting in the chair next to her. She doesn't even look at Rachel, let alone respond to her.

"Peyton, manners," I remind her.

Rachel lifts her hand casually. "It's okay, Mom. I'm friends with a lot of children."

"Hello," Peyton says softly.

Rachel may be friends with a lot of children and knows how to read them. My daughter, however, was taught to respect elders. Rachel isn't much older than me, but that doesn't matter.

"I know you feel scared about today. Most people are very nervous on their first visit. I want you to know this is a safe place. We're going to talk and get to know each other today." Rachel smiles sweetly.

"I'm crazy. That's all you need to know." Peyton sniffles and my heart breaks.

"No, Sweetie." Rachel leans down so she's looking Peyton in the eye. "You're not crazy. You have some big emotions you've never felt before. We're going to talk about it and help you find ways to handle those emotions better in the future."

Peyton drops her legs and sits up straight. "I'm not getting sent away?"

"No, Peyton. We're going to find ways for you to handle your emotions when you're angry and upset."

"Can you help my dad too?"

Rachel lightly laughs. "We'll do our best." She stands and holds out her hand. "Why don't we go to my office? It's more comfortable in there, and we won't have to worry about anyone walking in off the street."

"Can my parents come too?" Peyton finally glances our way.

"Of course. I would never ask you to talk with me alone unless you requested that." She offers her hand again. "What do you say, Peyton?"

"Okay." Peyton takes Rachel's hand and stands.

Rachel glances over her shoulder. "Mom, Dad, follow us."

When we get to Rachel's office, Peyton slides to one corner of the sofa. Aaron takes the other. The distance between him and Peyton today is really getting to him. Rachel sits in the leather chair beside her desk with a notebook on her lap and a pen in her hand. She's ready to work. How did my family's problems become someone's job?

"Peyton." Rachel waves a finger between Peyton and us. "What's going on here?"

Peyton glances at us and shrugs. Rachel watches her and Aaron for a few minutes. The awkward silence is unsettling. I'd speak up if I knew what to say to start things off.

"Why are you mad at your parents today?" Rachel lays her pen down and leans against the arm of her chair.

"I'm not mad," Peyton replies in a soft voice.

"Peyton, look at me." Rachel waits until she does. "This room is a safe place for everybody. We all have to be honest. If we're not, our time here is wasted. Do you understand?" Peyton nods. "Good. Now, you're clearly upset with your parents. The distance you put between yourself and them showed me that. Your dad isn't handling the distance well. So, I ask again, why are you upset with your parents?"

"I didn't want to come," Peyton admits.

"Thank you for being honest." Rachel picks up her pen again. "Now we can work on that. I'm guessing because of what you said in the waiting room, you've heard people who see a therapist are crazy and get sent to hospitals."

Peyton nods. Honestly, she's not the only one. We all have heard the same scenario and instantly believe it. It's joked about way too often in school. Kids aren't all to blame. Sadly, some adults still joke about it too.

"Only people who are mentally unstable have to go to a hospital. You aren't mentally unstable. You experienced some new emotions and didn't know how to handle them. Don't worry. It's perfectly normal. Even adults go through this." Rachel's focus stays on Peyton.

"Really?" Peyton looks hopeful for the first time today.

"Really." Rachel motions toward us. "I'm sure your parents have experienced some big emotions too."

The day Aaron bought Karlee's coffee comes to mind. I destroyed a display stand in the salon because I couldn't handle my emotions without some outward force. Aaron seems to fly off the handle when he's upset. Our daughter gets her emotional and anger issues honestly.

"I sure have," I mumble.

Rachel ignores me and continues to focus on Peyton. "You're having trouble being away from your dad. I know you just met him. Can you tell me what scares you?"

"I just got him. I'm afraid he'll leave and never come back." Peyton drops her head and rubs her eyes with her fingers.

Rachel hands her a tissue. I slide my hand close to her on the sofa. I want to pull Peyton into my arms, but Rachel gives me a little shake of her head.

Aaron leans forward. "Little Bit, I swear, I will never leave you like that."

"Can you not take your father at his word?" Rachel asked.

"Not all Dad's stay," Peyton replies softly. "Maverick Edwards' dad promised to stay, but he left anyway."

Oh my. Josiah and Brynn Edwards' story has been the town gossip for over a year. No one has confirmed the real reason Josiah left town. Brynn is still an emotional mess. They were a happy, loving couple with a seven-year-old son, or so everyone thought. One day, people noticed they only saw Brynn and Maverick around town. If anyone asked how Josiah was, Brynn blinked back tears and hurried away. Maverick is in Peyton and Jeffrey's class.

Josiah's brother Dalton plays baseball for the Mariners with Brady Maxwell. So far, the media hasn't caught wind of Dalton's family's troubles. It's only a matter of time before they do.

Megan hasn't posted it in her blog either. Of course, Megan's too busy publishing articles about Brady to even worry about the Edwards family. Several people believe Megan is doing it to get back at Beth for banning her from Beth's Morning Brew. She posted stuff before to rattle Beth's nerves. Since being banned, Megan posts something about Brady every couple of days. Some of her articles have to be her making up rumors. More than half of it is nonsense.

"It's not good to compare people like that. We don't know their entire story. It won't match yours at all. You should give your father a chance and only hold him accountable for the things he does." Rachel lightly taps her pen on the notebook. She hasn't written anything down yet. "Will you give that a try this week?"

Peyton looks at Aaron sheepishly. "You promise you're not gonna leave us?"

"I promise, Peyton Rose. I'm not ever leaving you two. My stuff is already here in storage. When the remodel is finished on my dad's house, we're moving in there. We're going to be the family we should have always been."

Peyton springs to her feet. "Really?"

I snap my head in Aaron's direction. "Really?"

"Really." He holds his hand out. He and Peyton shake on it.

Wait. That's not how things work. He can't just start planning our lives without asking me first.

"Aaron."

He gently grabs my chin with his thumb and index finger. "We'll talk about it later, Peaches. I'm not going to spend a day without you two again if I can help it."

But moving in together? That's a huge step.

"Okay." Rachel lightly claps her hands twice. She keeps eye contact with Peyton. "It sounds like Dad is serious. I believe you can trust him to keep his word." She flicks a sharp warning glance at Aaron. He nods. "I think you three should spend the rest of the day celebrating."

"Yeah," Peyton shouts.

Rachel spends the next twenty minutes teaching Peyton a breathing exercise to help her when she's upset, scared, or angry. Peyton insists Aaron practices them, too. He already knows how. He was taught these exercises in the Army. Peyton breaths in and holds for two seconds. Aaron gets four seconds. He promised to work on his anger issues, too. At least he's taking this seriously. I quietly practice along with them. Rachel notices. When our session is over, Rachel walks us to the waiting room.

"Pey!" Jeffrey runs to meet her.

I give Tara a hug. "I didn't know you were coming to Missoula today."

"Jeffrey insisted on being here when Peyton finished." Tara puts an arm around both kid's shoulders.

"That's awesome. Why don't we all go to Rainer Steak House and celebrate?" Aaron suggests. "My treat."

"Yes!" Peyton and Jeffrey shout.

Rachel waves to us as we leave. We have another appointment with her next month. Peyton has her card with an emergency number to reach Rachel if she needs her. The way she was with Peyton today, I see why Rachel comes highly recommended for women and children. I sure hope she can help my little girl.

Chapter Thirty-Nine

Aaron

There are better ways to spend a Friday night than in a little rundown bar. If I could choose bars, I'd be at Cowboys tonight. It's Girl's Night Out. Kennedy and Tara are going to hang out with their friends. Cowboys is safe. Noah ensures it is. Still, I asked Phillip and Aiden to keep an eye on Kennedy for me.

Kennedy and I have been butting heads all week. She's struggling to hang on to her strong, independent single mom status. I get it. It's who she's been for the past ten years. Even during their brief marriage, Mark wasn't there for her.

Sherlock has pulled everything he can find on Mark Bevins for the past ten years. He's pulled the family's history for three generations. The data shows a lot of money switching hands. None of it gives me a clue as to why Mark destroyed our lives. My ex-friend has some serious explaining to do. A few documents are sealed. Sherlock's working to get them open. He's not worried. Wish I wasn't.

Dropping my plans to move Kennedy and Peyton into my dad's house in Rachel's office wasn't my smartest move. It's another entry to my long list of mistakes. My plan isn't a mistake. How I delivered the news was. After a few minutes of staring into her eyes, I see the look of wanting. Her fight isn't real. I'll wait it out.

Tink sets a drink on the bar in front of me. It's just *Coke* with ice. Serving it this way lets the customers think I'm here to drink and to have a good time just like they are. Anyone paying attention would know it's not true. The Iron Rebels know it.

The biker gang is back early from their little adventure. Sherlock tracked their trip to Vegas through social media and their bank accounts. Every one of them are idiots. Their leader, Buzz, is the only one who tries to guard his privacy. He's a little harder to track, but Sherlock finds him.

"Can I get you anything else?" Tink slides the tumbler across the bar with her fingertips. Her eyes flick to the bikers sitting in the back corner for a second.

"How about a burger and fries?" Ordering food gives her a reason to talk to me more. The food here isn't terrible. I wouldn't ask for a box to go if I couldn't finish it. I slightly lift a finger and point to the other side of the bar. "Get one for my friend too."

Smoke sits in the corner on the far left side of the bar. I'm on the right. After working with him for two nights, I understand why they call him Smoke. One minute he's there. The next, he's gone. Tex stands next to the front door with his arms folded. He's not happy with bouncer duty. Jude sent me some help until Pete hires a few guys.

"How generous are you feeling tonight?" George asked from his claimed stool in the middle of the bar.

I grin and nod to Tink. "Make it three."

"What about the big guy at the door?" Tink tilts her head and looks over my shoulder at Tex.

"Get him whatever he wants when he takes a break." I'll be on bouncer duty when he does.

Tink hurries to the kitchen with our orders. She's been extra quiet since the bikers returned. If she knows these guys personally, Sherlock can't find the connection.

The Iron Rebels gang has dwindled to about a dozen members over the past three years. Apparently, the former members, which is about two dozen men, weren't happy when Buzz took over leadership. This little group believes their former members left to join other gangs, clubs, or whatever they call themselves, closer to their original hometowns. Sherlock, however, found them. They moved to Kentucky and renamed themselves. Can't say I blame them. Buzz is a jerk. He's leading the Iron Rebels into some shady business adventures.

Fifteen minutes later, Tink returns to the kitchen and comes out with George's food. She sets a plate in front of Smoke. His eyes meet mine, and I nod. I don't know why, but Smoke won't eat or drink anything if he doesn't know where it came from. A couple of the ladies here have sent him drinks, trying to catch his eye for the night. When they aren't paying attention, Smoke slides the drinks to George. Tink brings me my plate and a bottle of ketchup.

"You wanna talk about it?"

"About what?" She sets three drinks on a tray for Misty, the only server here tonight. She's being run ragged by the customers. The other server quit without notice.

"Therapy."

We've been pretending we didn't see each other last week. Kennedy has dropped a few hints about the woman ahead of us at Rachel's office. She doesn't have to be afraid to ask me questions. All I can tell her about Tink is that she works here. Hopefully, it would be enough to settle her jealousy. Yeah, she's jealous, and some bizarre part of me enjoys it.

"Nope." She pours me another drink below the bar where the customers can't see. "You have a cute family, by the way."

"Thanks."

"The little girl yours?"

"Yep."

"You gonna marry her mama?"

"Just as soon as I can."

"Good." Tink sets my drink on the bar and walks away.

Smoke's half-eaten plate is on the bar. He's gone. A couple of the bikers are missing, too. I turn on my stool to look at Tex. He shrugs.

He's used to Smoke disappearing. My eyes lock with the gang leader. Buzz figured out Tex and I were working together. I'm not sure if he knows we're a security team or just extra help Pete hired. We've asked Pete and his skeleton crew of employees not to mention we're from Slone Security. It gives us a slight advantage and keeps the customers from being nervous. Fights happen when drunk men are on edge.

One of the missing bikers returns from the hallway leading to the restrooms. A woman in her mid-thirties wearing a miniskirt follows him back into the room. She's smiling, so whatever happened between them was consensual. I still don't see the other guy or Smoke.

"We got a problem, Bull," Smoke whispers in my ear.

I almost jumped off my stool. How did he get into the small space behind me without me knowing? Smoke and I are going to have to work out some kind of signal. This isn't cool. Okay. His ability to move about unnoticed is cool, but not when you're the unexpected victim.

"What?" I'm too startled to comprehend things. It's going to take a while to get used to Smoke.

"Door." With that, he blends into the crowd on the dance floor.

The table of bikers perk up. Whoever just entered the bar has their attention. I groan and glance toward the door. Surely, these fools aren't about to pull something. Tex is no longer standing casually next to the door. His eyes flick to me. He knows this is bad. My blood runs hot. Anger seeps from every pore in my body. Even without seeing their faces, I know the two women showing Tex their ID.

I have to do something before I explode right here. I pull my phone from my pocket, pull up a contact, and hit the call button. This is too important for a text message.

"Hey, man," Phillip shouts into the phone. The sound of the crowd at Cowboys almost drowns him out.

"I take it you don't have eyes on them." I'm going to lose my temper tonight. Breathing exercises won't help, so there's no point in trying them.

"Naw. They should be here any minute." He doesn't sound worried.

"They aren't coming." I snap a picture of the front door and send it to him.

For a moment, the only sound I hear is Jake Campbell's band. I silently count as I lift up my fingers: one, two, three.

"Oh, snap! You've got to be kidding me," Phillip shouts.

"Nope. It's real. I'll see you in twenty minutes."

"I'll be there in ten." Phillip abruptly ends the call.

My eyes follow Kennedy and Tara as they make their way to a small table along the front wall. Nearly every man in here watches them, the bikers included. If they go near my woman and her friend, Pete nor the law will have to worry about the Iron Rebels anymore.

Chapter Forty

Kennedy

"I don't think this was a good idea." My body tingles with a nervous energy.

All it took was one look around Pete's Saloon to know coming here was a mistake. The dozen motorcycles out front should have turned us around in the parking lot. I don't have a problem with people who ride motorcycles. During our town festivals, a few Christian Motorcycle Clubs and one of all cops have come to celebrate with us. Most of their members join in the games from the local stores. During the Memorial Day Festival this year, one of the biker's wives won the finger painting contest at the salon.

"You wanted to see where your man worked." Tara sits down across from me. "We'll have one drink and head to Cowboys."

That's exactly where we should be. We never should have turned toward Willows Bend. There's a fight in the bar nearly every weekend. Aaron's been working here for a couple of weeks now. I wouldn't step foot in this place if he weren't here.

"Hello, ladies. I'm Misty. What can I get you?" Our server looks to be in her early thirties.

"Whatever they want, it's on me." A rough-looking man in jeans, black boots, and a leather vest walks up behind Misty.

The man's sly grin gives me the creeps. He's clearly one of the bikers, and they're definitely not one of the Christian clubs or law enforcement. They must be why Aaron was assigned to this bar. Oh, this night will end badly.

"The ladies are fine." Aaron sets two beers on the table. "Everyone can walk away now."

Misty wastes no time in hurrying away. The biker stands tall and cocks a one-sided grin. He's shorter than Aaron. The night has gone from bad to worse, much, much worse.

"Aaron, it's okay." I grab his hand.

He gives my hand a little squeeze. His eyes never leave the biker. Aaron's hard glare has me cringing in my seat. The biker doesn't flinch.

"Didn't realize she was yours." The man slightly tilts his head. His eyes practically dance with excitement. He's not afraid of a fight.

"She is." Aaron's not afraid of a fight, either. "You should walk away now."

The biker holds his hands up in surrender. "Don't worry, cop. I'm going."

"I'm not a cop."

"Maybe. Maybe not." The biker grins wickedly. "Whatever you are, Pete never should have brought you here."

"Dawg! Let it be!" Another biker across the bar yells.

Aaron raises his eyebrow. "You should listen, *Dawg*."

"You should go back to Hayden Falls and stay there," Dawg counters.

"Dawg!" The other biker is on his feet.

"Walk away now or leave." The bouncer from the front door steps slightly in front of Aaron. Now, he's taller than Aaron.

"I'm going." Dawg holds his hands up again as he backs away.

"That's going to be a problem." Phillip is standing next to Tara's chair. We didn't hear him come in.

"Yep," Aaron nods.

"Phillip." Tara's quickly on her feet.

"Farm Girl, this isn't where you're supposed to be." Phillip puts a protective arm around his wife.

"It's my fault." I slowly stand.

The bikers watch every move we make. Aaron stops the staring contest with Dawg and turns to face me. He's angry, so so angry. I cower under his glaring eyes. If only I could slip between the cracks of the wooden floor and disappear.

"Peaches, you know this place isn't safe, especially for two women."

The guy from the door taps Aaron on the shoulder and leans closer. "They're planning something."

Aaron looks over his shoulder to the table of bikers in the corner. The five men sitting are leaning over the table whispering. Several more men stand behind them, leaning in to listen to the one who shouted at Dawg.

"Go back to the door. Be ready for anything." Aaron grabs the bottles of beer he set on the table and shoves them into Misty's hands as she walks by. "Give these to George." He wraps his hand around my upper arm. "Grab your purse. Time to go."

Normally, I'd protest being ordered about like this. The unsettling glances Tara and I are getting from the bikes, and the sense of danger in the room have me grabbing my purse as ordered.

The four of us follow the bouncer and pause long enough for him to open the front door. Misty sets the beers in front of an elderly man at the bar. He must be George. He smiles and nods to Aaron.

The bartender takes an order from Misty. She begins mixing drinks and setting bottles of beer on the serving tray. My mouth falls open. I nudge Tara with my elbow and flick my eyes to the bar when she looks at me. I'm not sure if she understands because we're quickly escorted out the door and straight to her car.

Aaron opens the passenger door and turns me to face him. He lays his palm against my cheek and searches my eyes briefly before closing his. He takes several deep breaths. I don't have to hear him to know he's counting and doing the breathing exercises Rachel taught Peyton.

He opens his eyes, presses his lips to my forehead, and wraps me in his arms.

After a few minutes, he steps back but doesn't let go of my arms. "Go to Cowboys and meet your friends, or go home."

Wait. We're outside now. The danger is gone. He doesn't get to order me around anymore.

"Look," I start.

"No," Aaron firmly interrupts. "This isn't open for debate. These guys are bad news. Even without them here, this place isn't safe. I wouldn't be here if it were. You know the reputation of this bar."

He's right. I do. Everyone within a hundred miles has heard the rumors from Pete's Saloon. Nearly every weekend, someone is arrested or sent to the emergency room, sometimes both. With Aaron here, I thought it would be okay to stop in and see him work. No one has mentioned trouble with a motorcycle club.

"We're going to Cowboys," Tara said.

"You'll follow them?" Aaron looks over my head to the driver's side of the car.

"Absolutely," Phillip replies.

"And I'll be behind him." Spencer Murphy steps out of the shadows. He and Phillip have become good friends.

"Everything okay out there?" Aaron asked.

"A couple of them are around back. One of yours is lurking in the shadows. I keep losing sight of him, though."

"I'm not surprised," Aaron mumbles, offering Spencer his hand. "Thanks, man."

"Not a problem." Spencer walks to his truck parked in the row behind ours.

"Try to enjoy the rest of your night. Stay where Phillip and Spencer can see you at all times. We'll talk later." Aaron's voice is much calmer now.

He presses his lips to mine. The kiss is quick, but I feel the emotion in it. He's worried, and he cares.

I nod in agreement. There's no point in arguing. He motions to the inside of the car and helps me inside. Phillip does the same for Tara. I look back as we pull out of the parking lot. A man walks up to Aaron.

They talk while watching us drive away. He must be the guy Spencer mentioned. Phillip pulls out behind us, blocking my view of Aaron. Spence follows behind him. Girl's Night Out at Cowboys won't be any fun tonight, but that's where we're heading. It's better than going home to an empty apartment. Peyton and Jeffrey are spending the night with my parents.

"Did you see her?" I face forward and stare out the window.

"Who?" Tara keeps her eyes on the road.

"The bartender."

"Not really. I just wanted out of there."

"It's her."

"Her who?"

"The little blonde from Rachel's office."

"So, he does know her." Tara's quiet for a long moment. "I'm glad you didn't ask him about her back there. It's probably nothing, but you should ask him about her when he gets home.|

Oh, I'll definitely ask him about the little blonde later tonight. I hate feeling jealous. I don't want to feel this way. Maybe I need to make a private appointment with Rachel.

Chapter Forty-One

Aaron

This night has been one disaster on top of another. I'm glad it's over. The highlight of my night was the text messages to and from my daughter. Peyton used both of her grandparents' phones to text me. I even got a few videos of her and Jeffrey. She adds a little pumpkin emoji so I automatically know the message is from her. It's freakin cute. I started adding a pumpkin pie slice to my messages to her. Peyton insists we keep doing it.

Phillip's truck is in the parking lot when I pull up outside Kennedy's apartment. Tara's car isn't here. Hopefully, that's not a bad sign. No one has messaged or called if there's been more trouble tonight.

Spencer's truck is parked in front of his sister's apartment. The loud music coming from inside isn't enough to drown out him and Beth shouting at each other. I figured Beth would be a handful this weekend.

Brady Maxwell hit the news channels this morning. He's having a great pitching season with the Mariners. Of course, his supermodel girlfriend was in the photos with him. It would be better on Beth if they'd use pictures of Brady on the field rather than his dating life.

The shouting inside Beth's apartment dies down. With any luck, Spencer has things under control for the night. He knows if he needs help during the night, he can knock on the door or call me. As of tonight, he's a new added contact as a friend and ally.

Cold chills run down my spine before I get to the apartment door. My hand automatically reaches for my gun as I spin around. It's been a long time since I've had to carry a gun. A quick scan of the area reveals nothing out of place. The only lights out here are the street lights around the parking lot and a few porch lights.

Crickets chirp, an owl hoots, and another animal cries out into the night. More than likely, it's a coyote. A gentle breeze passes through. It's the normal sounds of the night. Nature is undisturbed by any unwanted presence. The highway is clear. No cars pass by.

The eerie feeling could be my nerves playing tricks on me. Those bikers have me on edge, especially after they saw Kennedy and know she's mine. It wouldn't be so bad if two of them didn't pass me five miles outside Willows Bend. There are a few turns they could have taken to Walsburg, Missoula, or one of the other nearby towns. There's no guarantee they came to Hayden Falls. They know I live here, which has me even more on edge.

Night missions in the Army taught me not to brush feelings like this off. It's better to be safe than sorry. I shoot off a quick text to Spencer, Aiden, and Sherlock. The blinds move in the front window of Beth's apartment. Spencer gives me a thumbs-up. Aiden texts that Lucas and Leo Barnes will make extra rounds by the apartments tonight. Sherlock sends me a grinning emoji. The dude's just weird.

Phillip steps outside. "Everything okay?"

"Just an odd feeling." I walk up onto the porch next to him. We scan the area while I tell him about the bikers passing me on the way home. "Any problems here?"

"Not really. The fun was sucked out of the night, though. Girl's Night Out ended a couple of hours earlier than normal. Tara didn't feel right leaving Kennedy alone. We checked on her grandfather and came back until you got home."

This isn't officially my home even though I stay here now and not at the Inn. Sherlock refuses to give the room up in case my girl kicks me out. He thinks it's comical for some strange reason.

The Iron Rebels sucked the fun out of everybody's night. The atmosphere at Pete's Saloon darkened even more as the night went on. Tex and I broke up a couple of little disagreements. Neither of them involved the bikers. Something tells me they had a hand in starting those little shoving matches. Buzz watched with a little too much interest to see how Tex and I handled things. It's not clear yet if they know Smoke is with us or not.

"Thanks, man." He has no idea how much I appreciate him looking out for Kennedy. When he opens the door, I follow him inside.

Tara stands up from the kitchen table and gives Kennedy a hug. "I'll talk to you tomorrow."

"I love you. Thanks for being here," Kennedy says softly.

"Always. I love you too."

Tara walks over and takes Phillip's hand. He nods goodbye and leads his wife out the door. It's good Kennedy has a friend like Tara. I wasn't sure about Phillip at first. It hurt knowing he had a relationship with my daughter and I didn't.

"Do you want something to eat?" Kennedy won't look me in the eye.

Something's up. I didn't miss Tara's little glare as she walked by me. They've been talking, and I'm pretty sure I know what the subject was.

"No, but I'll take a cup of coffee if you have some." I point to the cups on the table she and Tara were drinking.

"Yeah. I just made a fresh pot."

She hurries to the cabinet and grabs me a mug. There's a lot of tension between us tonight. I don't like it. I walk up behind her and place my hands on her hips.

"Are you okay?"

She takes a deep breath and goes still for a moment. "You know her."

"Who?"

"The little blonde ahead of us at Rachel's."

I've been waiting for her to bring this up. "Yes. She's Pete's bartender and niece."

"You didn't say anything."

"I just met her. I don't know her story."

"You..." she pauses.

I know where this is headed. Maybe I should have spoken up and admitted to knowing Tink. Phillip's words about a woman being hurt in the past come to mind. I didn't purposely hurt Kennedy. Still, her heart has scars because of what happened ten years ago and everything since.

"Hey." I turn her around and lift her chin with my finger. "I know you thought I married a woman with blonde hair. I don't like blondes, if that's what you're thinking. You have no reason to be jealous of any woman, regardless of her hair color."

"She's skinny."

I firmly grip her chin. "What does that have to do with anything?"

"I'll never be that skinny. I can't even get back to the weight I was before." She drops her eyes, but I don't release my hold.

"There is absolutely nothing wrong with your body. You don't have to be skinny as a beanpole for me to love you. Your body is perfect. Your body carried my daughter. There will never be anyone as beautiful as you are to me. I only see you."

"Aaron." Her eyes begin to water.

"The only female that will ever come between us is our daughter. I love you, Peaches."

"You can't love me so soon."

"It's not soon." I cup her face in my hands. "I've loved you since we were teenagers. I lost you for a long time. I'm partly to blame for that. I shouldn't have refused your letters and those from my family. I'm sorry for my part in it." I lightly press my lips to the corner of her mouth. "I love you," I whisper.

She throws her arms around my neck and hungrily claims my lips with hers. Oh, yes. This is the fiery little vixen I remember. Kennedy Reed was a passionate girl. The woman clinging to me is about to own me all over again.

"Say it, Peaches." I kiss my way across her cheek to her ear. "Say the words."

"I love you too," she softly whispers.

I haven't heard those words from her lips in ten years. It's more than I can handle. I lean back just enough to look into her eyes. I see it. She still loves me. Something in me snaps. I grab the back of her head and clamp my mouth over hers.

She doesn't protest or fight in any way. Her arms tighten around my neck as she tries to pull me closer. Oh, I can help with that. It's time. She whimpers when I pull my lips from hers.

"Oh, Peaches, our night is just getting started."

Before she gains an ounce of her senses, I grab her around the waist and toss her over my shoulder. A promise is a promise, and this is one I won't break. I've been dreaming of this. I won't be sleeping on the couch or in a cold hotel room tonight.

"Aaron," she shrieks as we walk into her room.

"Yeah. Keep saying my name."

I don't know why she thinks her body isn't perfect. She was never a size six, and I have no problem with how her body looks now. I toss her on the bed and fall over her. She opens her mouth, and I quickly cover it with mine. Words aren't needed right now. Tonight, and for the rest of my life, I need her.

Chapter Forty-Two

Kennedy

Sliding out of bed this morning was hard—so hard. Last night was pure bliss. If I didn't know it was real, I'd swear it was a dream or a fantasy. Oh, it's real, all right. It wasn't a memory, either. Trust me. I've had plenty of those to haunt me over the years. Last night was better than every memory I have of us.

Aaron has been playful and very handsy this morning. He insisted on driving me to work today. My brain was still in an emotional coma from last night. I willingly went along with his suggestions and let him help me up into his truck.

Reality sets in as we drive toward town. My brain shifts from an emotionally induced coma to the responsible single mom. The emotional me gets shoved out, kicking and screaming, by the bossy me. I don't like bossy me at all right now.

He lightly squeezes my hand. I glance at our joined hands on the seat between us. He hasn't stopped touching me since he tossed me over his shoulder.

"It's okay, Peaches. Last night is nothing to stress over or worry about." He goes back to happily humming.

What? Is he serious? There's a lot to worry about. And how did he know I started stressing? He can't read me that well. Can he? Ugh! This is turning into a mess.

"Trust me." He lifts my hand to his lips.

His kiss is soft and tender. It brings back the emotional coma me. How can a kiss on the hand have this kind of effect on me? Bossy me is fighting a battle she has no chance of winning today.

Thankfully, he parks behind the salon. I don't know why I'm worried about people seeing us. Hiding is pointless. Everyone already believes we're together. My friends like the idea of Aaron and me picking up where we left off years ago. I seem to be the only one struggling with it.

A coffee from Beth's and a pastry from Sweet Treats would have been nice. Needless to say, we overslept this morning and didn't have time to fix anything. If I didn't have an appointment in thirty minutes, I would go in late today. As comfortable as I was this morning, I could have stayed in bed for a few more hours. Noon sounds like a great time to go to work.

"Aaron, we need to talk about last night."

"I prefer it when we don't use a lot of words." His cocky grin almost splits his face. He hops out of the truck and hurries around to open my door. "Come on, Peaches. It's a great day."

It is a great day, but we need to talk. We were a little irresponsible and very spontaneous last night. We can't do that again.

On the way to the back door of the salon, he snatches my keys from me in one hand and grabs my hand with his other. He doesn't want to talk seriously. He's riding the high from last night.

"You have an appointment soon. Let's get you inside." He unlocks the door and pulls me into the back hallway.

"Aaron, last night."

"Was wonderful." He leads me into the front of the salon without looking back.

"Oh, my gosh!" Lindsey squeals.

"You're officially back together!" Savannah yells.

All my girls scream and shout. Even their customers are excited. Connie Green grins wickedly. This will be all over Hayden Falls in less than thirty minutes. How could they tell anything happened by just looking at us?

"Good morning, ladies," Aaron says.

"Aaron."

He pulls me to him and takes my chin in his other hand. "You're not overthinking this and ruining it. Don't you dare say last night was a mistake. It was a lot of things, but never a mistake."

If everyone in the salon wasn't sure something happened between us last night, they know it now.

"We…"

"We're great. Better than great. Everything is perfect. I will not let you tear it down."

"But…"

"No, Kennedy." His eyes narrow. His expression turns serious. I hate taking the happy feeling from him. "There's no if, and, or buts. We've been given another chance. Most people don't get that. I'm not letting it pass by. I'll fight for it, for you, and for our family."

"Family?" I whisper.

"Yes, Peaches. We're going to have the life and family we dreamed about in high school." He shrugs one shoulder. "Yeah, it looks a lot different than we planned, but it's finally happening." His face drops. "Unless you don't want that dream anymore."

"I do." Admitting it lifts a thousand burdens off my shoulders.

"Good." He lightly presses his lips to mine. "We'll talk about the serious stuff later. Today, can you just be happy and ride this wonderful feeling with me?"

"I think so." His twinkling blue eyes have me melting at his feet.

"It's okay to just feel for a while." He gives me another light kiss. "Last night started some wonderful things for us."

"Like what?" I can't help but to lightly laugh at his childish wonder.

His lips turn up into a slow, knowing grin. His eyes now sparkle as they bounce back and forth between mine. This is the playful, fun-loving teenage boy I fell in love with.

"We'll discuss the list later. But..." His hand moves to my stomach. "The main reason is, in nine months, I'll be holding our son."

"Aar..."

His mouth covers mine in a possessive kiss. He can't be serious. This cocky fool believes he got me pregnant in one night. He can't possibly be that sure. Can he? I mean, I'm not on birth control, and we weren't careful last night. Oh my gosh. There is a chance.

My girls are screaming and clapping again. Phone cameras snap all around us. I might as well prepare for the gossiping biddies to flock to the salon within the hour.

Aaron abruptly breaks the kiss and releases me. I sway and catch my balance, only to lose it when Tara slams into me and throws her arms around my neck.

Aaron's unaffected. He opens the front door with a huge smile on his face. "Come on in, ladies. You're right on time."

Chloe Hamilton walks in with two to-go trays of drinks from Beth's. Andi Crawford is right behind her with a couple of boxes from Sweet Treats. Connie Green almost breaks her leg to get out the door. I'm not sure she realizes she just handed Lindsey a twenty-dollar tip. It's usually only five. Lindsey shrugs and pockets the money.

"You ladies enjoy your treats." Aaron dangles my keys. "I'm headed to the hardware store to get copies made of these." He winks at me and walks out the door.

"What's all the excitement about? It can't be because Aaron got you coffee and Sweet Treats." Chloe hands the drinks to Hope. She starts passing them out.

"Kennedy and Aaron are back together," Jade replies.

"Well, duh." Andi sets the pastry boxes on the front desk and opens them. "Everyone already knows that."

"Well, it's *official* now." Jade grins and wiggles her eyebrows.

"And Aaron says there's a baby on the way," Savannah adds.

"What?" Andi gasps and spins to face me. "Is it true?"

"Andi." I lift my hand and roll my eyes. "It's been less than twelve hours. He's dreaming. There's no way to know this soon."

"But it's possible?" Tara smiles.

"Don't you ladies have work to do?" I don't want to talk about this anymore.

"Were you safe?" Lindsey asked.

"Not every time," I admit.

"Oh my gosh!" Andi squeals and throws her arms around me. She practically pushes Tara out of the way. "You don't need videos after all."

"Of course, I don't." I playfully shove her away. "And if I ever hear you mention those types of videos again, I'm telling my brother and Zane to never speak to you again."

Andi gasps, and her mouth falls open. That's what I thought. I had a feeling she had her eye on Zane Gallagher for a while now. Andi Crawford will never mention those inappropriate videos again.

"Well, I, for one, hope you are. Peyton would love a little brother or sister," Tara says.

"And Aaron is right. You shouldn't question things. It's okay to feel. Besides, you two belong together." Savannah gives me a hug. "I'm so happy for you."

"Thank you." I take the to-go cup from Hope and walk to the side window.

Aaron is talking with Aiden and Spencer on the sidewalk in front of the hardware store. His job scares me after seeing those bikers. Being a security guard isn't just walking around businesses, making sure they're safe at night like I used to imagine. Aaron will be putting himself in dangerous situations at times. I'm going to have to find a way to come to terms with that because I do love him.

I place my hand on my stomach as I continue to watch him through the window. Is he right? Is there a baby? I sigh and smile.

Oh, I do hope there is.

Chapter Forty-Three

Aaron

"Do you want someone to go with you?" Phillip walks with me around the square.

"Noah's trying to work it out so he can go, and Jude is sending Tex with me."

My assignment this morning was at Crawford Bank. Sherlock was updating the security system and wanted me there in case something needed to be done manually. I'm not great with computers. Thankfully, the cameras only required a minor adjustment to get the best angles—those I did without help. Sherlock talked me through the system's little glitch. Please don't ask me to repeat those steps. It'll never happen.

Our girls are waiting for us at the diner. Working in Hayden Falls has its perks. I get to see Kennedy during the day. We walk along North Main Street rather than going through the center of the town square. Kennedy's salon is on the opposite street.

"Noah isn't guaranteed, and Tex is from work, not a friend," Phillip points out.

"Are you volunteering to go?" I chuckle.

"I am. You shouldn't do this alone."

I wouldn't confront Mark Bevins alone. Well, that's not true. If I could get him alone on a country road or in a dark alley without witnesses, I'd gladly confront him alone. The way my luck has run with situations that could lead to a fight, I'm not taking the chance.

"You wanna go as my friend?" I smile and nod to Ms. Taylor as we pass her in front of the barbershop. She watches us from the corner of her eye, looking for gossip, no doubt.

"I am your friend." Phillip nudges me with his elbow. Yeah, he is. "Even if Noah goes, I'm going too."

"Okay. We leave early Wednesday morning." In two days, I'll look the man who destroyed my life in the eye.

"We staying the night?"

"Nope. Our flight will leave Missoula at nine in the morning. The return flight from Denver is at five." It gives me more than enough time to do what I need to do. I'll have Sherlock add an extra ticket for Phillip. I'm pretty sure Noah isn't going to miss this.

"Does Kennedy know you're going?"

"She does."

"And she's okay with it?"

"At first, she wanted me to let it go. I can't do that. Now, she's gone quiet about it." We cross over North Main Street and walk past Beth's Morning Brew. Quinn Martin is at the front counter in Sweet Treats. He's not there for just pastries.

"That's not a good sign."

He's not wrong. Kennedy has gone so quiet on the subject that it concerns me. If I didn't know any better, I'd swear she's up to something. What? I have no clue. At least the situation with the bikers has calmed down a little. They haven't mentioned Kennedy or Hayden Falls to me again. I'm still on edge and watch them closely every night. They're not men who'll let things go so easily.

Smoke got close enough to record a couple of them talking behind Pete's last night. A big drug deal is planned soon. They didn't give the details away. It was enough for Sherlock to call his friend with DEA. They're on standby and ready to move. I figured out they were dealing drugs long before Sherlock confirmed it. It's not the type of situation I want to get involved with, but these guys are too close to my hometown. They gotta go.

"I'll see if Tara knows what she's up to."

I burst out laughing. "Of course, Tara knows, but it's not happening. Those two are too close for one of them to give the other up. Besides, it'll just get you in hot water with your wife."

"True." He chuckles. "I don't wanna be in the dog house. I like it when my wife is sweet on me."

He can stop right there. I don't need any details about his wife's sweetness. I'm happy for him, but some things we don't share.

We pass Frozen Scoops and get ready to cross over South Main Street to Davis's Diner. Water splashes over me, stopping me in my tracks.

"What the?" Phillip jumps back. He got wet, too, but my right side is drenched.

I shake my arms to knock off some of the excess water and turn to face the culprit. An old man with a tattered hat and scruffy beard stands on the sidewalk beside the ice cream parlor, holding a bucket. The once contents of the bucket are all over me. I can't believe this idiot is still alive, let alone standing in front of me.

"Mags, why did you throw water on me?"

"I just emptied my bucket," he replies like this is totally normal.

I hold my arms out to the side. "But on me?"

"Not my fault you walked into it."

"What are you doing?" Phillip asked the old man.

"My community service," Mags replies.

My eyes widen. Community service? Do I even want to know why he has to do community service? I look to Phillip. He shakes his head. Nope. I don't wanna know.

"You're community service is throwing water on people?" He seriously has me irritated.

"No. That would be dumb," Mags snaps.

"Mags, what's going on?" Lucas Barnes walks up with a duffle bag in his hand. He's heading to the gym.

"Just washing this sign like your dad told me to." Mags points to the picture of a historic Hayden Falls on the side of the ice cream parlor wall.

"You didn't have to throw your water on me." Great. Not only was I soaked, but the water was nasty.

"Didn't see ya." The old man doesn't care.

"There's a drain right there." Phillip points to the street drain less than three feet from Mags.

As mad as I am about his stupidity today, there's something I want more. "Where's that animal, old man?"

Lucas holds his hand up. "Aaron, you and Phillip move along."

"No." I shake my head and glare at Mags. "Where's it at?"

"You stay away from my dog!" Mags shouts.

"That's not a dog, old man. It attacked my daughter and Phillip's son. Where is it?" I demand.

Lucas quickly gets between us. "Aaron, we'll track it down soon enough. Go to the diner."

"You leave him alone, too!" Mags shoves Lucas in the back.

Lucas whirls around and points his finger in Mags' face. "You're doing community service because you hit me once. Shove me again. I'll handcuff you and take you in. You'll do more than community service this time."

"Leave him alone!" Ms. Taylor shouts from the middle of the town square. She rushes toward us with her arms flying above her head. Wow. She can move fast for an old woman. "Police brutality! Leave him alone!"

Lucas slaps his hand to his forehead and mumbles, "Not today."

"You ought to be ashamed of yourself." Ms. Taylor swats at Lucas but doesn't touch him. She loops her arm around one of Mags' "Come on, Mags. We'll tell the Sheriff about this."

The three of us stare in disbelief at the oddest couple I've ever seen as they walk toward the Sheriff's Office. It's one of the craziest moments I've ever experienced. How did those two ever become friends?

"Will they get you in trouble with your dad?" Phillip shakes his head.

"No. Dad will talk them down." Lucas digs into his duffle bag and pulls out a t-shirt with the Sheriff's Office logo. He offers it to me. "Here. Borrow this so you can go to lunch. I can't do anything about your pants."

I take the shirt. "Thanks."

I could go to the Inn and change clothes. Most of the water is on my upper body. This will do for now. Kennedy and Tara are waiting for us. Kennedy has to be back at the salon in less than an hour. I'll wash up the best I can in the restroom at the diner and get a shower after we eat.

"And don't worry. We'll get that animal. I won't stop until it's caught." Lucas tosses a hand up as he heads toward the coffee shop.

"They better catch it soon." Phillip looks me in the eye. "If I see it, I'm killing it."

"We should have our own private hunting party," I suggest.

"I'm already doing that around our place. We can spread out a little more if you want to join me." Phillip grins. He's not listening to the Sheriff's request.

"Yeah. Let's do that." I turn toward the diner. "Now, let's go have lunch with our girls."

Chapter Forty-Four

Aaron

Three hours ago, I kissed Kennedy goodbye and headed to the airport with Phillip and Noah. Tex was waiting for us in the parking lot. Peyton was sound asleep when I left. I kissed her forehead and left a note on her nightstand. Kennedy was way too calm this morning. I'm not sure what's up with her. She won't talk about Mark with me anymore. I'm deeply concerned, but I'm not sure what to do.

The two-hour flight to Denver, Colorado, felt more like ten hours. I'm a bit anxious and on edge. This is one meeting I'm not dreading. I'm ready to face my ex-friend.

My phone rang right after we boarded the plane. The flight attendant just ordered us to put our phones in airplane mode. Sherlock would have to wait. The man has the uncanny ability to call or text at the worst moments.

After landing in Denver, the four of us head straight to the car rental counter. While Tex gets the SUV, I turn my phone back on. It immediately lights up like a Christmas tree. Apparently, Sherlock doesn't care if you can't answer him or not. I have eleven text messages from the man. Before I can open the first message, my phone rings.

"Sherlock, you need to calm down. We just landed. I'll read your messages in the car."

"No time for that," Sherlock says quickly.

"Okay." I lightly laugh. "I take it this is important."

"For you, it is," he replies.

I freeze. What could have happened while we were on the plane? I tap Tex and hold up my finger. We won't need a car if we need to turn around and fly back to Montana.

"Is something wrong with my family?" The first thought that comes to mind is the Iron Rebels. If they showed up in Hayden Falls and did anything to my family, I will hunt every last one of them down.

"Everyone is fine at the moment. They're just not all where they're supposed to be." Sherlock is great with computers. His conversation skills are lacking. His reply doesn't settle the feeling that's twisting in my gut.

"You need to be a little more specific, man."

"Your girlfriend is in Denver."

"What?" Now, I'm extremely confused and even more on edge. "How's that even possible?"

"Well, if you would have answered your phone before you took off, you would have known she was on the same flight in coach." Sherlock's tone makes it sound like this is all my fault.

We were in first class. As far as I know, none of us even looked in the coach section when we boarded and exited the plane. I run a hand down my face and over my beard. This cannot be happening.

"Are you sure?" Please, let him be wrong for once.

"The passenger list has Kennedy Reed in seat 28C." He's sure.

"Thanks, man. She couldn't have gotten far. We'll find her." I end the call.

"What's up?" Phillip asked.

"Get the car. We'll meet you out front," I tell Tex before turning to my friends. "You two come with me. Kennedy was on our flight. We need to find her."

Phillip jabs his finger at me. "That's what they were being secretive about."

Noah laughs. I glare at him. This is not funny.

"Sorry." Noah holds his hands up. "We'll find her. I just think it's comical with all your *new resources* you didn't know your girlfriend was on our flight."

If he keeps this up, I'm moving Phillip to best friend status. If this were anyone other than Kennedy, I'd agree with him.

"Come on." Phillip taps my shoulder twice. "She'll need a taxi. We'll head to the pick-up zone."

The pick-up zone is full of people and taxis—Kennedy is nowhere to be found. Trust me. We checked in the windows of every taxi out here. By the time Tex gets our rental car and pulls up in front of us, we know it's too late to stop her.

"She's obviously heading to Bevins Technical Solutions." Tex pulls out of the airport and turns toward downtown Denver. "We'll catch up with her there."

"Before or after she confronts Mark?" Phillip asked.

"Does it matter? She has a right to give that lowlife a piece of her mind." Noah's sitting behind Tex. He gives me a firm nod.

Kennedy does have a right to confront Mark. She shouldn't be doing it alone, though. The file on my lap contains information she doesn't know about. Mark Bevins is not the man I thought he was. There's no telling what he'll do if Kennedy goes off on him, and I'm pretty sure she will.

The ride to Mark's office takes forever. Tex leads us through the front doors. The young receptionist looks him over and smiles. Her eyes never leave Tex as she calls upstairs. She likes what she sees. She doesn't seem to notice the rest of us. The women at Pete's Saloon looked at him this way, too.

"Mr. Linwood, you may go on up." She waves toward the elevators. "Mr. Bevins is expecting you."

Bevins Technical Solutions is one of the smaller buildings in Denver, with only ten floors. From the looks of things, they're not hurting. There's a small lab here. Sherlock found a huge complex connected to the company ten miles outside the city. The offices here are on the eighth floor. The building's floor plan confirmed the top two floors are apartments for the family.

We exit the elevator and walk up to another receptionist. I guess the one in the front lobby isn't enough.

"Good morning, Mr. Linwood. Mr. Bevins had an unexpected visitor. He'll be with you in a moment." This receptionist smiles sweetly at Tex, but she notices the rest of us.

Mr. Jed Linwood and his associates have an appointment with Mark Bevins to discuss a new technical merger on video gaming equipment for die-hard fans. Sherlock is a genius to get us this meeting. However, Tex and I know nothing about video gaming equipment.

"You can't be serious!"

Kennedy's shout stops everyone from working. Heads pop above and around cubicles, glancing toward the hallway.

"Which office?" I push past Tex. Jude said to follow Tex's lead, but I won't on this.

The receptionist springs to her feet. "Sir, you can't go in there."

Tex steps in front of her to keep her at her desk. "Which office?" he demands.

"You are unbelievable!" Kennedy shouts.

"Never mind. We'll follow her shouts." Noah's on my heels.

Kennedy's shouts lead us to the third door on the right. I shove it open and barge in. Kennedy is standing on this side of a huge marble-top desk. Mark stands behind it, glaring at her. Two older men stand behind him. One is his father, whom I met years ago. The other is his grandfather. I only know him from the pictures Sherlock sent me.

I wrap an arm around Kennedy's waist and pull her into my side. "Hello, Peaches."

"Aaron, I…"

I place a finger on her lips. "Shh. Not now."

"What's the meaning of this?" Craig Bevins, Mark's father, demands as my friends hurry into the office behind me. Phillip closes the door and leans back against it.

"We have an appointment." Tex grins at Mark.

"You're Mr. Linwood?" Craig Sr., the grandfather asked.

"Yeah, but we're not here to discuss gaming equipment." Tex moves to go around the desk. I grab his arm.

"Then why are you here?" the Grandfather asked.

Noah takes Kennedy's arm and guides her to one of the leather chairs in front of the desk. He stays by her side with his hand on her shoulder.

I place my hands on the fancy desk and lean toward Mark. "Because he destroyed my life." I shake my head. "He doesn't get to get away with that."

"Aaron." Mark steps back and runs his hand through his perfectly styled hair. "That was ten years ago. There's no need to talk about it. Everything worked out fine."

Kennedy jumps to her feet. "Everything did *NOT* work out fine!"

"Look." Mark's father steps forward. "I don't know what this is about or what it has to do with my ex-daughter-in-law. But you gentlemen should leave before I call security."

"We are security." Tex shows them his ID.

The two older men look at each other. Mark takes a deep breath and runs his hand through his hair again.

Craig Jr. ignores the rest of us and looks at Kennedy. "My family would like to see my granddaughter."

"What?" Kennedy narrows her eyes at Mark. "You didn't tell them?"

Mr. Bevins speaks before Mark can. "I don't know what happened between you and my son. Your failed marriage shouldn't allow you to keep Peyton from us. This company pays you two thousand dollars a month for child support. We deserve to see Peyton. The only reason we haven't taken you to court for custody is because Mark insists we don't. He thinks it's best for Peyton to come to us someday."

"Custody?" Kennedy looks as though she may faint any second. "You want custody of my daughter?"

"She's our family too," Craig Sr. says.

"No. She's not." I take the file Tex hands me. "Peyton Rose Reed is my daughter." I point to Mark. "And he knows that. I went into the Army. My friend here sent me a letter a couple of weeks later. He said my girlfriend was seeing someone else. She got pregnant and was marrying the guy. He said my family and friends were laughing at my stupidity. They thought I should never come back to Montana."

"That's not true." Noah is ready to rip Mark apart.

I continue, "He told Kennedy I married a little blonde I met while in boot camp. He then offered to marry my girlfriend with the promise of giving her baby a name and that he'd take care of them for the rest of their lives."

"Aaron." Mark holds up his hand.

"Is that true?" His father asked.

"It's not what it sounds like," Mark insists.

"No. It's worse than what it sounds like." I open the folder.

"Why?" his father asked.

"His trust fund and access to the more departments in the company could only be granted before his twenty-sixth birthday if he was settled down with a family." I pull out the document and toss it on the desk.

Kennedy slowly steps forward. "You lied to us and cost my daughter nine years without her father for money?"

Mark bites the inside of his jaw and looks down. Oh, I'm not done.

I pull out another document with photos and drop them on the desk. "He gave Kennedy a one-time settlement of twenty-five thousand dollars to annul their marriage. The two thousand dollars you think you're paying her goes to Cassandra Garrison for child support for Mark's illegitimate son. Adam is about to turn nine years old."

"You had a child with Cassandra Garrison after we told you to stay away from her?" Craig Jr.'s face turns red.

"Do you know who she is?" his Grandfather asked.

Oh, let me have this honor. "Cassandra Garrison is the granddaughter of Albert Tifton, the founder of Tifton Technology, your company's oldest and biggest rival." I toss another photo on the desk. "Last night, Miss Cassandra Garrison's family announced her engagement to Mr. Roland Stanburg IV, the great-grandson of the founder of Stanburg Legal Offices in New York."

Mark gasps and snatches up the photo.

"They will bleed us dry!" his father shouts.

Tex's phone dings. He opens the message and shows it to me. Phillip and Noah look over my shoulders.

"Do you know what this means?" Tex is playing dumb.

Sherlock: *The cameras are off. Turn the older two away.*

My friends move without saying a word. Phillip moves in front of Kennedy and starts backing her toward the door. Noah and Tex walk over to the elder two Bevins men and turn them away from Mark.

"Gentlemen, we should calmly talk about this," Tex says to the father and grandfather. Noah just grins.

Mark sees the danger and starts toward the door. I quickly block his path.

"I don't have to do anything to you legally. The Tifton's and Stanburg's will come for you and your company sooner than you think." I tilt my head and grin. "But I take pleasure in this."

I draw back my right fist and punch him in the face. Blood spews from his nose. He screams and falls to the floor. And that's how we leave Mark Bevins. I hurry to Kennedy and pull her to my side. My friends surround us as I escort her to the SUV. Things are settled here. It's time to go home and start the life we should have begun ten years ago.

Chapter Forty-Five

Kennedy

The girls and I are booked solid this weekend. We've had a steady stream of customers since everyone found out Aaron was back in town. We're overbooked today and tomorrow. A few ladies have begged me to open on Sunday, but I won't. A few of the girls are accepting customers at home on Sunday. I don't have the extra space in my apartment to set up a mini salon like Savannah and Lindsey do. It's okay. Sunday is my day with Peyton. I won't give my time with her up for not-really hair emergencies.

Aaron says I get an entire room in his father's house for a home salon. It's already being worked into the remodel. The room was going to be a surprise. Aaron asked Savannah for a list of the equipment I needed. He walked us through the house yesterday, showing us what our future home would look like. I still can't believe I've agreed to move in with him.

Peyton loves her room. Aaron is sparing no expense to set it up the way she wants it. The room next door to hers is being set up for Jeffrey.

Aaron is warming up to the little guy, but he says they're getting too old to share beds during sleepovers. He's really trying, so I give him this win. Jeffrey's thrilled to have his own bedroom in our home.

Peyton was so excited yesterday. She hurried ahead of us, looking into every room. The furniture and decorations aren't there yet, but we can see Aaron's vision for our home together. Peyton found the only closed door on the first floor and opened it before Aaron could stop her. Surprise! Home salon revealed early. I'm not disappointed at all. Now, I get to decorate the salon exactly how I want it. It's a sweet gift. I'm not sure how often I'll use it, though. I'm not giving up the salon in town.

Peyton and I arrived at the salon an hour early this morning. Naturally, we stopped by Beth's and Sweet Treats. No, my child doesn't have coffee. She pleads with me to let her try a cup, but a nine-year-old doesn't need to be a caffeine junkie like her mom. She has a fancy chocolate milk with whipped cream and chocolate drizzle on top.

Beth goes out of her way to make the kids feel special. She has a kid's menu and changes it up each season with drinks to match the grownup versions. Beth gives so much to our community. I wish she and Brady could work things out. They should be together. Beth shouldn't be here going off the deep end and mourning a relationship she never had. Brady shouldn't be in Washington State dating a supermodel. Something needs to change, for Beth's sake, at least.

The Fourth of July is Wednesday. This week is what most of us call a special holiday. Independence Day is a special holiday on its own. However, when it falls in the middle of the week, Hayden Falls celebrates the weekend before and the one after. Peyton and Jeffrey aren't dancing at the town festival this time, but the high school girls are. They're one of the reasons we're overbooked this weekend.

"I can't wait to go to the lake." Peyton hops out of the car with her drink and the bag from Sweet Treats.

"I thought you were looking forward to all the games around town." I dig my keys out of my purse as we walk up to the back door of Kenny's Kuts.

"I love the games, but I love camping too."

Every year, at every festival, she bounces from booth to booth and game to game. It doesn't matter to her if she wins a prize or not. Peyton loves everything about our town festivals. She loves camping trips with my brother even more. Camping is extra special now because her dad is here. Aaron is already at the lake helping set up our campsite.

"Do you think E and Baby Caleb will be there?"

"No, Pumpkin. They're not camping with us this time."

Or ever again if E has anything to say about it. Camping will have to be a father-and-son adventure for Aiden when Caleb gets older. I hope they have a daughter someday so E will have someone at home with her while her guys go camping.

A strange feeling comes over me as I push the back door open. It feels like pins and needles cover my body. The alarm pad by the door doesn't light up. That's odd. The salon is dark. The low overnight lights we leave on aren't working. I flip the switch by the door. The hallway lights don't come on either.

"Mama?" Peyton senses it, too.

"Stay here, Pumpkin."

"No, Mama." She drops the Sweet Treats bag and grabs my hand.

"I'm just going to check to see why the lights aren't working."

"Don't, Mama." She drops her drink and grabs me with both hands. "Please, don't."

The fear in my daughter's big blue eyes is enough to stop me. Peyton pulls me back through the door. I grab her hand and run to the back door of Enchanted Stitches. Aunt Susie's car is here. I frantically pound on the door until she opens it.

"Oh, my goodness. What's wrong?" Aunt Susie hurries us inside.

"The lights aren't off in here." Peyton wraps her arms around my waist.

Aunt Susie's eyes narrow. "You don't have power?"

"No." I shake my head. "It feels weird."

I can't confirm this is an emergency, so I call the Sheriff's Office instead of 911.

"Sheriff's Office. How can I help you?"

"Miss Ruth, can I speak to a deputy, please?" My voice trembles.

"Kennedy? Are you okay?" Do you need emergency services?" Miss Ruth asked in a hurry.

"We're okay, but something is wrong at the salon. The security panel wasn't working, and all the lights were off. Peyton and I are at Enchanted Stitches."

"Good. You two stay there, and I'll send the boys right on up." Miss Ruth ends the call.

By 'the boys,' Miss Ruth meant everybody she could find. Within minutes, South Main Street and the street behind the shops are swarming with deputies, firefighters, and every nosy person in town. Aaron and Philip dropped what they were doing at the campsite and burst through the back door of Enchanted Stitches ten minutes after I called Miss Ruth.

"Daddy!" Peyton flies into his arms.

He lifts her onto his hip like she weighs nothing and rushes to where I sit at a small table in the back room. His free arm pulls me from the chair and against his chest. For a long moment, he says nothing and nuzzles his face in my hair.

"Are you okay?" His eyes bounce back and forth between mine.

"We didn't go inside." I lean back enough to kiss his cheek.

"Are you okay, Little Bit?"

"Just scared, but I did what you told me," Peyton replies.

"Good, girl," Aaron praises.

"What did you tell her?"

"Daddy said if something ever felt off to trust my gut instincts. I'm supposed to stop, turn around, and leave," Peyton replies.

That's why she wouldn't let me go further into the salon. "Good job, Pumpkin."

"You two stay here." Aaron sets Peyton down next to me. "I'll be right back."

Before he reaches the back door, Aiden and Spencer walk in. My eyes drop to Aiden's hands.

"The place is trashed." Aiden hands a ten-pound weight wrapped in a rebel flag to Aaron.

"You can go in after Lucas and Leo get through dusting the salon for fingerprints," Spencer tells Aaron.

Aaron growls and goes to throw the weight across the room. Phillip rushes forward and grabs his hand and the weight.

"No, man. You can't do that." Phillip stands firm, holding Aaron in place. That's not an easy thing to do. I have an even greater respect for Phillip now.

"It's obvious who did this." Aaron locks eyes with Aiden.

"It is, but we need proof." Aiden sighs.

"Kennedy, did your cameras get anything before they were destroyed?" Spencer asked.

"Oh, my gosh. I forgot about the cameras." I quickly open the app on my phone. The guys circle around me to watch the video. My hands tremble so badly Aaron has to hold the phone. My heart drops. The last image on the recording is a man dressed in black, wearing a ski mask. He takes my inside cameras out with a baseball bat. At least three more men dressed the same were inside the salon with him. One of them picked the lock on the back door, allowing them to enter with ease.

Aaron's phone rings. "Sherlock, I was about to call you."

"Kenndy, will you send me a copy of that recording?" Spencer points to my phone.

"Of course." My hands are still trembling as I email the security video to Spencer. I'm more focused on listening to Aaron's call.

"I want two systems like Phillip has at the bank delivered today. Include studier doors and stronger locks, too." Aaron paces as he listens. "Thanks, man. I'll be here waiting." He ends the call and turns to me.

"I don't need a security system like the bank." I'll admit I need something better than what I have.

"I've never had one," Aunt Susie adds.

"You're my family. I'm protecting you." Aaron gives her a hug and walks over to me. He places his palm against my cheek. "And I'll die before I let anything happen to you, Peyton, or our son."

"Son?" Aunt Susie's eyes widen.

Everyone in the room pauses. This is the first time he's mentioned a baby in front of his aunt.

"I'm getting a brother?" Peyton bounces on her toes.

"It's too soon to know." I shake my head. No one needs to get their hopes up.

He leans close. "You know you're pregnant. It's why you stopped ordering alcoholic drinks."

Tara has been the only one to notice. Or, at least, I thought she was the only one. It's true. I have been cautious since he so boldly claimed we were having a baby.

"This is so exciting." Aunt Susie claps her hands. "We have to celebrate."

"It's only been a week. It's not possible," I cry.

"Let's just go take a test." Aaron grabs my hand. Peyton leads us out the front door.

"Aaron."

"Nope, Peaches. We're going to see Doc Larson."

I protest all the way to the doctor's office. Aaron doesn't stop, and Peyton happily talks about her little brother. I hope we have another girl. It'll serve them both right.

"Hey, Doc," Aaron calls out as we approach the front window.

Doctor Dylan Bennett looks up from the file in his hand. "Hello. How can I help you today?"

"We need a pregnancy test," Aaron states proudly.

Doctor Bennett opens the door, and we follow him to a room. He hands me a cup. "I'll need a urine sample."

"Nope. She needs a blood test. We're not far enough along for a pee test. We could have gone to the drugstore for that." Aaron sets Peyton on the patient's bed with me.

Doctor Bennett rolls his eyes. "I'll be right back."

"Make sure there's no towels," Aaron mumbles.

Doctor Bennett pauses at the door and looks over his shoulder. His eyes narrow, but he doesn't say anything. He doesn't get it. Somehow, Aaron knows about the handsome Doctor opening the door on Katie Hamilton when he was wearing nothing but a towel and lots of water. It was before Katie and Miles got married, by the way. The ladies around here love the story about Mr. BMW in a Towel. Some of Doctor Bennett's female patients were perfectly healthy. The women in this town can be ridiculous.

Time slows after giving the doctor a blood sample. I'm the only one who's nervous. Aaron and Peyton are already making plans for our new baby. It feels like an hour until Doctor Bennett returns. It was only minutes. He hands Aaron a piece of paper with the test results. The doctor's face is unreadable. Aaron's is very readable.

"Here you go, Peaches." His face lights up, and his body vibrates with excitement.

I stare at the test results in awe.

"You're approximately a week along," Doctor Bennett informs me.

My tear-filled eyes lift Aaron's dancing blue ones. "We're having a baby." How did he know?

"Yes!" Peyton shouts.

Epilogue

Aaron

Every third song Jake Campbell's Band plays is slow and sweet. The line dancers aren't happy. The couples and the guys hoping to get lucky tonight aren't complaining. I slipped Jake fifty bucks to make it happen. The song choices are Jake's. I just wanted every chance I could get to dance with my girl.

"Are you happy?" I whisper in Kennedy's ear as we gently sway on the dance floor.

"I am." She lays her hand against my shoulder. I savor every second of her being in my arms.

"Having fun?" I love the smile she's had since Friday. After getting over the shock of finding out she's pregnant, Kennedy smiles all day.

"Yes."

"But you're tired." I feel bad for having her on the dance floor.

"A little," she admits.

She stopped line dancing an hour ago. I should have taken it as a hint. She was still laughing with her friends, though. I didn't want to take that away from her. Her face looked drained when we started this dance. It's time to call it a night and take her home. Well, to the campsite. It's the Fourth of July, and we're camping all week.

Friday night, Kennedy was an emotional mess. I tried to get her to stay home, but she insisted on camping. Naturally, we turned our first night of camping into a huge celebration with steak dinners. Aiden and Miles didn't mind doing the grilling. Several people came to the party but went home later. E Maxwell was one of those people.

Everyone was heartbroken to see the inside of the salon. Everything was smashed to pieces. Kennedy and all her girls cried. They had a right to. Savannah and Lindsey have salons in their homes. Customers who couldn't wait were moved there. The rest were rescheduled. We were able to get the front room ready for the festival today, thanks to the wonderful people of Hayden Falls pulling together. Sherlock rush-ordered the new equipment. Kenny's Kuts will officially reopen on Friday.

The Iron Rebels haven't been to Pete's Saloon this week. We can't legally prove they destroyed the salon, but we know it was them. Their little calling card left no doubts in anyone's mind. Sadly, it's what can be proven in court that matters to our justice system. Not to worry, Sherlock seems to find ways around a few legal loopholes.

The DEA got close to their drug deal on Saturday Night. Not close enough to make an arrest, though. Sherlock has tracked the bikers to Idaho. They're still too close for my liking.

The new security systems for Kenndy and my aunt are up and running smoothly. They have a direct line to the Sheriff's Office, Slone Security, and an app on my phone. The new doors and locks are in place, too. Getting in won't be so easy anymore.

"Why don't you say goodnight to your friends, and we'll head to the lake?" I guide her through the crowd back to her table of friends.

"We're going to go. I'm a little tired," Kennedy says and hugs each of the ladies in her group.

"I'm ready, too." Tara looks exhausted. Phillip wraps an arm around her and starts toward the door.

One of the Barnes brothers runs through the front door. He makes a beeline to Lucas and Leo. They sit back-to-back at tables with their own group of friends. All three Barnes brothers rush out the door. Half the men on the upper level go with them.

"Wonder what that's about." I'm mainly wondering to myself.

"I don't know, but Luke was in one of his hyper moods. It's bound to be something crazy." Kennedy leans against me.

The men rush to the opposite side of the parking lot. Lucas and Leo are cops. They can handle whatever the problem is. My girl needs to get off her feet. I help Kennedy into my truck and drive through town. One of her hands rests on her stomach. Alarm shoots through me.

"You and Baby Bailey okay?"

She lightly laughs. She won't let me give our baby a boy's name yet, so Baby Bailey it is for now.

"We're good." Her loving smile warms my heart. "Are you sure this is what you want?"

I almost stopped in the middle of the street. Where is this coming from? Phillip's words during Memorial Day come to mind again. Kennedy's been hurt in the past. As Phillip does with Tara, I have to treat Kennedy extra gently when it comes to matters of the heart.

"I'm sure." I reach for her hand.

We pass the lake and head toward my dad's house. I have something to show her. Hopefully, I can put some of her fears to rest tonight.

"Did you forget something at the house?" She knows where we're going.

"No, but I have a surprise for you."

We ride in silence the rest of the way to the house. I can't wait for this remodel to be finished. I'm ready to move my family into this house. This house was a happy place for my dad and me. It'll be where my children grow up.

"Is the salon ready?" Her face lights up as I help her out of the truck.

"Almost."

This surprise is extra special to me. Hopefully, I didn't overstep and take something from her.

I unlock the front door and take her hand. The living room is ready except for the furniture. Kennedy and Peyton will pick out all the furniture for the house. Well, except for this one room. If I got this wrong, we can change it.

We pause in the hallway so I can punch in the code to let the security system know we're here. After the break-in at the salon, I added a system here, too. Nightlights are in every room and down the hallway. My family will never stumble around in the dark.

She narrows her eyes as I lead her upstairs. "If we're here to be romantic, I'm not in the mood."

I stop and pull her against my chest with one hand. My other hand cups her cheek. She's tired. I see it in her eyes. This is too tempting, though.

I press my lips to the corner of her mouth. "Are you saying I can't get you in the mood?"

Her eyes flutter. "Mmmm."

"That's what I thought." My lips cover hers. When she moans again, I deepen the kiss. Before we get too carried away, I pull my lips from hers. "This is wonderful, but it's not why we're here."

"Okay," she says breathlessly. I love the effect I have on her. "Then why are we here?"

I lead her to the door next to ours. Peyton's room is across the hall. "For this." I push the door open and flip on the light.

Kennedy's mouth falls open when she enters the room.

"Aaron."

"Is this okay?"

She walks across the plush carpet to the wooden crib. Her fingers lightly slide over the oak stain finish. She takes in every detail. She silently moves to the matching changing table and rocking chair.

"I'm sorry. I haven't decorated it yet. I wanted you to do that. Peyton would enjoy helping, too." I clasp my hands together, unsure of what to do.

"Aaron." She spins to face me. "This is amazing. I love it."

That's my cue. I close the distance between us and place my hands on her hips. "I hope this shows you how serious I am about us. If it doesn't, maybe this will." I kneel on one knee and hold up the ring that's been in my pocket for two weeks. "I love you, Peaches. I wish I'd never joined the Army because doing so cost me you and Peyton.

God's given me a chance to have you back. I'm not taking this chance for granted. I've wandered the world a broken man, unsure of where I belonged. With you, I know I'm finally home. Will you marry me?"

"Of course, I'll marry you," she replies through tears.

I slide the ring on her finger and stand. She is my home. Her body trembles in my arms. It's okay. These are happy tears. Plus, I've already been warned by Aiden and Miles that pregnant women cry a lot.

"We can get married at the courthouse next week if you want," I suggest.

"No." She looks up at me. I wipe a tear from the corner of her eye with my thumb. "I want to marry you at The Magnolia Inn on August twenty-first."

Tears sting my eyes now. "You want to get married on my dad's birthday?"

"Yeah. If that's okay." Her sweet smile will get her anything she wants. "In a way, it'll seem like he'll be there with us."

"I'm sure he already is." Being in the house makes me feel like I'm close to my dad again. "And thank you. August twenty-first is perfect."

"Now, we should go tell Peyton. She's going to be so excited. It'll take us hours to get her to sleep tonight." She tries to step out of my arms.

"We'll go in a moment. Right now, I need this."

I press my lips to hers again. Right here, with this woman, in this house, in this town, is where my home has always been. I was a fool ten years ago and let a lie cause me to lose sight of what mattered the most. Never again. Kennedy's been lost and wandering, too. Together, we're finally home.

Hello, my lovely Reader,

Thank you so much for reading Finally Home. I hope you enjoyed Aaron and Kennedy's story. Just like you, this series means a lot to me. Your love for these characters keeps me writing more books. Some of my favorite characters are in Hayden Falls. Check the Follow Me page for ways to connect with me, and let me know who your favorite characters are. I can't wait to hear from you.

If you started the series with this book, you got a few spoilers about a few of the other couples. I hope you go back to *Forever Mine – Book One* and start with Aiden's story. If you enjoyed this book, will you please leave it a star rating and/or a review? Reviews don't have to be long. Just say what you liked about the story. If you're not comfortable with written reviews, a star rating helps. I'd really appreciate it.

If you like my books, I'd love to have you on my book launch team. I can help you get a free eBook copy of my books. Join me on Facebook at Debbie Hyde's Book Launch Team.

Thank you again for reading Finally Home – Book Seven. Book Eight will be coming soon. Any guesses on who it'll be?

Blessings to you,

Debbie Hyde

Follow Me

Here are places to follow me:

Sign up for my Newsletter:
www.debbiehyde-author.com

Facebook Page:
Debbie Hyde Author

Facebook Groups:
Debbie Hyde Books – This is my reader's group. I hold giveaways in the group often.
For the Love of a Shaw – This group is dedicated to the series. I hold giveaways here, too.
Debbie Hyde's Book Launch Team – I would love to have you on my book launch team! The team gets all my book news first. They sometimes help with cover designs. The Team can get FREE ebooks for an honest review. Join me today!
The Fireside Book Café – This is a book community group with various Authors and books from every genre. We hold Giveaways here, too.

Instagram:
www.instagram.com/debbie_hyde_author

Twitter:
Debbie Hyde5

TikTok:
debbie_hyde

Hayden Falls

Forever Mine ~ Book One
Aiden and E
Today, I'm going home to a town that wrote me off years ago. Home to watch the woman I love marry someone else. I'm not going to survive this.

Only With You ~ Book Two
Miles and Katie
My career was strong and sure. My personal life was a mess. My only regret was keeping her a secret. Winning her back won't be easy, but I have to try.

Giving Her My Heart ~ Book Three
Jasper and Hannah
The dance teacher annoys me at every turn until she twirls her way into my heart and my daughter's. Now, I need to find a way to get her to stay.

Finding Home ~ Book Four
Lucas and Riley
I was the fun brother until my twin almost died in a fire. Now, I'm a mess. Then she came along. I'm charming, but am I enough for her to stay?

Listening to My Heart ~ Book Five
Phillip and Tara
My family took the biggest part of my heart from me. A piece I didn't know existed. After nine years, the woman who holds every piece of my heart returns, bringing a huge secret with her. This time, no one will keep me from her.

A Hayden Falls Christmas

Spend Christmas in Hayden Falls. Enjoy a short story about the five couples we've met, plus two of the town's beloved families.

Falling for You ~ Book Six

Lucas & Hadley

I'm a career-minded cop. I wasn't looking for love. When my nosy matchmaking brother gets involved, my favorite barista is all I can see.

Finally Home ~ Book Seven

Aaron & Kennedy

If I had known joining the Army would cost me her, I never would have enlisted.

Book Eight is Coming Soon!

The Dawson Boys

Holding Her ~ Book One

Harrison & Tru

Losing her destroyed me. One letter gave me hope. Like a man on a mission, I went after her.

I Do It For You ~ Book Two

Bryan & Dana

Slow, steady, and sweet isn't always the best way to go. Did I wait too long? Did my plan fail? I don't know, but I'd do anything for her.

Everything I Ever Wanted ~ Book Three

Calen & Daisy

"Get out!" I've shouted those words every day. Does she listen? Not a chance. She challenges me. She tests me. How did she become everything I ever wanted?

Book Four is COMING SOON! Expected by August – November 2023.

For the Love of a Shaw

When A Knight Falls ~ Book One

Gavin & Abby

A battle at sea with a notorious pirate leaves Gavin Shaw wounded and far from home. He will battle his long-time enemy more than once when he falls for his nursemaid. Will Abby marry the wrong man to save an innocent girl?

Falling for the Enemy ~ Book Two

Nate & Olivia

Nathaniel Shaw takes a job to prove his worth to his father. He loses his heart to the mysterious woman in his crew only to discover she isn't who she claims to be.

A Knight's Destiny ~ Book Three

Nick & Elizabeth

Nicholas Shaw is a knight without a title, but he's loved the Duke's sister for years. When Elizabeth needs protection and runs away, rather than sending her to her brother, Nick goes with her.

Capturing A Knight's Heart ~ Book Four

Jax & Nancie

Jackson Shaw isn't bound by the rules of society. He's free to roam as he pleases until he stumbles across a well-kept secret of Miss Nancie's. Will Nancie guard her heart and push him away? Or has she truly captured this knight's heart?

A Duke's Treasure ~ Book Five

Sam & Dani

Samuel Dawson, the Duke of Greyham, has loved Lady Danielle Shaw for years. When Dani stumbles into his darkest secret, Sam has no choice but to steal her away.

A Knight's Passion ~ Book Six

Caleb & Briley

Caleb Shaw feels lost, alone, and misunderstood. The past haunts his mind. While running for his life, he devises a plan to save Briley. The bluff is called, trapping them together forever.

A Mysterious Knight ~ Book Seven

Alex & Emily

Alexander Shaw had no light, peace, or love if he didn't have her. The day she sent him away almost destroyed him. Emily's trapped in her father's secrets and can't break free no matter how much she wants to. Alex will risk his life to free hers.

Other Books by the Author

Forest Rovania series: Middle-Grade Fantasy

Written with: Nevaeh Roberson

Jasper's Journey ~ Book One
Forest Rovania's only hope begins with an epic journey.

Women's Christian:

Stamped *subtitle:* Breaking Out of the Box
Her *subtitle:* Beautiful, Loved, Wanted, Matters, Priceless!
Her: Beautiful, Loved, Wanted, Matters, Priceless! Guided Study Journal.

Blank Recipe Cookbooks:

My Thanksgiving Recipes
Store all your holiday recipes in one place. Choose from 4 cover designs.
Burgundy, Orange, Peach, and Cream & Burgundy.

My Halloween Recipes
A great place to store fun children's recipes.

Background Cover Photographer

Thank you to the wonder Carrie Licano Pichler! Carrie is the photographer of all the cover backgrounds for this series. Every picture is from the beautiful state of Montana. Carrie does Landscapes, Portraits, and Weddings. If you're in Montana, please connect with her. You won't regret it! Be sure to thank you for these cover photos.

You can find her at:

Website: carriepichlerphotography.weebly.com

Facebook Group: Carrie Pichler Photography

Acknowledgments:

Thank you to my awesome *Toon Blast* gaming friends, Four!, Pit, and Mags! You guys gave me some great character names for this series. Stay tuned! I'm sure those guys will be doing a lot more throughout the series!

Thank you, Carrie Pichler, for being our Montana Photographer for this series. All the background photos are really from Montana. Carrie is an amazing photographer!

Thank you, Nancie Alewine Blume, for being my beta reader.

Thank you, Wendy (Winnie) Sizemore, for bouncing story ideas with me.

A Montana School Transportation Law from the 1960s stated that if a student rode a horse to school, the principal had to take care of it. This law has been used for Senior Day pranks in Montana several times.

A very special thank you to the members of the *Facebook* group *For All Who Love Montana.* Your stories are so great! If you liked or commented on the post for stories, I have included your names here. It meant a lot to me that you took the time to share with me. Christine Migneault, Tammie Duran, Jim and Coleen Larson Done, Andrea Phillips, Joy Rasmussen, Kelli Vilchis, Sandra Stuckey, Sarah Jobe, Gracene Long, Dennis Fabel, Deb McGann Langshaw, Janice Berget, Ruth Collins Johnson, Roxanna Malone McGinnis, Shawn Wakefield, Alan Johnson, Judy Shockley, Danielle Mccrory, Larry Campbell, Maureen Mannion Kemp, Nancy Ray, Jerry Urfer, Kris Biffle Rudin, Holly Good, Vic Direito, Mozelle Brewer, Joseph Hartel, Cheri Wicks, Stephanie Schuck-Quinn, Travis Frank, Kamae

Luscombe, Dianne Eshuk Ketcharm, Patty Ward, Tina Griffin Williams, Steve Kline, Jim Lidquist, Christina Mansfield, Glen Hodges, Teri St Pierre, Lalena Chacon-Carter, Eric Wolf, Jennifer Ahern Lammers, Marilyn Handyside, Lynnette Graf, Arianna Dawn Fake, Cody Birdwell, Doug Jeanne Hall, Mary Thomas.

About the Author

Debbie Hyde is the author of the Historical Romance *series For the Love of a Shaw*. The seven-book family sage begins with Gavin in When A Knight Falls. She is currently working on *The Dawson Boys* series and the *Hayden Falls* series. Both series are Contemporary Romances. A couple more series are in the works.

Debbie has a love for writing! She enjoys reading books from many different genres, such as Christian, Romance, Young Adults, and many more. You will always find wonderful, clean stories in her fictional writings.

She enjoys using her talents in cooking, baking, and cake decorating when not reading or writing. She loves using her skill as a seamstress to make gowns, costumes, teddy bears, baby blankets, and much more.

Debbie started Letters To You on Facebook after God put it on her heart to "Love the lost and lead them to Jesus." This wonderful community of amazing people allows her to continue her mission to Just #LoveThemAll.

Debbie would love to hear from you and see your reviews!

Made in United States
Troutdale, OR
11/15/2024